MW01232014

SHADOWS IN TIME

Book one of the Shadows Stories

R. A. Lura

Library of Congress Control Number:
2008937633
ISBN 13: 978-0-9820562-3-3
ISBN 10: 0-9820562-3-0

Raular Publishing
www.raularpublishing.com

To Matthew & Jessica

PROLOGUE

The heat of the doctor's office assaulted Matilda in a sharp contrast from the bitter winter gales that she had just forged through. The small bundle of life in her arms lay all too still, almost lifeless, as she approached the receptionist to announce her arrival. Fear constricted her chest, making each breath laborious as she peered into the pale, wax-like cheeks of the infant in her arms. Her sweet little Caitlin; how small and helpless she appeared in the layers of fabric that surrounded her. Just last night her screams of despair where so powerful that Matilda was hard pressed to remember that Caitlin was barely six months old.

Matilda had named Caitlin after her cousin back in Ireland. She and her cousin Caitlin had been like sisters while growing up in the quaint countryside in county Cork. She recalled, with a smile, the laughter and joy that had filled her childhood years. Oh how she longed for the years gone by.

Matilda and her dear cousin had lost contact when Caitlin moved to America with her husband, Tommy, five years earlier, but had acquired Caitlin's address just before she and James started their journey to

America.

Her cousin was living in the hills of Pennsylvania; not far from Manhattan, actually. Matilda longed to contact her and let her know that they where close again and that she had a namesake, but James would have none of it while they where in such dire financial straits. His pride was a blessing in some ways and a curse in others.

Anger for her present situation welled up and her smile was lost to an anguished contortion. Having had such a happy childhood herself, she had vowed that her babies would know the same. She did her best to shield young Nora from the poverty and hardships that filled their days since arriving in America. The trip had been long and hard, filled with false promises and hopes. She prayed for her family's happiness and success in life and longed for financial security.

Matilda and her husband, James, had only recently immigrated from Ireland. A proud man, when the promise of housing and a job at his uncle's friend's factory had not been fulfilled and their meager funds dwindled as he scrambled for shelter and work, he refused to seek help from any federally funded assistance program; leaving the family to survive on what was left of his meager wages from the job he had managed to secure at a local shoe factory; after his thirst had been quenched at the neighborhood bar, of course.

The doctor's fee was probably going to take most of the money she had available to her for the week's supply of food and goods, but she could not risk ignoring her precious Caitlin's health. Her daughter was seriously ill; there was no doubting that. A doctor was needed and that was all there was to it. She would deal with James and his old fashioned ideas of natural healing and how doctors are a waste of good money later. For now, she would focus on the little darling in her arms and believe that her prayers would be answered and they would be fine. A long sigh of frustration was released as she thought of her plight.

"Mama, it's cold out here, can I come in?"

Matilda turned in response to the small voice belonging to her oldest daughter, Nora. Nora's big brown eyes pleaded with want and a touch of fear; fear of what, maybe of loss? Children could be insightful and intuitive, especially in Matilda's family lineage. Even though she had done her best to shield her eldest child, perhaps Nora sensed how serious their plight was.

Nora's bright strawberry blonde curls scattered around her face, glistening with the moisture of the melting snow. She was almost lost in a worn and faded blue wool jacket, a pair of bright multicolored, predominantly orange mittens with matching scarf, and a hat. They where a gift from Grandma Maloney. Grandma Maloney made a new set for everyone each Christmas. The family had grown to look forward to, and rely upon, Grandma Maloney's contribution to their winter warmth. The wave of sadness that passed through Matilda was almost consuming as she wondered what the future held for her dear little Nora.

"Yes darling, come in and sit down in that chair." Matilda's thick brogue was barely above a whisper as she directed her daughter to the empty corner of the room. With her free hand, Matilda helped Nora free herself from the constraints of her woollen outer wear, which was rapidly becoming heavily laden from the melting snow.

Nora settled back into the chair and looked around the room with her brown, doe-like eyes. Three of the four walls where lined with chairs that where occupied by patients waiting to be seen. They seemingly paid no notice to the newcomers, each absorbed in their own misery and plight. A man with beady red-rimmed eyes looked distressfully from behind the handkerchief that was covering the majority of his face. His obvious misery caused Nora to shrink for fear of catching his ailment as her mother approached the nurse who had appeared behind the reception desk.

"Excuse me, please. We have an appointment with the doctor." Matilda's voice was barely audible.

"Name?" The nurse bellowed, without looking up.

"McNevin, Matilda McNevin." The nurse looked up, making a quick assessment of Matilda before she scowled with disdain and looked back down at the schedule book. "I have a Caitlin McNevin; no Matilda."

Matilda sighed, frustrated with the obvious prejudice that the nurse was emanating. Was it her poverty or nation of origin that bothered this rude and self-important woman? She held the comment she longed to make about the nurse's arrogance at bay, knowing it would not help the situation. "I am Matilda. My baby is Caitlin McNevin. She's... she's quite ill."

"Sit down. I'll call you when the doctor can see you." The nurse's eyes never left the paperwork on her desk as she clipped her orders to Matilda; waiting until Matilda had settled in the chair next to Nora before looking up and briefly scanning the room. She smiled warmly at an elderly woman and nodded congenially at the man with the red rimmed eyes before scowling darkly when her eyes met Nora's. Nora quickly hid her face in the sleeve of her mother's coat.

The nurse picked up a file and walked from

behind the reception desk. "Mr. Roberts, follow me please."

The red-rimmed eyes of an elderly, oversized man squinted as he smiled in satisfaction while he heaved his weight out of his chair and stabilized his balance before following the nurse down the short corridor and into the examining room.

Matilda settled in for the long wait. Her body felt exhausted and achy. She closed her eyes and allowed herself to drift off and reminisce about the happier times and the life she had led in Ireland. Matilda was reveling in memories of the warmth, gaiety and excitement that she experienced at the last festival she attended before they had foolishly left her beloved Ireland, the Feast of St. Michael, when her attention was yanked back toward the infant she held in her arms as the buxom nurse in crisp white attire, abruptly ordered them to follow her into the pediatric examination room. The nurse barely harbored a look of disdain for the haggard looking trio as they trailed behind her into the small, bright room.

Nora gaped in awe at her surroundings; such bright and vivid colors! The wallpaper sported cartoon animals of all shapes and sizes. The table where her mother laid her sister was located in the center of the room, allowing the doctor freedom to move around it. A teddy bear mobile dangled above one end of the table, offering entertainment for small patients.

Nora sucked the warm air into her lungs as her eyes opened even wider to view the tall man in a white jacket entering the room. Ignoring her, he walked briskly toward the table and immediately began to examine her baby sister, Caitlin.

Matilda and the doctor spoke in hushed whispers. Nora sensed panic in the voice of her mother and concern in the voice of the doctor.

"Will she be alright doctor?" pleaded Matilda. She wanted to know, yet was afraid of the answer.

"Time will tell; time will tell. I am sorry you didn't get her here at the first onset of the fever. We have seen cases, when treated early enough, where the patient escapes any repercussions to the body and grows up strong and healthy. But this child is barely breathing and her heart sounds weak. I will give you something to keep her comfortable and we will start her on an antibiotic and then we pray. That is the best I can do for you."

Nora grabbed the hem of her mother's coat as she looked in the corner of the room at the two brilliantly glowing women standing in the corner. Their beautiful longs gowns shimmered of a pastel rainbow when they moved, yet appeared linen white when still.

She tried to get her mother's attention to point these beautiful ladies out, but to no avail.

The women looked down at Nora with warm and friendly smiles. Their eyes twinkled with a starlight effect. The scent emanating from them was of a flower she had smelled long ago. It was the scent of honeysuckle; like what was growing outside her baby sister's window. As they approached, the scent grew stronger.

Nora looked down at the hems of their gowns and was amazed to note that they where a few inches above the floor. She could see no feet under their gowns and wondered how these ladies where able to float like that. They stopped in front of her and she experienced a warm, soothing feeling of comfort that she had never felt before. It was so peaceful and gentle. Nora's head became light and it was difficult to focus as the glowing women continued on toward the baby on the table.

The doctor and her mother remained deep in conversation; oblivious to the women picking up her sister. Oddly enough, Nora felt no urge to speak. She remained planted in one spot, dreamily watching the two women as they raised their arms, holding Caitlin high toward the ceiling. Her sister was silent and motionless.

As the women lowered the infant, enormous glowing wings of brilliant gold appeared from behind their backs and enfolded the trio. It was difficult to know how long they remained like that. Nora seemed lost in time and space, mesmerized by the vision before her. Her mother and the doctor kept on talking.

The glowing women lowered their wings and placed the small child back on the table and she moved slightly while a small whimper from her tiny lips immediately caught the attention of the doctor and her mother. They seemingly ignored the glowing ladies who stood quietly and watched as the doctor examined Caitlin one more time. He turned to her mother, pleased and surprised with his findings.

Matilda began to cry and Nora reached up to comfort her teary eyed mother. She received a loving hug as her mother's gentle voice in her ear whispered, "These are tears of joy, my darling. Your sister will be fine. Caitlin will be fine!"

As they turned to leave the room, Nora looked back for one more view of the two beautiful glowing women, but saw no one. They had left as quietly as they had arrived. She made no mention of them to her mother and as time passed by, the beautiful glowing ladies became a faded memory.

~

One month later, while checking on the peacefully sleeping infant, Matilda peered into the room to discover a bright glowing woman bent over Caitlin's crib. The woman's billowing dress rippled with the colors of a pastel rainbow as she slowly passed her hands over the infant. She reminded Matilda of an angel from one of the fairy tales her mother had entertained her with during her childhood. Not feeling compelled to enter the room, she dreamily returned to her bed for the most complete and deepest rest she had experienced in years. When she awoke in the morning, Matilda recalled her dream and smiled.

ONE

The brilliant sun glistened off the morning dew of the roof top of the old nineteenth century, Pennsylvania estate house. Caitlin had risen early to survey the damage the years of neglect had done to the structure. Although the weathered exterior cried out for paint and there where random spots where the wood along the awnings appeared as if it would crumble to the touch, as well as several windows that where broken and those that where not appeared to be crammed into the wall at an angle, the structure itself was still solid and sound.

Caitlin held her head to the side and at an angle, as she viewed her dream house. Catching herself at this, she gave a slight chuckle. Purchasing this charming estate house only a few short weeks ago was a dream come true for her and she was not at all deterred by the immense work that needed to be done. Her friend, Arthur, had assured her that the structure, although needing much work, was basically sound. She was young and healthy and full of excitement and fully intended to take pleasure out of giving this fabulous old beauty a face lift!

The shrill whinny of her chestnut mare, Emma, caught her attention and she whirled around just in time to move out of the way of the racing beast. I really must do something about the fencing here, she thought.

Emma pranced proudly around her, rutting the soft moist ground with her hoof marks Spring was everywhere. The mountains were streaming the excess water from the melted snow down to the valley below. It appeared her house was in direct line and the ground stayed soft and moist as a result.

Caitlin reached up to pat Emma's muzzle as the mare gently shoved her owner off into the direction of the barn. It was feeding time and Emma new that if she did not prompt Caitlin out of her daze there may be no breakfast! Caitlin had a way of drifting off for long periods of time, with little recall of what had occurred or of the time that had passed. After having been with Caitlin for six years, Emma had become familiar with this and simply remained persistent in her efforts to regain Caitlin's attention, especially now that she was no longer in a stable and could not rely on others to step in when Caitlin stepped out!

The pungent smell of old cow manure that commingled with fresh horse manure flew at Caitlin as she entered the old barn. The stable had long been torn down, leaving only the dairy barn for shelter. The far corner had been cleaned and converted to accommodate Emma, but the major portion of the barn was still in dire need of cleaning and renovating. Bales of precariously balanced hay peeked down from the loft.

The tiny mouse skirting across the floor produced a startled squeal from Caitlin and she jumped back, shuddering. But Emma never flinched from the drama before her. The mare had grown accustomed to the response her mistress always had at the appearance of little things scurrying around her. She impatiently nudged her feed bucket in an attempt to bring Caitlin back to what was priority; breakfast!

Caitlin's body trembled. She had always had an unexplainable fear of mice and snakes. She was unable to control her reactions when one was in sight. Her friend Sally had offered repeatedly to treat these fears with hypnosis, but she had never taken the time. As her heart struggled to regain a steady beat, she thought that perhaps it was time to give Sally a call and take her up on her offer.

As she scooped the grain into Emma's feeding bucket, a quick flash of something moving caught the corner of her eye. Chills covered her body as she looked around and could find nothing there. "Again!", she moaned out loud. "I'm so tired of this, when will it end?"

Caitlin had seen things through the corner of her eye most of her life and although mice and snakes unnerved her, these chance sightings were little more than an annoyance. She returned to the task of feeding her mare and then wandered slowly back to the house. Today was the day she was going to go into the village to take a look around.

Caitlin had moved into the house over a month ago but had not yet ventured into the small village that rested in the heart of the valley, five miles east. She had been content to and explore her new home; riding Emma to the country store one mile away to purchase any of the staples she might need.

Caitlin was a tall girl of Irish descent. Long firelight curls hugged her face and fell well below her shoulders in wild abandonment. Her large, finely muscled frame afforded her the strength to accomplish daunting tasks that most women would buckle under. Yet, for all her strength and power, she managed to retain an air of femininity that brought men flocking when she was near. She was once described as being very charismatic; not only to the male gender, but in general. People either gravitated toward her, or they remained distant and in awe. There seemed no in between.

Caitlin had the type of personality that made her easy to get along with. Those who did not where generally controlling and frustrated at the lack of response they got from her. She sported a *'live and let live'* philosophy that most control freaks found unappealing.

Mitch was one of those control freaks. Caitlin had met him through a colleague of hers about two years ago. His solid, muscled body drew her attention long before he had crossed the room. Mitch's bulk was fluid and graceful beneath his white linen shirt. His rolled sleeves exposed broad strong forearms, coated with thick dark curls. When he shook her hand in greeting, she felt him struggle to maintain an easy pressure; as if at any moment he could squeeze the life force out of her. The chemistry between them was undeniable and they quickly fell into a passionate affair that lasted about eighteen months.

Eventually, Mitch began to place demands on Caitlin that she found undesirable and she slowly to pulled back. The more she pulled back, the stronger Mitch tried to hold on. It was not long before the relationship soured and the two went their separate ways. Unable to accept this, Mitch has made persistent efforts to reunite.

Unfortunately, their romance may have ended but their work relationship had not and he was now telephoning her about their most recent project.

Caitlin held her stomach with one hand as she verified it was him on her caller ID and raised the receiver with the other. She found her conversations with Mitch more and more unsettling as time went by. She often pondered over the fascination of how someone can be so incredibly wrapped up and taken by an individual one day, and the next day be completely repulsed by even the sound of their voice.

Taking a deep breath in resignation, Caitlin answered flatly, " Hello Mitch."

"Well, I see you at least have caller ID out there in no man's land. How interesting. And what other modern amenities might we find? A sink? A toilet? Running water?" There was no denying the sarcasm in Mitch's voice.

"Okay," she sighed, "You got your dig in for the day. So, what's up. Did I leave something out of the envelope I expressed?"

"No, the drawings where fine. You're a true artist." Caitlin was lulled into a false sense of easiness by Mitch's flattery, until he continued. "I was just sitting here thinking about the great time we had last year in the mountains at Charlie's cabin. Do you remember?"

Caitlin remained silent. She should have known that Mitch would not stop with a simple complement. He was so bent on getting his own way that he sometimes acted like an obsessed man. And, since it was Caitlin who ended the relationship and not Mitch, he was determined to get her back.

Of course she remembered. It was wild and sensual. She often thought back on that time. But it was time to move on and make new memories. What was the point in this conversation? She was just about to ask when he broke the silence. "Hello? Caitlin? Are you there?"

"Yes I'm here and yes I remember. What's your point?" Her tone was a little more brisk than she had intended.

"I just thought it might be nice to take another trip back there. Just you and me, like the last time. Or we can take William and Hilary if you insist."

There was something in Mitch's voice that made Caitlin leery. His words where friendly enough, but there seemed like there was a hidden motive behind them. Until now, she had looked at Mitch as annoying, but harmless. But now, she just did not know. The feeling she was experiencing was one of fearful apprehension; something she could neither justify or explain.

A cool breeze came from out of nowhere,

causing Caitlin to shiver uncontrollably. She glanced around in time to catch the curtains flowing in the living room, even though the windows and doors were tightly closed. The right side of her body shriveled, taking most of the chill, while the left remained relaxed. She made a mental note to check the windows for proper insulation before the cold weather set in.

"No thanks Mitch. I have a lot to do here before I go back to work full swing. And besides, I'm privileged enough to be able to enjoy the beautiful country side right in my own home. I don't need to climb to a mountain top to do it! But you go ahead and go... it will do you good, I'm sure." Caitlin responded warily. The chills where still plaguing her right side. Where was that breeze coming from?

"Well", Mitch sighed, obviously aggravated with being turned down again. "I guess I will be the judge of how beautiful your countryside is myself. Even though you haven't paid me the courtesy of an invitation since you moved in, William has asked me to drive out with him for the weekend so that we can go over the Wiley account. It seems he needs my input. So, we can pick up on this conversation again later:"

Caitlin's stomach contracted as Mitch's words assaulted her ears. He sounded like a cat baiting his mouse. How frustrating!

Well, she sighed, there was nothing she could do about it. She should have known better than to start a relationship with a business partner. Now she had to pay the price.

"And where are you staying?" She blurted out coldly; frustration filling her words.

"What kind of a question is that? Don't you have room in that big house? How many bedrooms are there, anyway? Oh yes, eight, correct? And you would be so rude as to make me stay in a motel, out in God know's where?" There was a chuckle in the undertone of his voice. He had managed to get to her and was savoring every minute of her irritation.

The chill that covered Caitlin's right side became an unbearable freezing ache. She wheeled around to get a sweeping view of her surroundings. It was approaching summer, yet this cold felt like winter! As her eyes swept the room in search of the source of the draft, she stopped, motionless, as if the cold had frozen her solid. Not even her eyelids would move as she looked directly into the eyes of an elderly man dressed in a flannel shirt and denim jeans. His large brown, clouded eyes scowled, yet she did not feel frightened; for she knew the scowl was meant for Mitch and not her. She did not know why she knew; she just knew.

When Caitlin finally blinked her eyes, the old man was gone.

She regained her faculties and snipped at Mitch, "I have to go. Stay where you like."

Caitlin slammed the receiver back into the cradle. The breeze had stopped and her body was warm again. What had just happened? Who was that man and where had he come from" And better yet, where did he go? Her mind was racing.

Her legs were feeling weak and shaky as she ran frantically around the house, checking all of the windows and locks. She opened closet doors and pounded on the walls in them, listening for a hollow sound. Sometimes these old houses had hidden rooms. Maybe this house had a hidden room and this man was living in it!

The remainder of her day was spent searching for the mystery man. After combing the entire house, attic and cellar, she proceeded to investigate the outbuildings. Her nearest neighbor was quite a distance away and there had been no signs of anyone coming up the driveway. This man had to be on the property somewhere. But where?

It was dusk before her search was interrupted by William's Cherokee bouncing down the drive with Mitch cursing his indignation loudly.

Emma raced up to greet them, kicking her heels with wild delight. William smiled affectionately. He enjoyed the beauty of this magnificent beast. The setting sun created shadows that bounced off the Emma's powerful muscles as she flexed them proudly. She was a beautiful sight.

William leapt out of the jeep and began stroking Emma's neck as she pushed him off balance with her nose. Laughingly he put a little more swing behind his stokes, understanding her commands completely. He often joked that she was half human.

Mitch got out of the vehicle more cautiously than William. He was not fond of animals, particularly ones that were larger than he was; not to mention the fact that this one was more than a little strange. Whoever heard of a horse that wandered around free like a dog? This was one of the little quirks about Caitlin that drove Mitch crazy. She insisted on treating her animals like they where people. He was about to make a sarcastic remark when he saw Caitlin running toward them down the drive.

"William!" She squealed with delight as she flew into his arms. The muscles in Mitch's face hardened as he stood in the background watching. *She's never greeted me like that*, he mused.

"Hey sis!" He laughed. "Damn girl, you're sure getting skinny! What have you been doing, eating grass with Emma?"

"Oh, yes, I noticed just this morning that my clothes are getting a little loose. But, you know how hard it is for me to keep the weight on and on top of that I've been pretty preoccupied around here. I keep forgetting to eat. For the last few days I've been keeping Emma's feeding schedule, since she's so good about reminding me. So when I feed her, I feed me. It works!"

"So, does that mean that we all have grain for dinner?" Mitch growled, barely able to contain his hostility. When he was away from Caitlin, he missed her unbearably. But, when he would find himself in her presence he could not hold down the hostility he felt over her rejection of him.. Which, of course, made things worse between them. It was a vicious cycle.

William turned towards Mitch, with Caitlin still cradled in his arms, and quietly, but in an authoritative manner, stated, "We will behave like adults this weekend, all of us. Let's try our best to get along. The Wiley project is due on the first and we are no way near being ready for presentation... so... let's get this monkey off our backs and get back to enjoying life!"

Caitlin and Mitch had been glowering at each other while William was working at keeping the piece. Suddenly, Caitlin let out a long groan. "Oh no! I am so sorry! I can't believe this!"

"What?" William asked smugly, as if he already knew the answer.

"I got involved with something this morning and I don't know where the time went! I never made it to town like I had planned and I have zip for dinner! Oh, God, how could I be so stupid. I'm so sorry." Caitlin pulled away from William in despair. This was a common reaction for her when she was upset with something she had done. More than once, William had joked about it with Caitlin, telling her that she needed no critics because she was critical enough.

William winked at Mitch as he reached into the back seat of the Cherokee and produced Chinese take out. He held it proudly before Caitlin while they all smiled.

At that moment, Emma interrupted to remind them that, at feeding time, she came first. They all laughed and Caitlin told her brother and ex-lover to go to the house while she followed Emma to the barn, assuring them that she would not be long.

As the men entered the old estate house, a bitter chill swept over Mitch. It was the feeling of winter in late spring; a feeling that permeated his bones, making him more than a little uneasy. He surveyed the small entrance way, looking for the source of the draft, but found nothing. *Caitlin must be positioned on the hillside where there is a cross current or something*, he mused, as he entered the living room.

TWO

Mitch had woken up with a stiffness throughout his body. His sleep had been choppy and uncomfortable and his every muscle ached. He had experienced a cold chill throughout his body all through the night. He scowled as he entered the room where Caitlin and William where already sitting enjoying their morning coffee.

The early morning sun shining through the French doors of the breakfast nook brought out the charm of the old estate home. Caitlin was working on restoring the woodwork to the original look and had discovered a method of repairing and cleaning the wallpaper from a "how to" show on public access television. She beamed proudly at her handiwork as Mitch surveyed the surroundings. Knowing that Mitch was not appreciative of anything that was old, she doubted that he would appreciate her efforts or see the value in the restored rooms.

"There's coffee in the kitchen," Caitlin announced brightly, "and some croissants with butter and jam. If you want oatmeal or eggs, help yourself."

Caitlin observed Mitch as he quietly turned

toward the kitchen. His strong muscular body rippled when he walked and his unruly curls where in need of a good combing; although there where signs of an attempt by him to bring some semblance of order to them by possibly running his fingers through them. His pants where crisply creased and his Armani shirt gleamed of newness. He was indeed a contrast to this old house with its faded wallpaper and worn wooden floors.

William's violent coughing seized Caitlin's attention. She paused briefly in confusion as she looked into his face. Her brother's eyes where watering and his cheeks where a bright red trimmed in white. His thin lips, that peered out beneath his strawberry blonde mustache, where turning a deep purple. He was choking on his food! She raced behind him and began the Heimlich maneuver, giving thanks to Nora for insisting she take CPR in high school.

The food was dislodged and William slowly returned to his natural state, feeling a little sheepish that such a thing had happened.

Mitch, who had returned to see what all the commotion was about, stood before William with coffee in one hand and croissant in the other. "Are you alright man?"

William responded with a wave of his hand and a meek smile as he held up the magazine he had been flipping through. Mitch laughed hysterically when William pointed to a full page picture of a nude woman. Shaking his head, he snatched up the magazine and walked out onto the patio to view it more fully. The wicker chair moaned under his bulk as he eased himself down.

"It serves you right, William." Caitlin scowled, as she went about cleaning up the dishes. "Didn't you see enough of that when you where dating Susan?"

"I'm in shock that she would do that," William mused, "She was such a prude when we where together. What the hell happened?"

"That was three years ago, brother dear. A lot can happen to a person to change them in three years. Besides, I said it then and I still say it. I think the prude thing was a show for you and you alone."

"Well," chuckled Mitch from the patio, "there's nothing prudish about the chick now. Damn William, are those real?"

"I guess," William grumbled, a little put out to have this hulk of a man out on the patio drooling over the woman he once loved. The woman he still loved; or at least he thought he did. "I'm going to take a quick walk outside. Does anybody want to join me?"

Caitlin and Mitch joined in a simultaneous "I will". The two stopped and looked at each other before they gave a quick chuckle and followed William outside.

It's a shame Mitch has to be such an idiot, Caitlin mused, *there are times when he can be so cute. If only he would drop the control thing.'*

Caitlin walked contentedly behind the two men, observing the drastic contrast between them. Mitch, with his dark hair and incredible brawn and William, fair and slender.

The trio decided to investigate the old logging trail that wandered up the west side of the wooded hillside. Caitlin had been curious about it since she had first arrived but the realtor had been firm with her warnings about the perils that awaited anyone who ventured down the path. Although Caitlin felt the realtor was being a little dramatic, she was still wary about exploring the path alone. If there was really an abundance of lifeless trees and sliding boulders, as the woman had stressed, it would be irresponsible not to travel in pairs; just incase of an injury. So, she had waited for William to arrive before exploring the forbidden territory.

Caitlin found it hard to believe that the path could be in such a condition, since the property bordered on State land. Didn't they take better care of the land than that? Surely the realtor was exaggerating. More than likely she had been getting her kicks trying to scare the city folk.

The morning sun had barely penetrated

the thick foliage along the path. The trees
overhead created a covering that allowed the
sun to peek sparingly through them. The
ground was moist from the morning dew,
still thick on the ground. Caitlin's feet sunk
into soft ground, layered with compost from
fallen leaves and branches. There where animal droppings along the path, which she
assumed were from the deer that came out
each morning to graze.

Loud crunching came up behind her and
she turned to see Emma casually following
along. Caitlin smiled at her mare. She was
such good company that Caitlin had to remind herself that this was a horse and not
a human. Noticing that Emma was in full
tack, Caitlin shrugged at her negligence.
She had been almost in saddle for an early
morning ride when William had called her
in need of his breakfast. She had fully intended to return to Emma for that ride, but
obviously forgot. But, Emma seemed not to
mind and Caitlin would make sure to remove
it as soon as they returned to the house.

As they approached a small clearing, William pointed out a wooden structure that
resembled a tiny house. As they made their
way closer, they recognized it to be an old
well house. Delighted with their discovery,
Caitlin ran on ahead, with Emma not far behind.

It was obvious, by the amount of decay to

the wood and the plant life that had grown around the structure that the well had not been used in a long time.

"Be careful Caitlin!", William called, "You don't know how sound that thing is. And with all this junk on the ground, there's no telling what you're stepping on."

Before William had finished his warning, a loud crack echoed off the hillside, the ground opened up, and Caitlin disappeared. The only sign that she had been there was the small patch of her torn shirt that had caught on the wood as she fell through. Emma reared, squealing loudly while backing up quickly to free herself from harm's way.

William raced, panic stricken, toward the gaping hole in the ground that contained his sister while Mitch froze in his tracks, completely taken aback by the scene before him.

Staring in disbelief, visions of Caitlin flashed before Mitch. He saw her laughing at the fountain last spring, completely immersed in the brutally cold water as she squealed with delight. He thought of her soft pale skin as she lay beneath him, soft pillows framing her childlike face. He remembered her racing through the fields on Emma, her long curls flowing in wild abandonment.

William's bellowing cries brought Mitch back to reality and immediately into motion. He plunged forward.

"Caitlin! God, I can't see her! My God! Oh God!" William turned to Mitch frantically, "Mitch, run back and call for help! Call 911. Call 9-1-1 and hurry!"

Caitlin's mare would have been hard pressed to keep up with Mitch as he pushed his sculpted body into action while William collapsed into a ball on the ground.

~

Caitlin stroked Emma's neck while she watched Mitch stare into the leaves of the trees. How fascinating! The trees where acting as a movie screen and there she was in full view. She saw herself in that cold fountain. She recalled fondly how he had tried to coax Mitch into the water with her, trying to convince him that it was not as cold as it really was, but he would not take the bait.

Then they where making love. Mitch's incredible body was covering hers. She always felt so small when she was in his arms.

And then, oh the freedom of wings underneath her body as she and Emma raced through the fields. It gave her a feeling of wild abandonment.

William's tormented cry caught Caitlin's attention and waves of sympathy filled her. She longed to reach out and comfort him, but her body would not obey. Suddenly very cold, she snuggled Emma for warmth as she watched her brother agonize at what had just happened.

As Mitch flew past her, his muscles working at optimum. She drew a deep breath of despair as she saw her brother fall to the ground, seemingly lifeless.

"Oh Emma," she cried, "I have to help him, but I can't move. I don't understand it!"

To her surprise, as she looked into Emma's eye words formed in her mind and she knew they where the words of Emma. She felt waves of energy penetrating her forehead as she and Emma communicated. "You are out of your body mistress, you must return before you can help your brother. Go back to your body. I will help to pull you out. I have a rope on my saddle. Do you remember? Go back now and we will help you."

Suddenly, the world was a flash of light. Bright colors of the rainbow flew by in tiny flecks. Caitlin was reminded of driving through an intense snow storm, except the snow was colored. Pain shot throughout her rib cage as she gasped for air.

~

A small cry escaped Caitlin's lips that causing William to raise his head. "Caitlin honey, are you okay?" He cried out as he cautiously crawled closer toward the edge of the hole.

A loud crack shot out beneath him and he backed up quickly.

At that point Emma was behind William, pushing his back with her nose and working her hoofs into the ground. William turned to her and she threw her head toward the rope fastened on the side of the saddle. He stared at it blindly, unable to think clearly. Emma whinnied and tossed her head more aggressively. William finally got the message and reached for the rope. He tied one end around his waist and the other onto the horn of Emma's saddle.

To William's recollection, Emma had no training for what he was about to ask of her and he prayed for help. He prayed to the beautiful Angels his sister Nora used to tell him about when he was a little boy. "Please, if you are really there watching over my Caitlin, please help me. Please." He fought back the tears as he buried his face in Emma's neck who was impatiently working the ground and tossing her head.

William made the sign of the cross over his chest, took a deep breath, and began to slowly feel his way down into the depths of the well. It was dark and foul smelling from an abundance of decay. The jagged edges made an easy grip for him as he inched his way down deeper.

A soft breeze floated past him, carrying with it the sweet scent of honeysuckle. The refreshing difference gave him a boost of energy and optimism as he proceeded downward, calling for Caitlin as he did.

"Help me," Caitlin's moan was barely above a whisper. The pain in her chest prevented her from drawing enough air into her lungs for her to cry out much above a whisper. She could only hope that her brother could hear her. The rank smell in the bottom of the well was making her stomach queasy. She moved her hand and it nudged the remains of a raccoon that had met its fate here, not fortunate enough to have rescue. She shuddered with repulsion when she realized what she was touching and quickly pulled back her hand.

It seemed like eternity before William reached Caitlin. He growled with disgust as he kicked the decayed remains of the raccoon aside and knelt beside his sister's body. She seemed so frail and lifeless. He cradled her head in his arms and whispered gently, "I'm here honey, I'm here. I'll get you out."

William tried to remember how he had learned to tie a rescue noose in scouts. Damn, how was it done? He began playing with the rope, panic mounting. Suddenly a calm swept his body and his hands just began maneuvering the rope around his sister and then himself. It was as if they had a life of their own. He lifted her gently to him, wincing with the cries that escaped her pale lips, and commanded Emma to start backing up.

To his surprise, Emma smoothly and steadily worked the rope, leaving little for William to do except cradle his sister as they gently where pulled to the top. *Amazing,* William thought, *Emma is pulling us with the grace and power of two big draft horses*! Again, the beautiful soothing scent of honeysuckle swept past him.

The sound of his Cherokee coming up the path got clearer as Emma continued to pull William and Caitlin to safety. Leaves and mud flew as Mitch screeched the vehicle to a quick stop and leapt out from it. He rushed to help Emma during the final stages of the pull.

As William and Caitlin came into sight, Mitch reached forward and grasped Caitlin beneath the arms. He lifted her high, like a tiny child, and lowered her gently to the ground. Mitch then turned to William and lifted him out with equal ease. Beads of sweat coated Mitch's face and his breathing was labored. He had not stopped to think about what he was doing. He had just kicked his body into gear and done what needed to be done. Now, as he rested for the first time since the nightmare began, his muscles cried out from the strain. He had heard of situations where people had used super human strength and where even able to lift things like cars up in a crisis and he had just experienced that ability now. Mitch fell back onto the soft moist ground ignoring the tiny leaves and twigs that pierced through his clothing.

William bent over Caitlin, nervously. Her face had a pale grayish appearance and her lips where a faint purple-blue. He feared that if she did not get help immediately, they would lose her. "Did you call for help?" He barked, a little more gruffly than intended.

Mitch let the tone of William's voice slide, since he too was tense, and answered briefly, "Yes, they should be here any minute. Should we take her to the house? I don't know. What do you do in a situation like this? Should we move her, or wait?'

"How hard was it to get the jeep up here? Can they make it?" William looked anxiously at the muddy path.

"Not easily, I was sliding in this slimy shit a lot." Mitch shook his head. He doubted the ambulance would be able to get up the hill. They would be foolish to try.

William was having the same thoughts. "Then, let's take her back to the house. I don't want to risk them getting stuck coming in here. Come on, help me get her into the back of the jeep. Lower the back seat, will you?"

Mitch rose to his feet and did as asked. He

no longer had the speed or the power in his body and it felt like he was pumping lead through his veins as he struggled with each movement.

Mitch completed his task while William pulled a blanket from the back of the Jeep and spread it onto the ground, near Caitlin. "Let's carry her in this Mitch. Maybe it will help to balance her weight and not jog her as much. Help me get her on . Here, you take that side."

They eased Caitlin onto the blanket. As the two men wrapped her tightly, their hands brushed and William grabbed Mitch by the wrist in a firm hold. Their eyes met. William's expression of gratitude and friendship caused a lump to form in Mitch's throat and he muttered quietly "Come on buddy, On the count of three". William released Mitch, nodded and they carefully moved Caitlin into the back of the Cherokee .

THREE

Caitlin lay peacefully in her bed. She had been released from the hospital that morning and it was wonderful to be home. Her sister Nora, who had flown in from Arizona the a few days before, entered the room with her hands tightly gripping the bed tray she had prepared for Caitlin. The aroma of Nora's home made chicken soup and freshly baked bread filled the room. Caitlin's senses where instantly aroused and her stomach announced it with a loud rumble.

"Yum, Nora, that sure smells delightful. I can't tell you how bad that hospital food was." Caitlin giggled as she watched her sister struggle with the heavily laden tray. "Careful, Nora, you're spilling my salvation. You never where good with carrying trays. It's no wonder they fired you from that waitress job at Johnny's café."

"Pick on me and I'll send you back to the hospital," Nora teased. Her big doe-like eyes twinkled with delight as she viewed her sister in the bed. Caitlin, who had just narrowly escaped death from the fall she took into the old well, was rapidly regaining her strength and vigor. Her once pale cheeks sported a warm, rosy glow. It would not be long before she was up and around again.

"Oh please, anything but that!" Caitlin feigned despair.

Nora gently placed the bed tray across Caitlin's lap and then busied herself by reaching behind her sister and patting more fluff into her pillow in an attempt to provide more support for her back.

Nora was the eldest of the three siblings. Since the death of their mother, Matilda, ten years ago, Nora, at the tender age of eighteen, had assumed the role of caretaker for her younger brother and sister. Despite the unexpected trials and tribulations that surfaced more often than she would have liked, she had handled it quite well and had somehow managed to keep the family together.

Caitlin was thirteen at the time of her mother's death. They never spoke about it and all of the pictures of her father had been removed from the house long before she was old enough to even know what a father was. Her mother was a nervous soul, who eventually grew to handle life's disappointments with the assistance of a bottle. Her mother's alcoholism and his own drinking habit, combined with his failure to succeed in the business world, eventually prompted Caitlin's frustrated and beaten father to disappear. Of course, this only served to drive

Matilda further into the sanctuary of a bottle.

Nora had learned early how to care for herself and her brother and sister. She was the only mother figure Caitlin could remember.

Caitlin watched her sister fondly as she bustled about the room; opening windows, shifting draperies and picking up loose clothing. She turned to Caitlin and smiled. "I had a lovely sleep last night, dear; except that there is a terrible breeze in my room. It's fine now, because it is soon to be summer, but I think you really need to tend to it before the winter months come." Nora reached forward and patted Caitlin's knee, "But we'll discuss that later, when you are well again. I have to go to prepare dinner, William is arriving tonight and will be like a bear if he doesn't have a nice meal when he gets here."

Nora loved drama and often slid it into her life experiences. Caitlin knew that William would be anything but a bear if there was no dinner ready, but being able to make believe seemed to comfort Nora; so she said nothing. William tolerated it as well. He had always felt a kind of pity for his older sister. She had been placed in a situation very demanding at such a young age. He felt her youth was taken from her, when she assumed the responsibilities of family caretaker. Maybe even before, since her mother had relied heavily on Nora to keep the house up and care for her siblings while she was alive. How Nora had managed to keep them together and not dispersed in foster homes after their mother had died, William never understood. Nora had certain things she placed on the 'do not discuss' list, and this topic was one of them.

"How is your novel coming along?" Caitlin asked quietly between spoonfuls of the delicious soup. "What's it about? I can't remember."

The novel is coming along fine, honey. In fact, it is almost done. And you can't remember what it is about, because I did not tell you. But nice try sweetheart!"

Caitlin heaved an impatient sigh and began to dive into her fare with even more gusto. She hated secrets. Nora had a habit of refusing to divulge the theme of her novels until they were in print. Then, Caitlin and William would get special edition copies. It was a sort of ritual with her that frustrated Caitlin. She could not understand where Nora was coming from with her superstitions. Just once she would like to be able to know the plot before hand.

Nora continued bustling about while Caitlin ate her food.   She loaded her arms with soiled clothing and she turned to Caitlin, "I'll be back to clear that away in a bit, honey. If you need anything before then, I placed a small bell on the night stand. Isn't that cute?"

Nora's giggling shifted to sweet singing as she made her way down the once majestic stairway to the laundry room with her bundle.

As Caitlin finished off the last of the homemade bread, using it as a sponge to absorb the remains of the chicken broth, she felt that all too familiar chill again on her body. When she looked toward the window, a flash caught the corner of her eye. Unable to follow to investigate, she could only lay there, barely breathing. Then he appeared. The same man who had appeared the day before her accident. He was standing still, completely still, watching her; simply watching her.

"Who are you?" Caitlin broke the silence.

The old man stood motionless.

"What do you want? Where did you come from?" The harshness in Caitlin's whisper hinted at the panic within her that was beginning to peak as the man continued to just stare. Who was this man and how did he get in here? Was he a thief, a rapist, a murderer? The fact that he just stood there, staring at her, was unnerving enough, but what were his plans? Why was he here?

Caitlin scrambled for the little bell that Nora had left on the night stand and began swinging it wildly. When she turned back to check on the man's response to this, he was gone.

"What's the matter?" Breathlessly, Nora rushed into the room. The way the bell had been ringing, she was not sure what to expect when she entered. The sight of her sister's pale, frozen expression stopped her in her tracks.

Nora looked in the direction of Caitlin's stare, but saw only the curtains flowing in the summer breeze. The sweet smell of honeysuckle filled the room. She did not recall Caitlin mentioning having honeysuckle on the grounds. Satisfied that all was well, she allowed herself a few moments to enjoy the sweet aroma that filled the room; which was why she did not immediately notice that the windows were still closed.

Seeing that Caitlin was obviously distraught, Nora made a mental note to remind her sister to have the house weatherproofed before winter before she moved to Caitlin's side and wrapped her in her arms.

By the time William had arrived a few hours later, things had calmed down and gotten back into order. Nora sat quietly on the patio watching the sunset when William approached her from behind and placed his hands on her shoulders. They remained as if suspended in time, neither one willing to speak and break the silence filled the air while they reveled in the beauty of the fiery orange ball as it slowly made its way behind the trees.

William had often marveled at such wonders of nature. When he was a small child, he would sit in Nora's lap while they waited for their mother to return home and watch the stars. Nora used to point out the constellations to him as she had learned them in school.

"It looks pretty clear out tonight. Let's open a bottle of wine and relax out here for awhile." William suggested, wrapping his arms affectionately around Nora's neck and resting his cheek against her cheek. "And, if you're a good girl, I'll let you tell me all about the stars; like you did when we where kids." He chuckled and he gave her a quick kiss on the cheek.

"Oh yea?" Nora laughed and lovingly patted her brother's hands. The bond between them was a warm and loving one. She was grateful that they had all remained so close. In so many cases like their's it has not been the case. "I feel honored." She rose and made her way to the wine rack in the corner of the dining room. "Let's see what kind of stock our dear sister has."

While the two siblings settled in for a quiet evening of star watching and wine, Caitlin was not so peaceful. She had fallen into a deep sleep, taking with her that disturbing feeling that she'd had since the man had appeared in her room that afternoon. She tossed uncomfortably as she relived the experience of the well.

For the first time since the accident, Caitlin recalled the way she was able to see Mitch's vision in the trees and communicate with Emma, as if she was human. She relived the piercing pain of re-entering her body and bolted up in bed; her entire body trembling as she gasped for air like she had done while in the well.

The room was abnormally dark and Caitlin could barely see her hand in front of her. Nora, feeling Caitlin needed as much undisturbed rest as possible, had taken great pains to tightly secure the drapes over the window to prevent any evening air coming in through the cracks and to help muffle any outside noises.

Suddenly, in the corner of the room, where she had seen the man standing, a glow began to appear. This time there was no fear in Caitlin as she watched a figure in biblical robes slowly and regally step out of the ball. It reminded her of the science fiction movies where the people travel through time and slowly re-materialize.

Unable to see anything but the robe, she sensed that this robed figure was a man. He glowed like firelight in such a way that she was surprised not to feel heat radiating from him. The faint smell of honeysuckle filled the air. She peered as best she could, but was unable to see the face that was protected by the hood of a rich, blue cloak; pulled down over it, as if to deliberately hide it.

"Hello?" Caitlin heard her words yet she never uttered a sound. The words seemed to be flowing from her mind, not her mouth.

"Greetings, my beloved. May the grace and peace of the eternal One be upon you." His words floated to her on petals of honeysuckle, creating a soothing calm throughout her entire body. And then the vision was gone.

Caitlin stared at the corner of the room while the light faded and the room went dark again. This time, she did not ring the bell on the night stand, but, instead, went peacefully off to sleep; the scent of honeysuckle filling the air.

~

Caitlin's body felt weightless as she drifted off to sleep. The dark room around her gradually receded and she soon found herself floating. Cloud-like wisps surrounded her. *I must be in a cloud. I can't see a thing. But I think I'm in a cloud.* Just then she felt a pulling on her shoulders, as if someone was pulling her down. She jolted slightly and then gave into the motion.

As she drifted downward, her surroundings became more visible. Beautiful lakes of an indescribable bluish green glistened and shimmered, reflecting the intense green of the leaves on the trees. The colors where clear and sharp; nothing like she had ever seen before. On the edge of the water stood the cloaked man. The brilliant fabric of the cloak glistened with what appeared to be tiny strands of gold and silver. When he moved he created a magnificent sight.

The grip on Caitlin's shoulders loosened and she found herself standing firmly in a field of flowers of incredible beauty and grace. Beds of roses without their thorns, coupled with lilacs and lilies, seemed to stretch on into nothingness. Oblivious to whether it was their season or not, they simply coexisted in this massive field.

As the flowers gently brushed her bare calves, she experienced a sensation of security and happiness that exceeded anything she had ever felt before. She felt so calm and tranquil that she vowed she could remain there forever

The figure in the cloak stood patiently watching her. Although he made no motion to her, she somehow new she should approach him. Slowly, and with surprising confidence, she worked her way across the field of luscious flowers to the edge of the water where he stood.

This time, his face was clearly visible. It was a gentle face. Clean and free of any facial hair and milky soft in appearance. It bore no wrinkles and seem free of worry or anger. His eyes where the deepest bluish green she had ever seen. They reminded her of the water that they stood next to.

As Caitlin approached him, he smiled and said softly. "Greetings my beloved. You are most welcome."

The fact that Caitlin simply stared at him in wonderment did not seem to trouble him at all and his twinkling eyes watched patiently, waiting for her to finish drinking in his sight. Finally, she responded, "Who are you and where am I?"

"I am Lael. I come from the council of twelve. This is not twelve in number, but in vibration. I have been with you since before your conception, my beloved, and I will continue to be with you while you walk this planet and thereafter. We are eternally bonded." His words where a gentle soothing song to her ears.

As she absorbed there meaning, Caitlin realized that Lael's mouth had not moved! He was communicating with her through her mind, like Emma had done. Only, this time there was no pressure on her forehead from the thought waves penetrating. The words floated gently and clearly into her head.

"I have been waiting for you to come, so that we may begin our work together." Lael continued, "But the wait has not been long, dear one. You are progressing nicely."

Caitlin had no idea what type of work he could

be talking about. She marveled at how she felt no fear in his presence. She actually felt incredibly secure. But, should she be so complaisant about things? Shouldn't she be questioning things instead of reveling in wondrous relaxation? Such as where was she was and exactly what the heck was going on? Who was this Lael and what did he mean when he said that he had been with her since conception and that they were bonded for eternity?

Caitlin knit her brows together as she tried to make sense of what was happening. Lael gave a little chuckle and gently swept his hand across her face. She felt a slight pressure, but not his touch. The scent of honeysuckle grew stronger as she closed her eyes to revel in the delight of the experience. Never in her life had she felt such joy; such peace and tranquility.

"My title and station is that of Master Teacher", stated Lael. "It is my task to work with you while you are in this growth process. I am honored to assist you in expanding your knowledge of the earth plane and the spiritual plane. Together we will grow." This time Lael's lips moved as he spoke the words. His voice was smooth and gentle, just as Caitlin imagined it would be.

"I'm not sure I understand", stammered Caitlin. She found it difficult to harness the thoughts and form them into sentences.

"This is natural, for you are just awakening to yourself. In time, you will become strong in your understanding and you will be able to share with others what you have learned. In the beginning, you will feel tired from our meetings. I assure you that this is temporary, so please do not be alarmed. You are loved, my beloved. And you are protected. No harm will come to you here. You may call on me at any time, for I am always near. Blessings."

Again Caitlin felt the pull on her body, as if someone was steering her through space. The beautiful surroundings faded and once more she found herself enveloped in what appeared to be a cloud. She hovered in the cloud for a moment before she found herself snuggled safely in her bed.

Caitlin quickly opened her eyes and looked around. The faint dust speckled streams of morning sun that were peeking through the cracks of the fabric barrier that Nora had created, accompanied by the faint singing of the birds, brought a smile to her lips. She stretched in a cat-like manner and rolled over, not quite ready to give up that feeling of euphoria and come back to reality.

~

The trio lived in harmony for the next two weeks while Caitlin steadily regained her health.   Nora and William dove into some much needed house repairs. Nora worked diligently each day, while William drove in from the city on the weekends to do his part.

They repaired a large hole in the fence, much to Emma's dismay, and finished the paint job on the porch that Caitlin had begun.

Caitlin had a slow and methodical way of working, which allowed for the brief *zone outs*, as she called them, that she would experience. Nora, on the other hand, was swift and to the point. She had completed an easy two month's work for Caitlin in the two weeks that she was there.

Nora did not hear Caitlin walking up behind her as she eased herself down into the wicker rocker on the patio, preparing to enjoy yet another magnificent Pennsylvania sunset. Her muscles, unaccustomed to the type of physical labor she had been doing, where aching and her movement was noticeably rigid.

"Are you hurting sis?" Caitlin spoke softly.

"Oh!" Nora jumped. "I didn't hear you coming. You startled me. Yes, I'm sore as hell. But I enjoyed it. I think I am going to see about going home soon. You're pretty well back on the road to recovery and I'm behind on my manuscript. Besides, you still have William."

Caitlin sat on the cool flagstone patio at Nora's feet and lay her head in her sister's lap. She always hated to see Nora leave. Arizona was so far away. "Oh, pooh. It's not fair. I was too sick to even enjoy your stay. Can't you stick around a little longer so we can do a few fun things together. Please?"

"I wish I could, honey. But I took off in such a rush that I left a lot of loose ends and my publishers are screaming for the final chapters of my manuscript. I really need to get back." Nora stroked Caitlin's soft locks while she stared absently out across the shadowy fields at Emma, who was peacefully grazing. "You'll be fine now. And I'll be back before you know it. I still plan on making my regular visit. Don't think this is a substitute."

Caitlin gave a childlike giggle and snuggled deeper into Nora's lap. They stayed there, each one deep in their own thoughts until the chill of the evening penetrated their clothing and they moved inside for warmth.

Nora took a long look around at the interior of the run down estate home. It really did have charm and would be quite a beauty once it was restored. The wallpaper spoke of days gone by. She could almost hear the laughter of the former owners. There where marks on the woodwork leading into the laundry room where they had measured the growth of a small child, from early years and into adulthood. The intricately carved banister boasted style and charm and the slight curve of the stairway leading up to the second floor added grace and elegance. What an unusual estate house for the north, Nora mused. It had the charm of a southern home. She was not aware of such structures on northern farms and estates. It seemed far too grande, even in its run down condition. She was pleased with the effect the little bit of work she and William had done. It was as if the house smiled with gratitude. It was a wonderful home with a friendly feel. Yes, she would be back, and would be happy to do so.

The next morning Nora was packed and saying her good-byes. She was sorry to leave her little family. They had succeeded in knitting together any gaps that may have formed from the distance and time away from each other in the few weeks that she had been there. But she was also ready to get back to complete her manuscript and her normal daily routine. She would be back in July and August; which was her normal time to visit and a welcome escape from the Arizona summers. Her bustling and fussing rang through the house as she did a last minute run with Caitlin and William on the do's and don'ts of life.

"Some things never change." Caitlin chuckled to herself.

It was decided that Caitlin was still not in the best of health to endure the grueling trip to the airport, so she stood waving as William chauffeured her eldest sibling off to destination, JFK.

As the jeep eased its way down the winding drive and tiny puffs of dust rose from beneath the wheels, Caitlin was unexpectedly unnerved as she listened to the silence around her. She could not explain the eerie feeling that came over her as she looked around at the stillness. Seeking the refuge of companionship, Caitlin dashed off toward a pacing Emma, who was clearly not appreciative of the repair work that had been done to the fence.

Struggling over the fence, Caitlin raced to her mare's side. The pungent aroma of the horse's body, mingled with the scent of grass and a hint of manure. Caitlin inhaled deeply, taking in as much of the familiar smells as she could while reveling in the comfort she immediately received for her unsettled nerves. She wanted to erase the gap of time that had elapsed between herself and Emma, while she was recovering from her fall.

Emma turned her nose deep into her mistresses side. The mild pressure to Caitlin's ribs brought a twinge of pain and she flinched.

Ah, I see you are still not yet recovered, my mistress. Emma's thoughts made their way into Caitlin's head.

"No," replied Caitlin, "Not quite, but it is much better."

The sudden realization that they where conversing telepathically sent Caitlin bolting backward. She fell on her buttocks and scrambled frantically backward toward the fence; confusion enveloping her. Her breathing labored and the threat of hyperventilating hovered. The mare stood quietly with her eyes gently observing Caitlin's reaction and then she turned to graze on the luscious rich pasture that awaited her. Caitlin remained motionless, stunned with disbelief of what had just occurred.

Regaining a semblance of composure, the startled young woman rose shakily and made her way back toward her mare. "Did you do what I thought you did?" Caitlin asked warily. But, Emma just kept on grazing, reveling in the juiciness of the rich green grass. "Emma! Emma!" Caitlin cried.

Emma raised her head and looked over, giving the impression of boredom. She was completely absorbed in the process of eating and was not desirous of any more attention from Caitlin. She turned her rump toward her mistress, relieved herself, and walked away; as if that in itself was a statement.

Confused and exasperated, Caitlin turned toward the house. She had experienced a firm pressure in the middle of her forehead while communicating with Emma and now her head was pounding. She decided to lay down until William returned from the airport. Perhaps this was just a hallucination of some type. After all, she had suffered a terrible shock when she fell and she was not quite recovered. Maybe she was just overdoing things today and this was a result of it.

Caitlin stopped at the top of the steps leading up to the broad wrap around porch and looked back toward the peacefully grazing mare. There was something familiar about the pressure she felt while communicating with Emma, but she could not quite place it.

As Caitlin stood motionless, a faint memory of a robed man and the scent of honeysuckle filled her head. *Oh yes*, she mused, *that wonderful dream*; and she turned to enter her house.

Making her way toward her bedroom, Caitlin decided that it would be best not to mention her dream or her telepathic experience to William. Some things where better kept secret. At least for now; until she understood and believed enough about what was happening to explain it.

FOUR

Spring turned into summer as Caitlin continued to heal and get stronger. She spent
her days doing light jobs and keeping contact with the main office via telephone, fax
and computer. Her tasks where easily per-
formed from home, which is why acquiring
this house in the country was possible.

Mitch had gone to Japan to meet with several perspective clients and work the kinks
out of an ongoing project. His return was
indefinite, which left a heavy work load for
William. Caitlin regretted not being able to
take some of the burden from him, but he
insisted he could handle it and that she
should focus on healing.

Although the peace and solitude was a
welcome change from the hustle and bustle
of Manhattan, it was beginning to wear thin.
Caitlin longed for companionship; someone
to talk to, laugh with and even argue with.
She decided it was time to get out a little and
break up the monotony. She would spend
the day exploring the quite little town in the
valley.

Caitlin sat down on the patio, basking in
the early morning sun. The lilting songs of

the birds serenaded her while she made a list of what supplies she would pick up in the small town that was only a few miles away. But, by the size of the list, one would be lead to believe that it was a long journey that was made only on a monthly basis at best. And that was probably very close to being correct!

Wearing a light gingham sundress and a broad rimmed straw hat, Caitlin headed toward the barn. She had managed to convert the shed attached to the southern end of the barn into a garage. It was probably meant to house the field equipment, but since she owned none, it did nicely as a haven for her little BMW convertible. Her face twisted in disgust as she observed how riddled with bird droppings the canvas of her car was. This was awful! She sure had not expected that!

Caitlin grabbed a broom and brushed as much of the dried droppings off the car as she was able. She then backed it up to the water hose and tackled the task of rinsing off the white dusty spotting while searching for signs that the ammonia in the droppings may have damaged the finish, shuddering with revulsion the entire time. There was something about bird droppings that she found repulsive; which seemed odd, considering she cleaned up after Emma every day. But, although she found birds beautiful to listen to and look at, she was cautious not to allow them too close to her. Their near-ness brought out a response in her that she found unsettling. William said it was a past life thing.

Satisfied with her work, Caitlin eased her-self into the driver's seat and started out the drive. Emma, unaccustomed to being left alone since she had been moved from the stable in Long Island to their country estate, raced wildly in the pasture. Her long mane and tail flowed as her lean muscles worked to keep up with the convertible. She reared and squealed loudly as Caitlin turned onto the macadam road and picked up speed. And then, with surprising aloofness, she re-turned to her grazing.

Watching her mare in the rear view mirror, Caitlin mused at what it must be like to be a horse. How did they perceive this vast world of ours? How quickly and easily they where entertained and bored.

She shook her head as a sudden flash of re-membrance of the telepathic communication she had experienced with Emma. Her mind went back to the scene of her fall, and she again remembered her experience of com-municating with Emma. Caitlin touched her forehead lightly to help shake the thoughts free so that she could focus more clearly on driving down the unfamiliar road toward an unfamiliar town.

The road was winding and hilly with ancient, tall trees lining it in a manner that gave it a stately air. Caitlin breathed in the fresh warmth of the air through her opened window. She decided her top must be dry by now and she would over to the side of the road so that she could put it down and really enjoy the sunshine of the day.

Searching for a suitable spot to pull over, Caitlin noticed a narrow dirt road leading off into the trees. She slowed her car down and slowly drove down the dirt road; making sure that she was far enough away from the main road to avoid any mishaps with speeding cars that might zoom by while she was lowering the top of her car.

As she stepped out of the car, Caitlin felt the familiar sensation of musty foliage beneath her feet and her thoughts flashed back to the day of her fall. She looked up at the sky through the trees and remembered her vision of Mitch's memories in the tree tops that day.

The sound of snapping branches quickly brought her back to reality and she turned to discover a beautiful deer standing completely still while it watched her warily, poised for flight at a moments notice. Caitlin tried to stay motionless, breathing as quietly as she could, while she locked eyes with the beautiful, statuesque creature. To her dismay, their encounter was cut short when she unexpectedly let go a riotous sneeze which sent the deer flying into the depths of the foliage; gone within a matter of seconds.

Caitlin did not notice the woman who approached her. She was just suddenly there. Her bulk blocking the sun's rays, creating a formidable shadowy outline. As the woman moved to the left, Caitlin was able to get a clearer focus on her. She was about Caitlin's height, but double her width. Her thick bosom heaved with each breath, as if laboring for stability. Flecks of gray topped off her once jet black hair that was worn in a long straight braid down the middle of her back, almost touching her waist. Although the sun was warm and the air a little sticky, the woman was completely dressed in flannel, from shirt to pants; yet, she appeared to be cool and relaxed. Although worn with age, her clothes sported a look of quality.

"That's a mighty pretty car ya have there, lass. What kind is it?" The woman's distinct Irish brogue echoed through the trees as she reached to touched the hood of Caitlin's BMW. "Your a lucky lady to be able to afford the likes of this! Ah, yes, lucky indeed!"

The old woman made her way toward the canvas on the top and exclaimed, "And a convertible, no less! Imagine that! I have never seen the likes of something this lovely in me whole life. I sure haven't! Where are ya coming from, lass?"

The enthusiasm of this unusual woman was infectious. "Oh, I'm coming from my home up the road. I moved here in the beginning of the spring and I'm only now getting out to explore the area because I had a terrible fall into an old abandoned well a few months ago and I'm finally feeling up to going out to explore. I had converted my utility shed into a garage and the pigeons pooped all over my car, so I had to clean and wash it off and needed to wait for the top to dry before I could put it down. I thought I'd stop here and put it down and then continue on my tour of the town while I enjoyed the sunshine and warm breezes!" Caitlin could not explain why she felt compelled to babble on about her car and the pigeon poop and the wet top, but it just seemed natural and expected.

The woman nodded intently, her clear grey eyes focused on Caitlin's mouth, as if absorbing and digesting each word as it was spoken. Her head shook in rapid agreement and a slight groan of empathy escaped her when Caitlin reached the part about the pigeon poop all over her car. There was something about this woman that Caitlin immediately gravitated to.

"Where are ya fixing to go? In two blinks

and a hand shake you're in and out of that
wee town. I'm headed there meself to do me
weekly food shopping. Perhaps such a geer
lass as yourself wouldn't mind hitching me
beside ya in this beauty? I'd love it, I would.
What do say lass? Can I lift with ya?"

"Absolutely!" Caitlin giggled. "I'd be delighted!"

"What a grande lilt of a voice ya have there,
lass. 'Tis music to me old ears, it 'tis." The
woman strained her bulk into the passen-
gers seat while Caitlin worked on lowering
the top. "So tell me, lass. Tell me all about
yourself. We're neighbors, ya know. It isn't
polite not to socialize, I know, but, I keep to
meself mostly. I'm getting on in years. Me
Tommy passed three years ago, God rest his
loveliness. And I just couldn't find it within
me to keep socializing with the townsfolk.
They pick on me something fierce; thinking I'm odd, ya know. Like, for example, the
clothes I wear. They think I should be out
of these!" She pulled at her flannel pants.
"Can ya imagine? In this heat? Why, everyone knows it absorbs the sweat and keeps a
body cool!"

"Really? Why I never knew that, how interesting!" Caitlin responded with genuine
interest.

"Ya didn't? Well, you're young. This kind
of knowledge comes with age. Give yourself
time, lass. You'll know as much as I do in

due time. Trust old Linnie. I don't fib. Old Linnie will teach ya everything she knows."

A nostalgic smile covered Caitlin's face as she recalled her childhood years. Her mother had called her Linnie. She said it was a nic name from the old country.

Linnie studied Caitlin's face in silence. There was a familiarity about her that she could not place, but she was certain it would come to her in time. "Are we ready?"

The jovial boom of Linnie's voice brought Caitlin back to reality. "Yes. Indeed we are."

~

Caitlin spent the day getting to know the area, with Linnie as her guide. The two woman where an unlikely looking couple. Yet, there was something about Linnie that Caitlin found delightful. She felt a trust and security with Linnie that was instantaneous. They shared stories about themselves and stories about people they knew and places where they had been. They compared likes and dislikes and discussed trusts and distrusts.

To Caitlin's delight, Linnie had a passion for animals that surpassed her own. On a whim, she invited the old woman back to her house to meet her Emma. It was an invitation that Linnie readily accepted.

As they approached the driveway, Emma pranced at the edge of the paddock. Her eagerness for her mistress was apparent.

"That's my Emma." Caitlin smiled broadly as she pointed to Emma with pride.

"Ah. 'Tis a fine animal indeed. And such a strong love for her mistress. Yes, yes... a strong love indeed." Linnie looked closer at the mare and scowled. "She hurt her foot? Ooooooeeeeee. That must have been painful!"

"No, she never hurt her foot. Why would you say that?" Caitlin's surprise made her words come out more curt than she meant for them to sound. She saw no indication in Emma's manner that would denote an injury anywhere on her body and, since she took such pride in the care she gave her mare, she was a little offended at the concept of an injury slipping past her.

If Linnie noticed the sharpness in Caitlin's tone she made no mention of it. "Stop the car missy and let me get closer to the beauty."

Linnie's mannerism was gentle, but firm. Caitlin pulled to a stop and they walked over to the fence. To Caitlin's amazement, Emma ignored her and went immediately to Linnie. Linnie scratched the mare's head and rubbed her ears with zeal. Emma's eyes closed as she reveled in the sensation. Then, Linnie stood back and looked directly at the mare. Time seemed suspended as neither one moved. Then the mare tossed her head high in the air and whinnied.

"How do ya get in there. Where's the gate?" Linnie craned her head from side to side searching. Instead of waiting for Caitlin's response, within seconds, she was climbing the wooden fence with the ease and grace of a cat, dropping lightly to the other side before immediately approaching the mare.

Caitlin was not as graceful. She hitched her sundress up around her thighs to free her legs for climbing. Her open toe sandals left her skin exposed to the weathered wood, necessitating caution against slivers. She hung clumsily over the top rail and froze, staring at the vision of this massive Irish woman and her lovely mare.

Linnie was again gazing steadily into Emma's eyes and again neither of them moved. Then, Linnie held her broad hand just above the flesh of the mare and began to pass it slowly over her muscular body.

She stopped at the whither and turned to Caitlin. "'Tis mighty painful here still, Lass. Why did ya say she wasn't hurt? She's plenty sore here, love; plenty sore. She says she hurt it when she was pulling you and your brother out of that big hole ya fell into. That's a lot of weight for her to pull on. She says she is thankful that the shiny lady helped because she wasn't sure she would have held up without the help! You sure are lucky to have such love from this beast. She's a beauty. And she sure does love you."

A startled Caitlin dropped to the ground with a thud. Her knees buckled out beneath her and she lost her balance, falling forward like a rag doll beneath the mare's stomach. This brought rolling laughter from Linnie. Her bright eyes watery from the intenseness of her laughter. Caitlin, realizing what a sight she was, joined in with Linnie. It felt good to laugh.

When they had calmed down again. Caitlin asked seriously, "How did you know that Emma hurt herself, Linnie? How did you do that?"

"I got the gift, honey, I got the gift. But, so do you. Here," Linnie reached for Caitlin's hand, "look at that hand. Can't ya see? You're a healer lass. You're a seer and a healer. It's easy to see."

Caitlin was almost overwhelmed with confusion. What was Linnie talking about? She wasn't a healer. She was an artist. She wasn't a seer. What did that mean anyway, what was a seer?. She closed her eyes and placed her fingers to her temples. Her head was pounding. Visions of the accident at the well swept before her and then there the vision of the cloaked man from her dreams passed before her. She groaned with frustration.

"Are your memories hurting ya? Not to worry, love, 'tis normal. It'll get easier as ya open up to the flow. Just relax now, Linnie's here. Relax... Relax." Linnie moved closer to Caitlin and placed a large and weathered hand on the small of her back and the other on her forehead. The roughness of Linnie's callouses did not seem to interfere with the waves of energy that flowed through Caitlin, leaving a sensation of peace and tranquility while pulling the ache from her temples.

"Oh Linnie," Caitlin moaned, "sometimes I think I'm going crazy. I see things, really strange and weird things. I see people who aren't really there! They just show up and then pouf... they're gone! I see movie like visions in the trees. For God's sake, I even sometimes hear my horse talking!"

"Now don't go getting all riled again lass. We just got ya relaxed! Nothing is going on here that is abnormal, ya see. 'Tis the way of our kind, that's all. 'Tis nothing abnormal. 'Tis nothing abnormal at all."

"I wish I felt that way. I don't understand half of what is happening. And when it does happen, I get scared. I can't begin to tell you how unnerving it is to have someone just appear in front of you. Just like that; from out of no where!"

"Well, that will stop when ya get a better grip on your gift. Ya see, ya need to control the gift. Take control lass, and then, ya won't be plagued with the surprises like that. If ya see someone 'twill be because ya want to see him. I'll tell ya what. Why don't I spend a little time with ya and show ya what I know? Would ya like that?"

"Oh, would you? And if I learn what you know the surprises will stop? The fear will end?" Caitlin's voice was full of hope.

Linnie wished she could be positive that learning would be all Caitlin needed, but until she better understood the girl's abilities and gifts, she really could not be certain. "'Tis possible, but I can't guarantee anything because that's not a good thing. That's your first lesson. Never guarantee anything, never. But most likely things will calm down for ya."

"Oh that's wonderful, Linnie. What a lucky day it was today. I do believe I have met my savior."

The relief in Caitlin's voice made Linnie hope she was right. She reached over and lightly pinched Caitlin's cheek before she walked back over to Emma and gently caressed her neck. Her expression gave Caitlin the impression that her mind was miles away; far away in time and space.

Caitlin remained silent, respectful not to interrupt the moment. Her heart was pounding with excited anticipation of the concept of becoming Linnie's student.

Linnie turned to Caitlin, smiling broadly. "The sun is down, the moon is out and I feel like howling! Take me home now, lass. We'll start your lessons the day after tomorrow. Good enough?"

Caitlin nodded agreeably as she leapt to her feet, feeling happy and satisfied with the turn of events.

FIVE

It seemed like time had never dragged on as long as it had for Caitlin while she awaited her next meeting with Linnie. She had found Linnie's company soothing, as well as interesting and lively; such a wonderful combination of traits. The woman's eccentric ways only served to make her more enjoyable.

The promise of learning from the old woman left Caitlin eager and impatient. She listened to the grandfather clock in the corner chime the hour. It was five a.m. and the sun was just peeking over the horizon. The slated kitchen floor felt cool against her bare feet as she made her way to the coffee maker and her senses heightened to the aroma of freshly brewed coffee.

Caitlin's movements where slow and deliberate as she filled her mug with the dark liquid. Mornings where always special to her. It seemed like the world was asleep and it was a time when she could be alone with her thoughts uninterrupted. Getting up at this hour was a habit she had acquired when living in Manhattan. Now, it was no longer necessary to rise so early to catch the peace and tranquility of the day, for she had that available around the clock. But the habit was a solid one and it was one she chose not to alter; not at this time anyway.

Not long after Caitlin had finished her second cup of coffee, the telephone rang. Its shrill ring shattered her peaceful state, causing her to jump and knock over a plant in the interim. "Shit! What a mess!" She exploded as she rushed to grab the receiver out of its cradle.

"Hello?" Caitlin's frustration was distinct.

"Are you okay, sis?" William asked hesitantly. He was accustomed to a bright and bubbly response when he telephoned and he was immediately on the alert.

"Yes. Good morning William. Nothing is wrong except that my clumsy butt tripped over a plant on my way to answer the phone and now I have a major mess on my hands. I was still recouping from the experience, that's all." Caitlin knew how nervous William was about leaving her alone in the country to live and she did her best to regain her composure and convince him that she was fine. It would not do to cause worry for him. Good lord, the poor man was on overload with work as it was. She did not need to create unnecessary anxiety.

"Okay. You know I worry about you out there by yourself. I was thinking maybe we should get you a dog or something. One that is trained. What do you think?" William seemed more concerned than usual.

"I guess that would be nice." Caitlin said. Not really focusing on her words as she tried to figure out the true meaning behind William's suggestion she get a dog. "I suppose it would be nice to have a household pet. Emma's great, but she can't come in at night and snuggle. Yes, a dog would be fantastic! Or a cat. Or, what about both? Do you think I should get both? Would that work? A dog and a cat together in the same house?" The more she talked about getting a dog and a cat. The more attached to the idea Caitlin became.

"A regular animal farm, eh?" William chuckled.

"Now you sound like Mitch." Caitlin's tone flattened.

"Oh, speaking of Mitch. He called from Switzerland." William chose to ignore his sister's change in attitude.

"Switzerland? I thought he was in Japan? Why is he calling from Switzerland?" Caitlin could not explain her sudden wave of anxiety.

"Well, you won't believe it , sis. He fell in love with this Swiss chick that he met in Japan and they eloped. Talk about a whirlwind romance. And he went to Switzerland to meet her family; or his new family, or however it goes." There was hesitancy in

William's voice.

So, this was the reason for the strange tone in William's voice. Although Caitlin and Mitch were no longer an item, William felt they were far from over each other. He hated to tell his sis about the sudden marriage, but it had to be done.

"No kidding!" Caitlin responded a little louder than intended as she worked at covering the myriad of emotions that were raging within her. "He always was incredibly impulsive. I can't believe he went so far as to marry though. After all, he's only been gone a month. How could he possibly know whether he wanted to marry her that quickly?"

"I know, sis, it's a bit weird. But then, so is Mitch at times." William had felt the same anxiety as Caitlin when he had heard the news and he could not understand or explain it.

"You're not telling me anything I didn't already know", Caitlin giggled. Flashes of memory of Mitch flew before her; like his silly habit of eating the crust of the sandwich first and creating a small circle to "pop" into his mouth for the grand finale'. He made eating a simple sandwich a ritualistic experience! He used to laugh and say it stemmed back to his childhood days. But he never went further with the explanation.

"Well, I have to say Caitlin, you sure are a sport about it." William mused.

"I have no reason not to be. After all, Mitch and I have been over for some time and I have no reason to be anything else!" Caitlin's voice was slightly higher than normal and she wondered if she sounded believable. Did William believe her? Better yet, did she believe herself? Was she really over Mitch?

"Well, I'm glad to hear it. I just hope the damned fool doesn't regret this later on. But, anyway, tell me what's on your agenda today? Are you planning anything fun and interesting?" William teased. As much as he enjoyed visiting his sister's home, he often wondered how she was keeping herself from going crazy with all that quiet isolation. He would be mad by now.

Caitlin proceeded to go into great detail about her plans with her new friend, Linnie. William listened intently with mild satisfaction. He was delighted to hear that his sister had managed to make a friend and he encouraged her strongly to cultivate it more. He did not feel comfortable with her being so isolated and alone. A friend near by was good.

~

Linnie arrived at the door just as Caitlin was placing the receiver in the cradle; startling Caitlin as she entered without waiting for an invitation. Oddly, Caitlin was not offended by Linnie's familiarity and accepted it as part of her eccentricity.

"All ready for the big day?" Linnie was bubbling with energy.

Caitlin could not help noticing a small glow around her new friend's body. As she peered at Linnie's long braid, she imagined the glow about her to be a halo. This brought a feeling of security and satisfaction to Caitlin, *What if she is an angel in disguise?* She mused, remembering the stories from her childhood.

"I'm really excited; and a little nervous. Just what am I going to be learning?" Caitlin replied.

Linnie bellowed over her shoulder as she led Caitlin into the living room. It was as if the statement would have more meaning and power to it if she used plenty of wind. "The basics, love. Just the basics. Then you're on your own. I'm no grand teacher. No lass, I'll teach ya the basics, that's all"

The two positioned themselves in on opposite ends of the sofa. Linnie reached into the bag she had been carrying and pulled out a white candle, oil, matches, a bag of dried leaves, sticks of incense and an incense holder.

When Linnie had arranged everything carefully on the coffee table, she turned to Caitlin. "Okay. I am going to start by explaining

this stuff to ya. These are the basics for the
first step to the gift. I want ya to pay close
attention to what I'm saying and doing. Got
it?

Caitlin nodded in agreement, unable to take
her eyes off the spread on the coffee table. It
seemed to pull at her from the chest up.

"Okay. Now, I am going to start with this
candle. 'Tis white. And ya should not meditate with anything but white in the beginning. The colors bring different stuff. That's
all ya need to know about it for now. We
can do colors another time. Just remember. Use only white candles. Got that?"

Caitlin nodded.

"Good. Now, I want ya to take this candle
and hold it carefully while ya rub some oil
on it. That helps to purify it and it will
also make it burn longer." Linnie grabbed
Caitlin's hands and gently pressed the candle in her palm while she dabbed a little oil
in Caitlin's other palm and then guided her
hands into action.

"Ya start in the middle an' work your way
to the ends. Like this, see?" Linnie's large
rough hands where remarkably gentle and
dexterous as they directed Caitlin.

When they had finished with the candle,
Linnie secured it in a holder and moved toward the bag of dried leaves. "This is called
sage, lass. 'Tis for purifying the energies in
the room and on yourself. Ya can grow it in

the garden. Now, I want ya to stand before me nice and straight with your arms out to your sides."

Caitlin obediently followed Linnie's instructions as she watched the old woman light the sage and blow out the flame. The small cluster of leaves billowed smoke while emitting a pungent aroma that resembled marijuana. Caitlin coughed slightly as Linnie waived the smoking cluster around her body. Linnie followed by doing the same to herself and then around the room. She placed the remainder of the cluster in an ashtray, allowing it to continue to smoke, and lit the incense. The smooth aroma of the incense curled and intertwined with the pungent aroma of the sage, creating an exotic blend.

Caitlin stared hypnotically as the sage eventually died away and only the incense remained. The room felt still and warm. It was as if a blanket of security had been placed over the entire space. As Caitlin, relaxed, the songs of the birds flittered through the open window, accentuating the sense of peace that was pouring though her.

"Now, lass, we are ready. I want ya to sit back in the chair. Sit nice and straight now. Put her hands in your lap. That's it, just rest them on your thighs, nice and peaceful. Now, close your eyes. I want ya to sit still and try to make your mind as still as ya can.

Don't control the thoughts. Just let them flow in and out. And stay that way until I say stop. Got it?"

Caitlin nodded, afraid that if she spoke she would break the magic in the room.

Time seemed to stand still as Caitlin's head grew heavier and heavier while the scent of the incense filled her nostrils. Her body experienced a floating sensation, similar to the one she had experienced when she had entered the clouds and met Lael. Oh, Lael... she had not thought of that experience in a while. She wondered if she would go there again. But, only the floating sensation occurred. She saw nothing but darkness.

"Time's up." Whispered Linnie, careful not to startle Caitlin.

"What? Already? It seems like we only just started." Caitlin exclaimed. Still feeling the effects of the meditation, her body was slow to move about.

Linnie chuckled. "That's normal. But we where quiet for almost an hour. That's a fact."

"Really?" Caitlin exclaimed. "Wow, I can't believe it. That's unbelievable." Her words were drawled with satisfaction as she stretched her body in a cat-like manner.

The room seemed a little chillier than when they began, so Caitlin walked to the window to close it. She was shocked to see the position of the sun in the sky. It had traveled quite far. They had indeed been quiet for a while.

Linnie stayed for a late morning tea and shared some of the area gossip, much to Caitlin's delight. She found the old woman unique and charming. Her speech pattern only emphasized her uniqueness.

When it was time for Linnie to leave, she handed Caitlin a paper containing the neatly typed instructions for meditation. They emphasized the necessity to burn the candle, sage and incense when doing this exercise.

The two women embraced and then Linnie was gone. Caitlin moved toward the patio with the instructions still in her hands and began to read them.

INSTRUCTIONS FOR MEDITATION

PREPARE THE ROOM; It is important that you clear the energy of the room before you meditate. This is easily done by burning either sage or cedar in the room. The negative energies will be neutralized, creating a positive environment. You should also cleanse your own energy field of all negative energy by passing the sage or cedar over you. Have a candle that has been treated with extra virgin olive oil *(or another type of anointing oil)* burning Make certain that, in the beginning, it is only a white candle. Remember that colors attract certain vibrations! The white will bring the good energy into the room and continue to transmute any negative energy. Burn a pleasant smelling incense to assist your senses in relaxing. This will also attract the spirit guides who are working with you, since they enjoy the smell as well. Keep your environment free of loud and startling noises. Take the phone off the hook or turn down the ringer while you are meditating.

STEPS::
1] Sit comfortably in a chair with your back straight. Do not cross your legs. If you are on the floor, have them out straight, if you are sitting, have your feet flat on the floor. It is not recommended that you lie down, as the temptation to fall asleep is too strong.
2] Allow your body to relax
3] Focus on your breathing. Taking slow and deliberate breaths.
4] Do not try to control the thoughts that are flowing through. If a thought comes in, do not try to hang onto it or release it. Let it run its course and move on. It is normal to have "chatter" occur in the beginning. Just relax and let the information and ideas flow in and out.
5] Take your time coming out of meditation. Do not rush, but allow your body to adjust to being alert again.

~

Still reading, Caitlin drifted off into a deep

sleep and remained there until Emma loudly announced it was dinner time. She rubbed her eyes, trying to get her whereabouts in focus.

The instructions for meditation had slipped from her hands. As she stooped over and picked them up carefully, a feeling of guilt swept through her. It was if, by letting them fall to the ground, she had shown some type of disrespect to a very sacred act. It was a feeling she could not justify or explain.

Caitlin quickly made her way into the library and placed the instructions carefully on her desk before going out to accommodate Emma.

SIX

Caitlin watched for Linnie eagerly each day, barely concentrating on her activities around the house. But, several days passed with no sign of the old woman.

Caitlin regretted not getting a phone number from her new friend. She did not even know exactly where she lived. When Linnie had asked her to take her home, she had insisted that Caitlin stop the car at the spot where they met and got out. Caitlin could see no signs of a house anywhere. She thought of going to town and questioning if anyone could direct her to Linnie's place, but somehow felt that the old woman would not approve. So, since they had made no specific schedule or plans for their next meeting, Caitlin had no recourse but to wait for her new friend to surface again.

~

Caitlin had been working diligently in her vegetable garden. The long straight rows of green where peeking above the rich dark soil with robust health. She straightened her back and looked proudly at them, remembering how, when she was a little girl, she had stared at the plants in her house and seen a ring of colors around them.

As soon as her memory appeared, so did the colors in her garden. She saw rays of lavender, pink, rich green, yellow and gold. The garden was alive with vibrant light circling the plants and darting back and forth. It reminded her of a light show she had seen in the city. It was beautiful! And then, as quickly as it came, it was gone.

The garden was quiet, peaceful and again the rows of green peeked above the soil; silently absorbing the nourishment from the sun, air and ground. She reached for the garden hose and sprayed the plants with gentle care while Emma frolicked playfully around the paddock.

Caitlin turned to watch Emma. Her mane and tail flowed freely as she leaped over the fallen tree and turned to do it again. Caitlin had decided not to remove it from the paddock since Emma seemed to take such delight in playing "leap frog" with it. She was definitely an unusual horse.

Sometimes Caitlin wondered what Emma would have been like, had she remained in the stable with the other horses. She had heard that a horse will act more aloof when it is with a herd. William often commented that poor Emma was confused about what she was. He was probably right.

Emma approached the fence, snorting and stamping her powerful hoofs into the soft earth. Caitlin turned the hose off and set it down. She walked carefully through the rows of vegetables to where Emma strained her head over the fence as she struggled to reach the delicious looking fare on the other side.

"Oh no you don't girl, that's people food!" Caitlin chuckled as she reached the horse and gave her a big hug.

"What's people food? Isn't food for everyone?" The child-like voice floated clearly across the garden.

Caitlin, startled at the voice turned around to see where it came from. There was no one in sight. In her haste, she had stepped back onto one of her tomato plants, breaking a bit of the stem.

As she reached down to see if she could repair the damage, she heard "That's Okay, the main stem is still intact. Just gently remove that broken part. Do it gently because plants can feel, and you wouldn't want to hurt it on purpose would you? But you must remove it because it will take too much strength from the rest of the plant, if you leave it. Just gently remove it from the stem... go on."

Caitlin stood up and looked frantically around but could not find the source of the voice. A tingling sensation started moving up the right side of her body and the hair on her arms stood erect. She rubbed her arm to relieve the sensation and continued to strain to see where the voice might be coming from. The thought of someone watching her from a hiding place was frightfully unsettling.

Closing her eyes, Caitlin concentrated on her own body's senses. No, this time there was no pressure in her forehead, so it was not coming from Emma. This time the pressure was slightly above each ear; between her ears and her temples. The voice was soft and she had a difficult time deciding whether it was a child or a young woman; but it really did not matter. The fact remained that someone was out there hiding on her and she could not locate her.

The birds sang gleefully and the bees buzzed past Caitlin as she continued her visual search for the female behind the voice. The radiant sun beamed warmth on her back as she stood with her hands over her eyes to shade them from the glare. The fields bent and swayed in the warm, gentle breeze that seemed always prevalent on the mountainside. The proud trees where alive with life. Their rich green leaves shook from the scurrying and bustling of squirrels and birds, but there was still no sign of anyone.

Giving up on the search, Caitlin decided to care for the tomato plant and pray that whoever it was out there hiding was friend-

ly and not some serial killer. She kneeled
down beside it and gently removed the broken piece of tomato plant from the stem. As
she held the plant in her hands, a warm vibration filled her. Caitlin knew, deep within
her being, that the plant was grateful for the
love and care she was giving and involuntary
joyful tears welled up within her and spilled
down her cheeks.

She sat down in the midst of the plants
and wept for no reason, except that she felt
like she was bursting with love. She felt as
if she was sitting in the middle of a field of
love instead of a vegetable garden and it was
a glorious feeling.

A flash of something moving caught the
corner of her eye and she swirled quickly to
see what it was. Again, the land was quiet
and peaceful with no sign of anyone or anything. This type of thing had been going on
for most of Caitlin's life, yet she had never
grown accustomed to it. Seeing or not seeing through the corners of her eyes gave her
an eerie and uncomfortable feeling. Not only
was she was very tired of it, but she was even
more nervous since she had still not located
the source of the voice that had spoken to
her.

Caitlin stood up, took a deep breath, and
wiped her eyes. Enough was enough! She
could either crumple in fear or get moving
and find out what it was that was zipping

around her place. It did not matter whether it was good or bad. She had to find out what it was. Of course, she hoped it was good, but it was too unsettling to have things flashing past her like that. It had to stop. So, if it was bad, she would deal with it when the time came.

The door on the tool shed creaked slowly, immediately catching Caitlin's attention. She moved cautiously toward it. The limbs of her body trembled as she carefully approached the small structure. She felt the pounding of her heart in the cavity of her head and her breathing thundered in her ears. She tried holding it to silence herself, but found it all the louder when she resumed breathing.

A rake leaned against the side of the weathered building and Caitlin grabbed it, feeling a little more secure having armed herself with some form of weapon.

Caitlin leaned against the side of the building as she struggled to regain control of her body. Beads of sweat covered her forehead and her nerves felt as if they where and trying to leap from her body. She was uncertain if her legs could support her one more minute.

Again the door creaked.

Gathering all her strength to prepare to enter the shed and ready to face and confront whatever it was that kept zipping around her property, Caitlin made her way toward the door. She was just about to enter when an enormous cat swept past her. The cat's piercing cry blended with Caitlin's shrill screeching at the startling confrontation.

Caitlin's screams continued long after the cat had disappeared into the tall grass of the fields. Her legs finally gave out and she crumbled to the ground, too weak to move. "That was the biggest cat I have ever seen." She mumbled, not caring about the fact that there was no one there to hear her. "That had to be the biggest cat I have ever seen; ever. What was it doing here? What kind of cat was it?"

Time stood still as Caitlin focused on regaining her composure. When her legs finally felt strong enough to hold her again, she pulled herself up with the help of the rake handle. Standing quietly while she steadied herself, Caitlin heard a faint cry; almost like a peep. Frozen, barely breathing, she strained her ears for the sound. When the cry came again, it was muffled, but distinct.

She walked cautiously into the shed and stopped with a start as vomit swelled within her throat. She hurried back outside and fell to the ground, release the bile in her throat and as well as the contents of her stomach. When she had finished, she leaned against the building and wiped at her face with her sleeve; still plagued by the sound of the small cry.

She steadied herself and started back inside, this time ready for what was on the other side of the door.

Caitlin entered the tool shed and swung the door withe open to allow as much light as possible. Although she dreaded facing the torment inside, she dreaded even more the possibility of stepping on it due to insufficient lighting. Her feet tread carefully as she avoided stepping on the remains of the animal. Fur and entrails were scattered around the floor of the shed and blood was spilled in large pools. It looked like a massacre had taken place.

Caitlin was surprised that such a thing could have occurred without her hearing anything. It was clearly a fresh kill. The thought quickly left her as she covered her mouth as more vomit threatened to spill out. The head of what appeared to have been a beautiful house cat lay before her. Its eyes stared blankly and its tongue protruded out of the corner of its mouth. Blood drenched the once fluffy gray fur and one of its legs lay not far away. Caitlin was shocked and horrified. She had to get out, she just could not endure the scene any longer. Racing out of the shed, she fell to the ground and vomited violently. Her body had a will of its own and even though there was nothing left in her stomach, it heaved and wretched anyway.

The action seemed to bring her relief and soon she was sitting with her back braced against the building, struggling at what to do. The crying was getting fainter, but it was still there. She knew that she had to reach whatever it was in there to help. But that meant again braving the horrible scene of blood and guts.

Caitlin closed her eyes and prayed for strength. Her head grew light and a feeling of euphoria consumed her. *We are with you our beloved, fear not, we are here. Go in and you will be strong. You will be strong.'* Caitlin recognized the voice of the man in her dream, Lael and she suddenly felt very empowered and ready.

Leaping to her feet, she entered the shed with deliberation. She moved steadily to the side cupboard without looking in the direction of the cat's remains. Pulling open a drawer, she reached in and yanked out a trash bag. She had left her gloves in the garden so she searched for another pair. When she found them, she pulled them on, still not looking around. Her hearing seemed more acute and the faint cry was more distinct. She was able to pick up the location without even searching.

Grabbing a small transplanting spade, Caitlin walked to the cat's remains and scooped them up into the bag. Surprisingly, she no longer felt the shuddering desire to vomit.

She was the only one to do the job, and the job had to be done. So be it.

When she had completed the task, Caitlin tied up the bag and set it outside the door before heading in the direction of the peeping cries. Pulling away some bags of garden fertilizer, she found a small bed of rags. There, amongst the rags, lay three small kittens who were barely able to walk. *These little creatures can't be only a few weeks old,* she mused. *What will happen to them?*

Caitlin pulled a small basket from a hook on the wall and shook out the dust. She scooped up the kittens, rags and all, and placed them gently in the basket. On her way out of the shed, she stopped for a moment and stared at the bag containing the remains of the mother. Her mind whirled with frustration. How cruel life is at times. How mysterious and cruel. What will these poor baby kittens do without a mother? What was she supposed to do with them? She knew nothing about how to care for them, absolutely nothing. She longed for Linnie.

The tiny creatures squirmed in the basket, snuggling each other for comfort and assurance. Caitlin noticed one was very lethargic, barely moving or breathing. She rushed into the house with her basket and set it on the kitchen table. Scurrying into the laundry room, she returned with a bundle of fresh rags for the basket. She gently took each kitten out and placed it on the table. They where more mobile than she had anticipated and made their way toward the table's edge, each in a different direction while their crying grew more pronounced.

Caitlin quickly dumped the basket upside down to remove the old rags. The jerking action loosened more dirt and dust from the basket and it settled on her table. She decided that this was a poor choice of location to do this, but it was too late to stop now. She reached for the kittens, barely catching one before it reached the edge of the table, and placed them back into the basket of fresh rags. The scent of their mother had left with the old rags and they cried out for her with loud wails.

"Well, it sure looks like you have your hands full there, sis. Where did you get these little critters?" Caitlin was so busy struggling to take care of the kittens that she had not even heard her brother arrive.

William came up behind her and slid his arms affectionately around her waist. She laid her head back against his chest, relieved to have reinforcement for the situation. "Oh William, it has been a nightmare! There was this enormous cat that was bigger than anything I have seen before! It killed the mother of these poor, helpless babies in the tool shed. What a mess!" Caitlin shuddered for emphasis. "And now I don't know what to do. I have no idea what to do with such tiny creatures. How will they survive? They need nursing, that's for sure." Caitlin moaned in despair.

"I see. Well, let's take care of these tiny things first, and then we can get back to the story of the big cat and the mama. Do you have any droppers in the house? You know, like an eye dropper?"

"Yes, I have one in the valerian jar. It's almost empty." Caitlin replied.

"Go get it and clean it out thoroughly. I'll warm up a little milk and we will see if we can get these kittens to quiet down". William released his hold on Caitlin and the two went about their designated duties.

Before long, the tiny kittens where satisfied and quiet. Caitlin smiled contentedly as she looked at the basket of sleeping beauties.

"So, now sis. What say we get ourselves a cup of coffee and go out on the patio while you tell me all about it. Start from the beginning and don't leave a thing out. Okay? This should be interesting." The two poured themselves some of the coffee that was still in the coffee maker from the morning and reheated it in the microwave, neither one seeming to mind that it was hours old. They made their way to the patio and positioned themselves comfortably. Caitlin began her story.

SEVEN

It was three weeks before Linnie came around again. Caitlin had abandoned her watch after the first week and had dove back into her day to day duties. The kittens had survived and where proving to be a handful. Caitlin had never been placed in a position of "mama" before and found it challenging. Between the care of the kittens, the duties of the household and its repairs, maintaining her work schedule with the deadlines and Emma, her days where full.

Linnie arrived late in the afternoon, just in time for dinner. She boisterously laughed and teased and carried on with Caitlin as if the two where long time friends and she had only just been there yesterday. Her response to the kittens showed little surprise, as if she had known of there existence all along. She held each one in her hands and did what she called 'scanning of their bodies'.

Linnie's visual abilities where as such that they allowed her to actually picture in her mind the inside of a person or an animal. Although she was not educated in the medical field, she was able to pick up on abnormalities in a body and instinctively know whether they required a doctor's care or a simple home remedy..

"This kitten's got a weak heart. I'm surprised he's managed to live. You must have given it a lot of love, lass. Indeed, you've got the touch!" Linnie stated as she stroked the tiny kitten and chuckled at its loud purr that seemed out of place.

"He had me worried, Linnie. I really am surprised he lived too. His breathing was so shallow. If William hadn't shown up when he did, well... I don't think any of them would have lived. I was at a complete loss as to what to do!" Caitlin's voice shook with emotion.

"Oh, I don't know about that, lass. Ya seem to have the knack for it, ya do. I think ya would have figured it out mighty quick if ya had to. Have more faith in yourself!" Linnie exclaimed.

There was a gentleness in Linnie's voice and eyes that somehow did not match the bulk of her body. Caitlin looked from the tiny kitten with the loud boisterous purr and then to the large bulky woman with her soft gentle voice and giggled.

If Linnie was curious as to the reason for Caitlin's giggle, she asked no questions. Instead, she gently placed the kitten on the floor, stood up with a cat-like grace and stretched. As she made her way to the living room, she called back to Caitlin, "Let's get to work". Caitlin followed obediently.

The robust woman had been carrying a large cloth bag with her when she arrived. Caitlin had not paid much notice to it until Linnie reached inside and pulled out a large, thick, leather bound book. She stretched forward to take a closer look. The book looked old. The edges of the binding where worn thin with use and the pages where brittle and yellowed.

Linnie handled the old book with loving care. Her large, bulky hands dexterously turned the pages until she found the section she was seeking. "This book has been in me family for generations. It tells the secrets of the ages. It tells the secrets of the gift. I want ya to have it, lass. I have no family to give it to, and the secrets can't be lost."

Linnie gently laid the open book on the table before Caitlin. The large print seemed to jump off the pages. The letters, where of Gothic style, were still clean and crisp. As Caitlin slid her hand over the pages, she felt a warm vibration in her palms. She quickly pulled back, startled.

Linnie threw her head back, her laughter coming from deep within her. She sat back comfortably in the chair and began to explain the history of the book. She told of her ancestors and their connection to the spirt world. She explained how her great, great, great grandmother had been a clan healer. The family had been revered at times and persecuted at others; but through the ages the gift lived on.

The two spent the rest of the day pouring through the book. Caitlin was amazed at how sensible, simple and clear the book was. It covered topics like the usage of herbs; how to read the tarot, and the even older Runes, plus connecting with your spirit guide and angels and others in the spirit world. There were sections on telepathy, vibrations and color usage. Caitlin squealed with excitement. She could not wait to sit down and read through its entirety. She asked Linnie if she had read it all and the old woman nodded. It was a staple in her family.

Linnie looked seriously at Caitlin for a long moment before speaking, "You gotta promise to take care of this book, lass. 'Tis older than you and I put together! Don't let anyone else touch it, ya hear? Not even your brother. Promise?" Caitlin nodded in agreement. There seemed something sacred about the whole scene. Like she was taking a pledge before God. She would keep the secret of the book close to her, until told otherwise.

Linnie got up to leave and Caitlin ran into the coat room to get her car keys, fully intending to drive her home. When she had returned to the living room, it was quiet.

The breeze gently tugged at the draperies through the open windows and the dusk outside them showed a bright orange skyline that outlined the tree tops. Caitlin looked around for Linnie, but found no sign of her. She had left as quickly and quietly as she had arrived.

Pausing only briefly to ponder on the mysteries of her new friend, she quickly settled herself in her reading room to further investigate the treasured book before her. She opened up the section on the Angels and began to read.

An angel is a heavenly being. There are orders of these angelic beings, they are as follows:

Sphere 1: These angels serve as heavenly counselors

      Seraphim - Serve closest to God

      Cherubim -Guardians of light

      Thrones - Guardians of planets

Sphere 2: These angels work as heavenly governors

      Dominions - Govern the activities of all angelic groups lower than them

      Virtues - Beam divine light to the planets

      Powers - The keepers of collective history and bearers of the conscience.

Sphere 3: These angels are heavenly messengers

      Principalities - The guardians of large groups, from cities to nations to multi corporations

Archangels - Tend to the larger arenas of
human endeavors. Commonly referred to as
Over lighting angels.
Angels - Closest to humanity, They are concerned with human affairs.

Fascinated, Caitlin quickly leafed through
more pages. She found connotations for in-
voking good spirits; and to her surprise, evil
ones. As she whispered softly the *Death Incantation*, a cold chill swept over her and her
temples started to throb.

She slammed the book shut and looked
around the room for a safe place to keep it.
Linnie had been insistent about keeping the
book above foot level at all times, so the mantle seemed the best place for it. She stood up
and paused, feeling the room sway slightly,
before walking to the fireplace mantle and
placing the book carefully on it.

Caitlin felt the hours of the day as she made
her way back toward the kitchen. She was
sure that was why she had felt light headed
when she stood up to put the book away.
She decided to make a cup of hot herbal tea
and snuggle up in her bed. The muscles of
her body ached and her eyelids felt heavy.

As she reached the kitchen, she changed
her mind about the tea, deciding she was too
tired to even bother making it. So, she shuf-
fled off to bed. It was only a matter of a minute or two before she was in a deep sleep.

~

Waves of light flew past Caitlin as she floated beyond the clouds. The wings of angels where all around her. She felt their light caress against her cheeks; like a gentle kiss. Peace and tranquility flowed through her and she felt safe.

There was a familiarity about where she was, like she had been there many times. Her body rocked and swayed as she continued to float, with no particular destination in mind.

The clouds parted and she was again in the presence of Lael. A smile formed on her lips as she looked upon him. Finding him here, amongst the clouds and the angels, somehow brought completion to the whole experience.

She was beginning to feel the bond between them. A familiar yet indescribable bond that was unlike anything she felt with anyone else. She did not question it. It seemed natural, and old, like they had been bonded forever. His gentle and caring eyes looked into hers. Caitlin marveled over how soft and deep his eyes were, as if there was a space within them that was a world in itself.

The love from Lael was strong. It flowed to her in waves that washed over her, creating a feeling of euphoria. Then, the clouds enfolded Lael and she was again amongst the wings of the angels, feeling pleased, loved and peaceful; although a little frustrated that Lael did not stay. Then the angels disappeared and the room went dark.

~

Caitlin sat up in bed and reflected on her dream. She felt a strong need to write down her thoughts and experiences. She got out of bed and went into the study, she sat at her desk and picked up a pen.

The words poured out of her, rushing forth so quickly that she could barely write fast enough. When she had finished, she sat back, feeling the a sense of pressure had lifted. Feeling satisfied, she returned back to her bed and immediately fell into a deep, comfortable sleep.

~

A loud crash startled Caitlin out of the warmth of her slumber. Taking a moment to gather her wits about her, she surveyed her bedroom for the source of the commotion. The morning sun was peeking through the window pane, announcing the beginning of another beautiful day. A slight haze of dusty particles hovered along the beam of sunlight that was tickling the faded oriental carpet on the bedroom floor. The room appeared still, almost frozen, as her eyes slowly focused from corner to corner. Again, another crash sounded, bringing a startled gasp from her lips.

Caitlin leapt from the bed, sliding into her slippers and robe with a quick graceful ease that required little thought and tiptoed quietly toward the door. She hesitated only briefly before peeking her head into the hall to look for intruders.

The long broad hallway sported memories of a time gone by. A time of grace and beauty and elegance. The faded wallpaper echoed laughter of children running from room to room playing the game of hide and seek. She could almost hear the clicking of the heels of the housekeepers through the years as they made their rounds, or the soft rustling of party gowns as the women made their way down the elegant staircase toward the adoring eyes of the men awaiting in the great room below.

At one time Caitlin's house was the main home of a great estate in the Revolutionary era. She did not know very much of its history, but intended to begin a search on it soon.

The crash sounded again and this time Caitlin was able to determine the direction it was coming from. It was coming from her reading room!

She hurried down the hall and stopped short at the doorway. Her mouth fell open, but not a sound passed her trembling lips as she slowly took in the scene before her. The room was in total disarray. The curtains where in shreds and the stuffing that was pulled out of the cushions of the sofa was scattered throughout the room. The once graceful antique etched glass door of the bookcase that covered the entire north wall of the room lay shattered on the floor. Pieces of the antique glass projected as far as the other side of the large room. It was as if an explosion had occurred. Papers lay scattered about, some loose and some actual pages of a book and long deep claw marks ran along the surface of the desktop.

The book that Linnie had given her lay propped on its side on the mantle, just as she had left it; completely in tact. It was the only thing in the room that seemed to have been spared. Caitlin rushed to it and hugged it to her chest as she lowered herself carefully onto what was left of the sofa. She stared in disbelief, unable to grasp what had happened to the room, or how it could have happened.

The loud wail of one of her kittens sounded as it pounced up next to her. She stroked the feline gently as she caught a brief glimpse of a dark figure flash past. And then the room went cold; so cold that she was able to see her breath. An icy chill crept up her spine, slowly, deliberately as she remained completely still; holding her breath and listening to the loud pounding of her heart in her ears while she continued to hug Linnie's book.

As if from nowhere a small black ball appeared. It hovered before her. Slowly, deliberately, it grew bigger and bigger. As it grew, it became more and more transparent, allowing her to see the figure inside it. When the black ball reached the size of a basketball, she gasped in horror. The creature inside it was like nothing she had ever seen before! She wanted to run but felt paralyzed. As the creature raised its head to look at her, she let out a shrill scream and the ball wavered slightly.

Not able to take her eyes off the creature in the ball, Caitlin could only watch out of the corner of her eyes as a bright white beam of light formed in the south corner of the room. Out of its brightness walked Lael.

Calmly, deliberately, Lael approached Caitlin until he stood before her, blocking her view of the growing black ball and its gruesome creature. His eyes were gentle as he asked quietly, "Do you desire my assistance?"

Caitlin feebly nodded her head, still too stunned by what was happening to do much else. Lael turned quickly, no longer serene in his actions. He raised his arms high above his head and spread his palms wide open before swirling them to form symbols in the air.

Bright light bounced everywhere as Lael spoke in a powerful, clear and authoritative manner, "By the power of the great One, I command that you leave!" He repeated this command three times, each time with a stronger and more forceful voice than the time before. Within moments the ball was backing away; shrinking until it was gone.

Lael turned back around and stood before Caitlin and addressed her in his usual serene mannerism. "Dear beloved, it would appear that you have unlocked the doors to darkness. We ask that you be more patient and cautious in your journey down the path of knowledge. All things in time, dear one."

Without warning, Lael raised his arms high above his head. This time he formed a small glowing ball of firelight. Its warmth permeated the room, warming Caitlin throughout her body and immediately calming her and bringing her back to her senses.

Lael's loving smile shone brightly as he bowed slightly before walking, in a regal manner, back into the beam of light.

The light disappeared, leaving Caitlin still hugging Linnie's book in silent stillness, until the sound of the purring cat next to her broke through. She rose slowly and walked to the door, stopping to take another survey of the shredded room before returning to her bedroom.

Caitlin set Linnie's book gently on the foot of her bed and turned toward the adjacent bathroom. She was in need of a soothing bath and time to think about what just happened.

As the old claw foot bathtub was filling, she turned to the mirror to examine her face. Her eyes looked hollowed and sunken. Her cheekbones protruded a little too much and her usually thick and lustrous lips appeared pale and thin. The coloring of her face took on a yellowish hue.

Caitlin turned on the water in the old pedestal sink and splashed the hot liquid over her cheeks in an attempt to add some color. Patting her face with a soft towel, she again examined herself in the mirror. This time, her eyes where bright, her lips full and rich and her skin a glowing pink. Her full cheeks radiated the ruddy health that she was known to display. She stood motionless for a moment before removing her pajamas and lowering herself into her steaming bath. She remained there for the better part of an hour.

The long soothing bath did wonders for calming Caitlin's trembling nerves and restoring her spirits. Bouncing, in her usual perky manner, into the kitchen, she swung open the refrigerator door and groaned. It was time to go to the store for more supplies. Horror of horrors, there was no creamer for her coffee!

Caitlin shut the door abruptly and leaned against it, her arms folded disgustedly over her chest. Her life had changed so drastically since she had moved into this house. Most of it was wonderful, but there where aspects of it that bothered her. And the inconvenience of not being able to run to the corner store or have something delivered was top on her list. She just could not tolerate coffee without creamer. She simply must have a creamer!

Caitlin's unsuccessful search for a non-dairy substitute in the cupboard persuaded her to have tea with lemon instead. She would have passed altogether, since she was a creature of habit and coffee was for the morning and tea for the afternoon, but after the morning she just had, some sort of caffeine jolt was in order.

After sipping her tea and munching on an English muffin, Caitlin decided to make the much needed trip to the local store for a few supplies. She did her major shopping on a monthly basis in the nearby city, but frequented the local country store or went into the small town for the basics such as milk and bread and creamer.

Caitlin saddled up Emma, excited about the prospect of bonding with nature for a while. She found riding Emma at a casual pace fantastic therapy for stress and tenseness.

As Caitlin gazed out over the hillside, the beauty of the day flowed before her with grace and ease. It was an incredible kaleidoscope of colors.

Sinking deeper into the saddle as she melded her body to Emma's graceful gate, Caitlin relaxed in anticipation of a peaceful journey to the local store. *It isn't such a terrible inconvenience after all,* she thought, *if I was closer, I wouldn't have been able to enjoy the beauty of this gorgeous day with Emma.*

As they reached a small grove of trees, Caitlin chuckled in amusement at a small family of squirrels as they scurried about collecting their nuts and taking them back to their nest. They seemed absorbed in their tasks and oblivious to the presence of Emma and herself.

The squirrels scurried in a frenzy when Emma picked up her gate, bringing Caitlin's attention back to the path ahead of them. Caitlin often gave Emma her head on their walks, allowing her to pick the pace that suited her mood at the time.

Caitlin prepared for the wild abandonment that lay ahead on the stretch before them. This was Emma's favorite spot. The ground was flat and solid, with minimal debris. It afforded an opportunity for Emma to put her powerful limbs into action. Caitlin's hair fell from the knot she had tied loosely on her head and flew freely about as Emma raced with the wind to the end of the stretch.

Out of the next grove of trees sprung an enormous wolf. Emma reared on her hind legs while Caitlin clung frantically for balance. The wolf seemed just as startled and it stopped, motionless before them, and stared.

Emma continued to rear and stomp, prancing away while Caitlin struggled for control. The wolf continued to remain motionless and stare and the horse and rider calmed a little. Finally Emma was under control, but still prepared to race away at a moment's notice.

A hazy feeling came over Caitlin as she watched the wolf raise up on its hind legs, in slow motion. As if in a fairy tale, its front legs grew shorter and its ears, which had been perked forward, grew long and floppy. Its long sleek wolf snout grew short and broad. As her haziness subsided, Caitlin found herself staring straight into the eyes of a giant hare! The wolf was gone!

Caitlin drew in a deep gasp as the hare rushed off into the grove, leaving horse and rider stunned and motionless.

Before she could regain her composure, a tall slender man appeared in the path before them. His sleek, fastidious attire emitted an air of prosperity. Emma's ears strained forward in an alerted fashion, uncertain whether she should stay put or run. Behind the man stood an enormous black steed. Its huge frame made Emma appear small in comparison. With its long silken black mane flowing casually, the steed tossed his head and flicked his tail; his broad nostrils fluttered as he moved closer to Emma.

The proud swagger in the stranger's walk, combined with the lock of jet black hair that fell teasingly over his brow, gave him a youthful appearance. But the steel grey eyes that bore into her spoke of wisdom and knowledge far beyond his years. A chill ran up Caitlin's spine and the hairs stood on her neck as she shifted uncomfortably in the saddle. She felt as if he was looking into her soul.

She cleared her throat uncomfortably when he smiled broadly; his bright white teeth glimmered in the afternoon sun. A pang of desire sprang through her loins making her blush with surprise. She had never responded in such a way to anyone before. Not even to Larry, who her best friend Sally swore had the body of a Greek God.

"Good afternoon miss, my name is Edwin. Edwin Holtz." He extended his hand toward her with a casual grace that was not reciprocated by Caitlin as Emma began to dance away from him. Edwin raised his eyebrows and stepped back. "It appears I have started your mare. My apologies"

"Emma, stop!" Caitlin sounded a little more agitated than she intended. Her nerves where completely unsettled and she was trying desperately to regain composure. She quickly surveyed this tall slender man. There was nothing extraordinary about him, so why was she reacting in this way? Maybe it was the way his eyes just bore into her. It made her feel exposed in some way. Yet, oddly enough, it also gave her a feeling of anticipated excitement. And the name, Edwin, it did not suit him at all.

Caitlin's agitation was steadily growing as Edwin's piercing eyes continued to watch her struggle to regain control of the increasingly frenzied mare. Caitlin had never seen Emma behave like this and was at a loss at what to do next.

Without knowing how, Caitlin found Edwin at Emma's head, holding her fast to quiet her. Although Emma settled down, she remained coiled in preparation to bolt, should the need arise.

The long slender fingers of this strange man's hand gently stroked Emma's neck and Caitlin watched as her mare visibly became more and more relaxed. Caitlin stared at Edwin's hands for a long time, unaware of the amusement in his eyes as he watched her. When she finally looked up, she was again taken aback by the intensity of those steel gray eyes.

Caitlin quickly shifted her attention to the black beast that was pawing at the earth behind him. "It appears your horse is anxious to get moving and I really must be on my way as well. It was nice meeting you. I'm sure we'll cross paths again."

Edwin's black hair tossed freely and his white teeth sparkled as he threw his head back in a hearty chuckle. "I'm sure we will, miss... ah... I'm sorry, I didn't catch your name."

"I didn't give it." Caitlin surprised herself with the crisp reply.

"Hmm.. That's right, you didn't." Edwin chuckled again as he bowed deeply.

Caitlin was suddenly ashamed by her lack of manners. "I ... I'm sorry. I don't know what got into me. My name is Caitlin and this is my mare, Emma."

"It's a pleasure to meet you Caitlin, " Edwin nodded his head toward the mare, "and Emma. And what, may I ask, brings you out into this remote part of the country?"

"We're on our way to the Roberts's country store for a few supplies. We moved into the Callaghan estate recently and this is the quickest way there"

"Ah yes, the Callaghan estate. If my information is correct, it's been vacant a long time. How did you find it's repair?"

"In need of it, definitely! But with some TLC and elbow grease, it's turning out to be gorgeous. I really enjoy the peace and serenity of the place."

"It's a bit secluded. That doesn't bother you?"

Caitlin squirmed uncomfortably. For a brief moment she had relaxed and allowed herself to enjoy the light conversation with this strange man, but his comment about her being secluded reminded her of her potential vulnerability. She looked at him long and hard, trying to read any hidden meaning behind the words, but his eyes never flinched and his smile never wavered. Either his comment was made in innocent interest or he had the best poker face she had ever encountered.

"No, actually we get company constantly. So I don't feel at all secluded. In fact. I value and appreciate any quiet time I might have!" She was lying of course. Other than an occasional visit from Linnie, the had been no company for some time; not even been a visit from William in two weeks! But she did not feel comfortable letting this stranger know the truth. And, besides, William was going on vacation soon and said he was going to spend it helping her with some repair work on the house. He was due to arrive at the end of the week. "I'll have to excuse myself now, er... Edwin. I really must be getting back or I'll be missed at home." Another lie.

"No problem. It was a pleasure to meet you and I'm sure our paths will cross again soon. In fact, I'm positive of it!" Edwin's twinkling smile didn't match the intensity of his steel grey eyes as he gave a mock bow and stepped aside to allow Emma passage.

Caitlin tipped her head in a short nod and gave a rather awkward smile in his direction as she spurred Emma into action. She could not get away from this man quick enough.

Again Caitlin regretted not knowing how to reach Linnie. So many frightening things where happening! She thought about her devastated study and the horrible creature in the ball and the wolf that turned into a giant hare right before her eyes! She needed to see Linnie. She needed to tell her everything that had been happening. Linnie would know what to do, she was certain of it.

To Caitlin's delight, as she approached the main road leading to the Roberts's small country store, she spotted Linnie. Her arms laden with groceries, she was making her way to a small cart on wheels.

Caitlin spurred Emma forward and was at Linnie's side in no time. She leapt down from the saddle and immediately set out helping

Linnie transfer the bundle of bags from her arms into the small pull cart.

"Ya came just in time, Lass. Old Mr. Roberts loaded me up, he did. But for the life of me, I had no idea how to undo what he'd done!" She stretched her back with relief as the last bag was placed in the cart. "Good lord lass, ya look as if ya have seen a ghost! You're all pale and frail looking. What's the matter?"

Caitlin opened her mouth to speak but before she could utter a word, Linnie continued. "Oh no, ya didn't! Of blimey, ya read the incantation for the dead, didn't ya?"

Caitlin was taken aback by Linnie's acute insight. "I... I'm not sure. I was reading a lot last night. I read something... let me think. It was something made me feel icy cold, so I stopped. But I don't know what I read."

Linnie moaned in despair. "Did ya forget lass? Did ya forget to pay attention to the markings on the pages? The markings tell ya where ya can't read! Did ya read the marked pages?"

Frustration mixed with fear and the implications of what she had done hit Caitlin. "I don't know! I don't know, Linnie!! Oh God. I don't know! I was just reading and reading and reading. I didn't look for markings. I... I just don't know."

Caitlin's eyes welled up as she realized that her fascination with Linnie's book may have been the cause for the nightmare she was now in.

Linnie reached out and brushed away a small tear that was trickling down Caitlin's cheek with her large hand. "Come lass, let's walk together while ya tell me what's been going on. It just so happens that I had a mind to pay ya a visit and I decided to pick up a few goodies for us to have while we visited. So, I was heading in your direction !" Linnie gave Caitlin a broad, reassuring smile. "We can start our visit right now."

The two women walked slowly down the path Caitlin had just emerged from. Caitlin pulled Emma while Linnie pulled her small cart. It wasn't long before Caitlin was deep into the story of the chain of events since she closed the book the night before.

Linnie said nothing as she listened intently to Caitlin's story.

EIGHT

The setting sun beamed bright orange as Linnie guided Caitlin down a long drive toward her home. After hearing Caitlin's tale of the unsettling happenings at her house, Linnie had decided it would be best that she stay there for a while. In need of some of her belongings, Caitlin was finally begin guided to Linnie's home.

The long narrow drive seemed never-ending as it wound its way up the mountainside. When they reached a clearing, Caitlin caught her breath. Never had she seen such a beautiful setting! A small white European style cottage nestled intimately amongst some large oak and apple trees in the middle of the clearing. It reminded Caitlin of an island in the sea. The tall grass swayed like ocean waves as they continued down the drive.

"It's like a whole different world!" Caitlin almost squealed with delight.

"Ah lass, 'tis that. Me husband built it, he did. He fashioned it after his house in the homeland. 'Tis such a lovely house and so sad that he wasn't long to enjoy it." Linnie's chest heaved an audible sigh. "Ah, well, such is living."

"You really miss him. I'm sorry."

"Eye, me heart bleeds daily. There is not a finer man you'll find. Now, I live me days waiting to join him."

"Linnie! Don't say such things!"

"Awe. Not to worry lass. But 'twill be me time soon. I saw it in a dream and he was waiting for me on the other side. 'Twas lovely. All bright colors and birds singing... Not to worry lass, 'twas lovely indeed"

"Stop Linnie, please. I can't talk like this. Please."

"Calm down lass, not to worry. Come on, let's go in and ya can meet me family." Linnie rolled the windows down and the car filled with a myriad of scents from the countryside.

"Family? I thought you said you had no one." Caitlin's tone showed her surprise.

Linnie threw her had back and laughed jovially. "Oh, I have a lovely family. But not the kind of family you would expect."

As the car slowed to a stop before the rounded oak door, a large collie came bounding around the building to greet them. Linnie got out and rigorously fluffed its fur.

To Caitlin's amazement, the lawn began to fill with animals of all kinds. Cats jumped down from the roof where they had been sunning themselves, while birds swooped down from overhead. A rabbit hopped onto the porch sniffing the air and a raccoon balanced himself along the drain pipes.

Linnie's eyes twinkled at Caitlin's response. "Come in lass and sit while I gather a few of me thing an we'll be off."

Caitlin followed Linnie into the house and settled into an overstuffed chair, smiling as the collie laid its head in her lap. Its soft moist nose pushed at her hands, demanding attention. Linnie seemed not to notice the scurry of the little creatures both in and out of her house as she gathered a few herbs and powders and put them in a pouch.

The scent of drying herbs mingled with the wild flowers, giving the room an inviting appeal. Their shadows danced as the remnants of the sun filtered through the leaves of the trees and the large airy windows. Linnie moved gracefully around the room as she continued to pack.

"What do you plan on doing with all those herbs and spices?" Caitlin found it hard to contain her curiosity.

"I don't know what I'll be needing at your place, so 'tis best to be prepared." Linnie completed fastening the clasped on the sack she had stuffed her herbs and spices into. "Now, let me get a change of clothing and we'll be leaving."

With her hands on her hips, Linnie stared at the collie with a concerned expression on her face. "Hmm, I have never left him for more than a day before. What to do?"

Caitlin did not hesitate. "Why not bring him with us. Can't he come to? I'd love it! He's so sweet."

"Ah, do ya hear that Samson? She says you're sweet!" Linnie threw her head back, laughing, while Samson placed his paws on Caitlin's lap and pulled himself up to cover her face with kisses. "'Tis settled then. Me pup will join us. Come on, old boy, 'tis time to be going."

Linnie closed up the windows and set two large buckets of food some type of animal food out on the porch. "This will hold the critters over until I get back." And they headed for the car.

Convincing Samson to enter the car took a some effort. But, in a few minutes everyone was settled and Caitlin was guiding the car back down the long drive.

Linnie reached over and scratched Samson's head. "'Tis an adventure for him, to be sure. 'Tis the first he's been off the property since the day he was born. Ah, me lovely pup, ya like me rubbing ya eh?"

Samson tried to climb into the front of the car, causing Caitlin to swerve onto the shoulder. As she regained a steady steering, she slammed on the brakes to avoid hitting an enormous wolf that stood before them. Its large yellow eyes stared into the car, unmoving, reminding her of her previous encounter while riding Emma.

Caitlin waited, wondering if it would remain a wolf, or turn into another giant hare, while Samson growled and snarled; fighting Linnie's powerful gripped as she struggled to control him.

The wolf showed no fear as it walked up to Caitlin's opened window. She rushed to closed it just before his moist nose reached the glass. He pressed his mouth against the glass, showing broad, pointed teeth; as his saliva ran down the window. Then, he backed away, threw his head high and howled.

Caitlin's heart pounded in her ears as the snarling and growling of Samson mixed with the piercing howl of the wolf. She shuddered from the chills that ran through her body and her legs felt weak. She was barely able to function as Linnie urged her to drive off.

Caitlin was too traumatized with the situation to notice a faint clip of panic in Linnie's voice. "Samson! You hush now! Come on, lass. Let's move out of here. Hurry up now!"

"Oh my God! What's wrong with him! I didn't think wolves approached people like this! Do you think he's rabid?" Caitlin's hands trembled as she put the car in drive.

"Let's just get and worry about it later!" This time Linnie's concern did not go unnoticed by Caitlin.

The wolf stopped howling and disappeared into the woods while Caitlin sped away in the direction of home. As they rounded a corner she swerved the car again. This time to avoid hitting Edwin and his horse. He seemed unruffled at the narrow escape and gave a bowing gesture as her car continued without stopping. Caitlin looked into her rear view mirror at Edwin and his black steed until they where no longer in sight.

"Darn fool. That's how accidents happen!" Linnie shifted uncomfortably in her seat and pulled Samson closer to her, still not willing to release her grip. She remained quiet and deep in thought the rest of the drive.

Caitlin was grateful for the silence. She needed time to digest the day's events. It was all too frightening and unreal. But it was real, wasn't it?

The sun had just dropped behind the mountainside when they turned down Caitlin's driveway. Emma raced to greet them, creating quite a response from Samson. Linnie had Caitlin stopped the car and she let Samson out to run and familiarize himself with the grounds, as well as Emma. The two animals danced and raced together in instant friendship. For a moment, Caitlin forgot about the day's events and fell into laughter as she watched them. Linnie remained more reserved, but still smiled.

Caitlin parked the car in the circular drive-way, near the front door, and immediately began pulling Linnie's belongings from the trunk. She filled her nostrils with the rich aroma of herbs and spices emitted from a bag as she lifted it.

Linnie grabbed what Caitlin left behind and closed the trunk. She did not immediately follow the young woman up the steps, but instead, stood for a moment and took in the feel of the place. There had been a slight shift in the energy since she had been there last and it left her feeling unsettled. Yet, she could not put her finger on exactly why.

Caitlin stopped at the top of the steps and turned to look at her. The two were silent while Linnie mounted the steps to follow Caitlin into the grand foyer.

"Okay lass. Let me take a look at the study room ya was telling me about. I want to see the damage from this mystery monster." Linnie dropped her belongings on the foyer floor and motioned for Caitlin lead follow her upstairs to the reading room.

"Oh, I just hate to think of that horrible sight. Linnie, there's nothing left untouched, nothing! The curtains, the leather sofa, papers, broken glass, it's like a war was fought in there!" Caitlin exclaimed as she led Linnie up the stairs and down the hall toward the reading room. As she swung open its door, she stopped, throwing her hands over her mouth to stifle a cry. Linnie rushed in past her and looked slowly around the room. Neither woman spoke.

Linnie walked to the window and opened it to let in the cool evening air. She tied back the draperies to allow as much air flow as possible. The sweet smell of summer permeated the room while a few moths rode the breeze and circled the lights. Linnie found a screen leaning against the wall and positioned it in the window before turning to Caitlin with a puzzled look.

"I... I don't understand it." Caitlin entered the room in disbelief. The warm, inviting glow of the desk lamp on the rich dark mahogany desk reflected the rays of light that bounced off the antique etched glass doors of the book case, its impressive mass covering an entire wall. All the books were neatly lined up on the shelves. The papers on her desk where left exactly as she had left them the night before when she write to ease her restlessness and the book that Linnie had given her rested peacefully on the mantle of the fireplace. There was no sign of the drama that had occurred early that morning.

"Linnie... I... I... But, it happened! I'm not imagining things, Linnie... It happened!!"

"Calm yourself lass. I'm not saying it didn't. But there is no sign of it now. And that's a

strange thing, wouldn't ya say? Strange indeed."

Linnie walked to the mantle and gently
picked up the "Book of Secrets". Caitlin
remained silent as she watched Linnie leaf
carefully through its pages until she found
the section she wanted. "Did ya read this
section lass? Is this what ya read?"

Caitlin moved next to Linnie to see where
she was pointing. As she looked at the pages
a cold chill crept up her back. She stepped
back so quickly that she lost her balance
and fell against the corner of the mantle and
then onto the floor. The pain between her
shoulder blades pierced her, making it difficult to breath. She fell to the floor wincing. Linnie bent over her to investigate. As
Caitlin looked up at her face, she glimpsed
the familiar form of that elderly man standing behind her. She reached out to point to
him, but Linnie simply took her hand and
lowered it, ignoring her attempts to speak.

"Never mind love, 'tisn't important. Now
let's get ya on the comfy sofa and I'll take a
look at what's going on in your back. Poor
lass, it must have frightened the daylights
out of ya. My oh My."

The old man stood motionless in the corner of the room watching the two women.
A look of concern covered his face, but he
said nothing. Caitlin struggled for footing as

Linnie pulled her up from the floor. As she settled onto the sofa and Linnie lifted her shirt to examine her back, she looked over for the man. He was no where to be found.

"Linnie."

"Yes love"

"Did you see him?"

"Who?"

"Never mind."

NINE

A week passed with nothing out of the ordinary occurred. Linnie had done a complete cleansing of the house and the surrounding property. She explained to Caitlin the necessity to keep the energies of her home and its surroundings balanced at all times. She insisted that if the energy was balanced, it would keep the negative forces from being able to remain, even if they did manage to break through the wall of protection that she had created.

Caitlin was thirsty for whatever knowledge she was able to acquire from Linnie. The old woman's presence in the house gave Caitlin a warm sense of security. And the best part was that she had not had an incident with anything out of the ordinary since Linnie's arrival. There was definitely something magical about this woman.

As they completed their daily meditation, Linnie reached for the bag she had packed at her home. She pulled out a small book. Its edges showed signs of usage and the binding was broken, barely intact.

"Today we are going to talk about the powers of the mind."

"Do you mean manifesting?"

"Exactly. Making things happen by will. Knowing your abilities and making good use of them."

"It seems so complicated. I struggle so much with what you are teaching me, Linnie. But I won't give up."

"That's the way lass, never give up. The day will come when it just comes naturally to ya, lass. Just keep learning and practicing and respecting what ya don't understand."

Linnie moved close so that Caitlin could see the writing on the pages of the book she held. "But you're right about it being complicated. It takes a whole lifetime, and then some, to understand. And then, ya still don't know it all."

Caitlin put her hand over Linnie's and looked at her with strong affection. She had grown to truly love this unique woman, even though she still did not know much about her. She did not even know her last name! She had asked one day and Linnie simply replied, "What's in a name? Names are for referring to someone who's not here. I'm here, lass. Linnie will suit me. There's no need for more than that."

Although she found it a strange response, Caitlin did not pursue it further.

Caitlin tucked her feet underneath her and snuggled into Linnie in a child-like manner as she settled in to listen to the words being read.

"There is only one mind, and that be the mind of God. Some call it spirit or universal intelligence, but it is God; the power of the mighty one. This mind is in all things on earth. In the life of man, the God mind lives. God life expresses through us, one and all. Since we all have the life power of God running through us, we all have the power of God to create! But this is only in accordance to what we believe, because we have free will to accept and reject. It is God's way to allow us this right. And it is also God's way to allow us to use our powers for what we want. So, if we are good, we are doing good with our gifts while making things happen. If we are bad, then it is the opposite."

Caitlin shifted uncomfortably as she remembered the happening of the prior week.

Linnie paused, watching for a sign that Caitlin was ready to hear more before continuing. "Learning to use it properly is the key; because man is using it all the time whether man realize it or not. Learning to use it properly will give you the results you desire, because God's power flows through you. It is a gift of his love to use as you want."

Linnie put the book down and positioned her body to face Caitlin. "Now, let's think of an example for a minute. If ya have a long beautiful sharp knife. Ya can do two things with this beauty. One is good and one is bad;

but 'tis the same knife. Look at the knife as the gift the Almighty One. Okay, now, ya are in a room full of hungry people and they all want to have the little bit of food ya possess and there is no extra. Have ya got the picture in your mind?"

Linnie waited for Caitlin to nod before continuing. "Now, with this knife ya can kill them off to keep them from taking your food and keep the food for yourself. Or, ya can slice the food up to make enough for everyone to have a little to sustain themselves while trusting in the Lord that there will be more food made available to ya. Now, one was bad, taking lives, and one was good, saving lives; but ya used the same tool. It was the same knife in both situations. Do ya understand lass?"

Caitlin nodded slowly. "I think I do. So, we have free will always and it is our decision what to do with our powers that determines what happens?"

"Ya might say that" Linnie sat back with a satisfied sigh.

"But I don't understand why God allows us to do harm with his tools. He is all powerful, so why doesn't he stop those who are doing harm?"

Linnie scowled and scratched her head. "Aye lass, that's a common question I hear, and sometimes ask meself. And I can only answer it to the best of me ability by telling ya that if he stopped us from using the tools the way we choose, then we'd lose our free will, now, wouldn't we?"

"Does that go for spirits too? Are they allowed to use the tools with free will too?" Caitlin's mind was racing with curiosity.

"Ah, indeed that's correct. But they have the advantage of having a better idea of what 'tis all about, this life and universe. They don't have to be like us and pick the information through the human brain to boot!"

"If that's true, Linnie, then why are there bad spirits? If they have an understanding about God and all the good there is available to them, why are they doing evil things? I don't understand."

"I asked the same thing meself at your age." Linnie laughed and stroked Caitlin's hair. "And I'll give ya the same answer me mum gave to me. 'Tis because when ya leave your body in death, ya still have your mind with ya. And because ya still are under the right of free will, ya have the choice of believing that ya should move into the light or not. That's why they send loved ones to get ya. Because ya relax and believe better. But, sometimes there is not a loved one to be found at your time and if ya don't have the faith to begin with, ya get scared, or angry and sometimes jealous that ya don't have your body anymore and ya wander the earth because ya refuse to go on into the light. Sometimes ya meet up with others who are feeling the same way as ya are and ya form something like an army that joins the evil one to get back at those who still have what ya want. Lots of things could happen after ya leave your body on earth. That's why 'tis good to pray for the poor souls who have passed on, to help their energies be balanced and to let them see the truth and go back to God's place. Do ya understand?"

"Yes, yes, I believe I am starting to. Oh Linnie, this makes perfect sense to me. So much more sense than what I learned as a child."

"Good. Now let's get back to the making things happen part. Everything in life exists in thought first. So, if ya think about it hard enough, it can happen for ya. Now people are doing this every day of their lives without understanding what they are doing. Take, for instance, the man who believes he is a loser. He wants to be a winner, but deep down inside he feels he is a loser. So, he gets himself a good job; a really good one now. And what do ya think happens? He fails at it. Why? Because even though on the outside he wanted it, he didn't believe he deserved it. So, he failed at it. If he had changed his thinking of himself, he would have soared!"

"Okay. But what about bringing money into your life, or a new love, or something like that? Would it happen just because you say it will?"

Linnie pursed her lips together and wrinkled her brow, "I guess the quickest answer is yes. Yes, as long as deep inside ya, that is what ya felt ya were worthy of and are ready for." Linnie tapped the side of her head. "Because it starts there, deep in the mind that is connected to God. And then ya gotta do what comes natural to help it happen. Like, get a good paying job or go out to meet people. Things like that."

"Ha! God helps those who help themselves." Caitlin beamed proudly.

"Aye lassie. Indeed."

"Okay, so if it is all in the power of the mind, then, why do people use candles and incense and rituals?"

"A couple of reasons, lass. The first one being to help get the energies flowing in the right way so it will make it easier to happen. Second being that they are asking for help from the spirit side, and that is the best way to please some the folks on that side. They respond nicely to the scents."

"I see. And what about all the blood sacrifices? Why them?"

"Again", Linnie sighed as if getting bored with the conversation, "'Tis because some of these spirits are bad and they fool the people into believing that the only way they will get what they're wanting is to do it that way. Remember, there's good and bad, greedy and generous on the spirit side too."

"Wow. This is all so fascinating!" Caitlin wiggled with excitement, ignoring Linnie's obvious desire to move on. "So the words in the book you gave me? The spirits respond to them?"

"Yep."

"I remember learning from you about our guardian angels and spirit guides. If that's true, why don't they stop the bad spirits from hurting us?""

They can only help if we ask for their help. Otherwise they have to sit back an watch. 'Tis a pity don't ya think?"

"Linnie, that man I keep seeing in my dreams? Do you think he is my spirit guide?"

"I imagine so. He said he's been with ya for many years, lass. That makes him special. Take some time to get to know him better. It'll be good for ya."

"Linnie?" Caitlin spoke hesitantly.

Noticing Caitlin's shift in body language and vocal tone brought Linnie back into the grove of the conversation. "Yes"

"If they can't help us unless we ask for it, how do you explain all the times people get help from some mysterious source and then call them miracles? I mean, if they haven't asked for the help? Why are they being helped?"

"Ha," Linnie chuckled, "you're full a questions, ya are. Okay. Well, that's because in their dreams or in their subconscious, or maybe even before they were born, they gave some kind of permission for certain kinds of help from their angels and their guides; like to save their life maybe. But, not to give them easy street through life. Do ya get what I mean?"

Caitlin placed her fingers to her temples. "I think so. It's really deep. I think I'll have to digest it a bit."

Linnie threw her head back in laughter and stood up. She walked to the mantle and placed the little book on top of the large book she had already given Caitlin. Caitlin smiled, knowing this was the signal that this book was at her disposal to read whenever she felt the desire.

Linnie turned to Caitlin and stretched her arms back over her head as far as they would go. "'Tis time to quit for that day."

"I agree. It's about time for dinner. What do you feel like having?" Caitlin did a mental survey of her kitchen cupboards while she waiting for Linnie's response.

Linnie had gotten to know Caitlin well enough to realize that food was not a priority for her and there was probably a minimal amount of supplies in her cupboard. "I'm thinking 'tis time to get off this land for a bit an go to town for dinner!"

"Oh! That's a fantastic idea? Where should we go?" Caitlin jumped up with anticipation.

Linnie smiled. She could never grow tired of her new friend's youthful exuberance. "Not too fancy, since ya know my attire. But, I know just the place for us. Come on, let's get ready to go"

TEN

As they where dressing for dinner, Caitlin was struck with the realization of how lonely and isolated she had actually become. It was good to be getting out amongst people. *When I was in Manhattan, she used to dream of being able to get away from it all and be alone. Now, I dream of being in the middle of the masses again. I guess Mitch was right. There seems no pleasing me,* she mused as she pulled the car into the parking lot of the Great Pines Restaurant.

The floor creaked under the strain of Linnie's bulk as they entered the dimly lit room. Linnie had guided Caitlin to an out of the way, rustic style, restaurant. She assured Caitlin that even though the surroundings where humble, the food was not. Caitlin did not mind. She was happy to just be out with a friend doing some socializing.

As they where shown to their table, she froze half-seated. Linnie followed her stare to Edwin Holtz, who sat with confident grace playing with the food on his plate. He seemed not to notice the two women being seated across the room. His rich, dark hair reflected the glow of the candle that burned in the center of his table.

Although Edwin was alone, there was evidence that he had a companion who had would soon return. He pierced the meat on his plate with his fork and almost threw it onto the plate across from him. At that point a slender young man returned and seated himself. The look of disdain on Edwin's companion's face was evidence that he no more wanted that piece of meat than Edwin did.

"Do ya know this fella?" Linnie asked quizzically.

"He's the one I told you about; the one I met that awful morning that everything happened. The one with the enormous black gelding. Or, at least I think it was a gelding." Caitlin hoped that she was able to disguise the trembling response her body had at the sight of Edwin Holtz.

"Ha, no matter. I'm wondering the same thing here." Linnie nodded as the man who had joined Edwin stood up to leave., obviously unhappy.

"Linnie!" Caitlin feigned shock. The two women laughed and giggled as they server took their order.

Still not aware of their presence, Edwin remained in deep thought over his food, while Caitlin and Linnie enjoyed each other's company.

Linnie had been correct about the food. It was simple, but delicious. They where deciding upon dessert when they found Edwin standing

next to them. "You really should try the peach
cobbler. It's delicious and fresh this time of
year."

Linnie assessed Edwin as he stood next to the
table. He seemed not to notice her, but kept his
cold grey eyes on Caitlin, as he bowed politely
and left the restaurant. There was something
about him that seemed familiar to her, but she
could not quite place it.

Caitlin looked pale when Linnie returned her
attention to her. "Lass, you're pretty shook up
by this man. How come?"

"I don't understand it myself. There's something about him that's creepy. He stares at me
as if he's looking inside me. Those eyes are...
I don't know." She refused to admit that not
only was she unsettled by his eyes, but she was
also embarrassed by the feelings that stirred
within her whenever he was near. "You were
staring at him in an odd way, Linnie. Your eyes
got small and glassy. What was going on?"

"I was just scanning him, love. I was looking
at his energy"

"Do you mean his aura?"

"Yes, that's exactly what I mean ."

"What color was it?"

I'm not looking for color, so much. That chang-
es in the blink of an eye. No, I was more looking at the flow of the energy passing through
him and around him. Ya can tell a lot about a
person by the way the energy flows with him."

The server came to take their order and both

woman laughed as they simultaneously asked for the peach cobbler. They also requested a little brandy in their coffee to top off the meal.

Edwin was correct about the cobbler, it was the best Caitlin had tasted. She was just finishing up the last of it when the server came with a note for her. She opened it, curious as to who would be sending her a note when the only person she really knew in the area was sitting across from her.

Caitlin's heart pounded in her eardrums, to the point of blocking all other sounds in the room, as she slowly read the bold handwriting. `I need to see you.  Meet me  at the clearing tomorrow at 3:00. Edwin.`

Linnie watched Caitlin read the note in silence before folding it up and placing it in her purse; making no mention of it. Linnie remained silent, waiting for Caitlin to speak.

Caitlin shifted uncomfortably in her seat, debating what to do. "When you where looking at his energy, what did you see?"

"His power." Linnie replied flatly.

"Huh?" Caitlin was lost to Linnie's meaning.

Linnie took a sip of her coffee before explaining. "He's a powerful man, love. And he loves his power. Be careful with this one."

"Why?" Caitlin wondered if Linnie already knew of Edwin's intentions.

"Well," Linnie drawled, "he's a man who goes after what he wants. And it looks like he wants ya, right?" She nodded toward the note in Caitlin's purse.

Caitlin looked away. "I don't know. It just says he wants to meet me tomorrow, but it doesn't say why."

"Well. Where did he say he wanted to meet ya?"

"At the same spot where we met before. At 3:00 tomorrow afternoon."

Linnie frowned. "Are ya gonna do it?"

"I don't know. I have to think about it."

"Maybe I'm old fashioned, but it seems to me that if he wants to meet ya, he should meet ya in a nice restaurant or some other respectable place. Why in the middle of nowhere? It doesn't feel right to me, no sir."

"Me neither."

"So then. What are ya going to do?"

"I don't know Linnie. I am curious, of course. But there's something very unsettling about him. And you're right about him wanting to meet me in the middle of nowhere. I think I should pass."

"Smart lass. Your mama taught ya well."

"Not my mother, my sister."

"Do tell?" Linnie shifted in her seat. If Caitlin did not know better, she would have thought that her last remark had upset Linnie. But why would it? Even so, she decided to proceed with caution. "There's nothing to tell, really. My father left when I was just a baby and my mother died when I was quite young. My sister took care of my brother and me. I don't remember my mother much. She was gone most of the time when she was alive. Nora said she worked all the time. And then when she died, Nora got custody of us. She's the only mother I really remember."

Linnie seemed to relax. "Ah, ya don't say! Such a thing for a lass to have to bear. How did your sister manage to keep ya together and all?"

"I.... I'm not exactly sure. We aren't allowed to talk about those days. She gets real upset when we try. She said some things are better left unsaid and that we need to let sleeping dogs lie."

"She sounds like a smart woman."

"She is. Oh yes, she is that! She's a writer, you know. Did I tell you that?"

"No lass, ya haven't mentioned her much. Where does she live again?" Linnie seemed happy with the shift in direction of their conversation and her voice grew soft and nurturing.

"She lives in Arizona, just outside of Phoenix. She has a beautiful house with some land on the dessert."

"Ya don't say! That sounds lovely"

"Oh yes, it is. I love going out there to visit her. But the truth is. I prefer the mountains and the trees over the dessert. Each has its own beauty, though. I guess it's just a matter of preference."

"Hmm, that's true."

"Have you ever seen the desert, Linnie?"

"Only in pictures, lass.   One day I plan on making me way west to see what there is to see."

"Oh, you should. It is wonderful; magical actually. The desert speaks to you with a life of its own. The last time I was there I took a balloon ride over the desert. What a sensation!"

"Like flying with the angels, was it?"

"Yes Linnie, you might say that. Like flying with the angels; fabulous."

Linnie and Caitlin simultaneously reached for the bill as the server placed it in the center of the table. Caitlin was just a little quicker and snatched it to her chest. Her insistence about treating Linnie to dinner went with little resistance from Linnie, who pointed out that it was necessary to be good at receiving as much as it was to be good at giving. So with that settled, the bill was paid and they left the restaurant.

The evening air was warm and inviting and the two women decided to drive with the convertible top down so that they could enjoy the sensation of freedom and the beauty of the star filled sky. As they pulled out of the parking lot, the full moon beamed down, causing shadows to dance all around them. The world took on a new life and Caitlin found herself searching for the earth fairies she had read about as a little girl, while they made their way home.

ELEVEN

Since Edwin had not given Caitlin any information on how to contact him, she had no way of telling him she would not be there. Feigning the need for a nap, she went to her room and paced. It was so tempting to go and see what he wanted, but she knew that it was not the smartest thing to do. If he had asked to meet her in the restaurant or even for a walk around town, she might consider it. But, not in the middle of nowhere. She could not believe that he would even ask such a thing. And, did she present herself as someone who would follow along with it? *Obviously, since he sent the note,* she mused.

The clicking of the clock on the mantle sounded throughout the room as she continued to pace. She wanted to open the French doors that led out to her small balcony, but feared Linnie, who was out in the lawn enjoying the afternoon sun, would see her and she was supposed to be napping.

She was not up to explaining her actions, nor could she explain her actions. It was like an unknown and unseen force was compelling her to go meet him and it took all of her will to ignore it.

But, dear Linnie rarely asked for explanations, anyway. It was more Caitlin simply blurting them out and Linnie quietly listening. The old woman rarely made a comment. Her convictions of 'live and let live' seemed even stronger than Caitlin's. But although Linnie had made no comment as to how she felt about Edwin, Caitlin sensed there was something she was not divulging; something that she knew and was keeping to herself.

The clock chimed three o'clock. It was too late now. He would be there waiting for her. She wondered how long he would wait before he realized she was not coming. It was an easy fifteen minute ride on Emma from her property to the spot where he wanted to meet her; add the time it would take to tack the mare up and it was at least twenty-five minutes. Even if she changed her mind and left now, she doubted he would still be there when she finally reached the spot. No one would wait twenty-five minutes, would they?

The nagging curiosity finally got the better of Caitlin and she snuck down the servant's stairwell and out to the barn to saddle Emma. Linnie watched in mild amusement as Caitlin made a feeble excuse about needing something at the store and Emma needing the exercise, and so it was a good idea to ride her to the store. She wondered if Caitlin really thought she bought the story. Chuckling to herself, Linnie returned to the book she had been enjoying in the shade of a gnarled and ancient apple tree.

Caitlin decided to ride Emma bareback. This would save her some time. It was not something that she was skilled at, but she had done it enough to feel she could manage.

As she put the bit in Emma's mouth, the mare tossed her head in anticipated response to Caitlin's excited demeanor. She pawed the earth when Caitlin climbed up onto the mounting stool. "Take it easy girl. You know I'm not good at this. Cooperate please!" As if she understood, Emma shifted slightly and settled down.

As horse and rider headed in the direction of the designated meeting place, Caitlin's urgency became more noticeable to Emma. The mare broke into an easy lope as they headed down the path through the woods. Caitlin felt the muscles of her mare blend in movement with her own. It was as if they had become one. The slight fear that she would not be able to stay on left quickly, replaced by exhilarated confidence. They where a team. They fit right. They felt right.

As they approached the edge of the clear-

ing, there was no sign of Edwin. Caitlin
slowed Emma down and looked around.
She should have realized that he would not
have waited. The disappointment that was
flowing through her changed to panic when
she spotted Edwin's enormous black gelding bending over his limp body on the other
side of the open field. She kicked Emma
into motion and flew to the ground before
the horse had completely stopped where he
lay.

Edwin was lying face down in the tall
grass. His breathing was labored, but
steady. Caitlin rolled him onto his back
and straightened his legs out. The lump
on his head was beginning to clot, allowing
only a small amount of blood to continue to
ooze. She pulled the scarf off her neck and
pressed it against his wound. The pressure
of her hand made him wince, even in his
dazed state.

As she debated on what to do, Edwin's
gelding began to fuss and strike at the
ground. Intimidated by such an enormous
beast, she was completely at a loss at
what to do with him. His massive bulk was
prancing nervously. Caitlin slowly stood up
as she decided on her next move.

She needed to quite the gelding down so
that she could, somehow, get Edwin back
onto him and take him someplace for med-

ical attention.   She held her breath and begged her heart to stop climbing up her throat as she timidly approached the gelding.

"Can I help?" A gentle, yet clearly masculine voice came out of nowhere.

"I don't know, I found him like this. I'm not sure what to do. I already moved him a little, wand I know that's the wrong thing. But, his face was jammed in the ground and he was having trouble breathing."

Thankful that she was talking to a real person and not some voice in the trees, Caitlin turned to face her newly arrived companion. She sucked in her breath in surprise. Never before had she come into contact with a more perfect looking man. His golden hair looked soft and refined as the light breeze tossed it whimsically. His blue eyes were lined with thick dark lashes; the envy of every woman, she was sure. Brilliant white teeth lined up in a neat row across his smile and his deep dimples only accentuated the chiseled look of his face. He stood tall and lean in a tailored shirt and jeans, carrying himself like a model during a shoot. He was completely at ease and confident with the situation.

"Hi. I'm Dominic." He extended his hand to Caitlin. "I was out for a walk and saw you racing with the wind, like an angel. So, I came to investigate. "You are..."

Caitlin quickly accepted Dominic's hand. "Caitlin. I'm Caitlin. And this is Edwin Holtz." Her attention returned to the gravity of the situation. "I don't know what happened to him. I found him here like this. I'm not sure what to do."

"Well, my wheels are parked over there, on the other side of the clearing. Shall I see if I can pull it over and we can get him loaded up and off to the hospital?"

Under normal circumstances, Caitlin would have found Dominic's comment of loading Edwin up, as if he was a bail of hay, offensive, but his overwhelming charisma had her so smitten that it went right over her head and she readily agreed.

Without waiting for Caitlin's response, Dominic sauntered back across the clearing. Edwin moved, making a feeble effort to sit up. He fell back as a loud moan escaped his lips, pulling Caitlin's attention back to him. "Oh, no... Stay still for now Mr. Holtz. You have a terrible egg on your head. Please don't try to move until I get some help and we'll get you taken care of."

"Who are you?" His vision blurred, Edwin struggled to focus on Caitlin.

"Why, I'm Caitlin. Don't you remember? You asked me to meet you here today."

"Oh yeah, Caitlin. Ha, you came after all." His week smile gave him a boyish look as he settled back down, awaiting the help she had promised.

It took some time for Dominic to come to the conclusion that he was not going to be able to maneuver his car across the clearing like he had hoped. There where too many ruts and hidden water patches. Before he found himself in serious trouble, he abandoned the idea and returned to Caitlin. "I'm sorry, but my car isn't going to make it over here. I couldn't risk getting it stuck." Dominic surveyed Edwin and heaved a sigh. "I'm just going to have to carry him out."

Although Dominic looked strong enough, Edwin was a few inches taller and practically dead weight. Caitlin looked at the distance Dominic would have to carry Edwin and creased her brows. "What about putting him on the back of his gelding ."

"Good idea." Dominic looked relieved. "Can you hold that beast steady for me?"

"I'll try." Caitlin took a deep breath to steady her nerves.

Dominic reached for the gelding's reins and handed them to Caitlin. Her heart pounded fiercely as she drew closer to the black beast. She had never been near so powerful a horse as this one and his seemingly wild actions made her apprehensive. But, to her delight and surprise, he remained docile while Dominic eased Edwin onto the saddle. He climbed up behind Edwin and held him steady while reaching for the reins from Caitlin. She handed them to him, saying nothing, and stood back to get a better look at the picture they made. It reminded her of a western movie.

Dominic turned the gelding in the direction of the car and Caitlin searched for a log to help her climb back onto Emma. "Leave it to me to ride without a saddle" she huffed. A large rock nearby offered just enough boost to help her on.

Dominic was halfway across the clearing by the time she and Emma caught up. Caitlin felt like she was riding a small pony next to them.

"My wheels are over there." Dominic nodded his head to the left.

Caitlin followed the direction of Dominic's nod to see a black Mercedes parked on the edge of the clearing, obviously the victim of traction trouble in the wet field. Its polished chrome glistened in the sunlight between speckles of mud. Caitlin let out a giggle at the thought of Dominic attempting to take a Mercedes across the clearing.

Dominic seemed not to notice Caitlin's amusement and he asked her to hold the gelding while he slid to the ground and lowered the still stunned Edwin. He half carried, half walked Edwin to the Mercedes and eased him into the back seat. Caitlin noticed the blood had started to steadily flow from his wound again.

Dominic closed the car door and stretched his back before moving toward the driver's door. "I'm not from around here, actually. I am just passing through on a little vacation. Do you know where the nearest hospital is?"

Caitlin was taken aback when she realized she had been ogling Dominic's fine physic. "Yes. Yes, of course."

"Well, maybe you should ride along to keep me from getting lost." Caitlin's admiration had not gone unnoticed and Dominic's eyes twinkled with amusement.

"What about the horses?" Caitlin held up the reins she was holding, grateful to take the attention away from herself.

"I'll tend to em." Caitlin whirled in surprise as Linnie walked up next to her and took the reins of the black gelding. She was already pulling a reluctant Emma behind her.

"Linnie? Where did you come from?"

"I decided to stretch me legs is all. And a good thing I did." She looked long and hard at Dominic, but said nothing. Caitlin assumed she was also appreciating his good looks.

Dominic shifted under Linnie's stare before regaining his composure. "Good. It's settled then. Come on... Caitlin, right? Let's get this poor fellow some care."

"Okay. Thanks Linnie." Caitlin smiled appreciatively at Linnie.

"Not a problem, lass. Go on with ya." Linnie's face was like an emotionless mask, but her tone of voice was gentle and nurturing.

Caitlin decided to ride in the back with Edwin and see if she could reduce the oozing of blood with some pressure. As they drove along toward the hospital, she compared the two men. Both had a rugged beauty about them, equal in his own right. Edwin, with his dark almost sinister looks, were in stark contrast to Dominic, who appeared angelic. And indeed he was a gift from the heavens today. She did not know what she would have done if he had not come along.

Dominic watched Caitlin tend to Edwin's wound in the rear view mirror. "Your friend took a nasty fall."

"Yes"

"Is he a close friend?"

"No."

"No?"

"We've only just met, actually."

"Hmm"

"Hmm? What is meant by that?" Caitlin clipped out the words.

"Oh... Nothing. And really it isn't my business. I'm just making small talk, don't get upset."

But Caitlin was upset. She knew herself how strange it must appear that she had only just met this man and was going to meet him in the middle of nowhere. But, after all, it was the twentieth century.

Edwin stirred and draped his arm over Caitlin's slender legs. His hand slowly caressed her strong calf. At first she made move to remove it, but then changed her mind. He was in a peaceful state right now, so she saw no harm in allowing him this small liberty. He probably did not even realize what he was doing and, actually, it felt nice.

Remembering she was the navigator, Caitlin returned her attention to the road in front of them and motioned for Dominic to turn left.

As they pulled into the emergency room entrance way, Dominic turned and asked Caitlin how Edwin was doing. She could not help responding to his handsome charm with a broad flirtatious smile and, to her delight, he returned it with an equally dazzling one. For a brief moment, Caitlin forgot where they were they were and why they were there. But, Edwin's moans quickly brought her back to reality.

Sliding out of the back seat, she gently moved his head off her lap and laid down on the seat. He raised his hands to his wound and groaned. It was comforting to Caitlin to see that he was coming around. He had been in that dazed state for the better part of an hour. Caitlin was not a doctor, but she did not think that was a good sign.

As Caitlin entered the emergency room reception area to get help, Dominic helped Edwin sit up. The motion of sitting created a renewed pounding in his head and Edwin wailed in protest.

"That's a nasty bump you have there. Do you remember how you got it?" Dominic's voice sounded concerned, but his eyes twinkled with amusement.

"Ah," Edwin replied, "I'm not sure. Something hit my head. Aarrrggghhh! It hurts!"

"I'll bet it does."

A emergency room attendants came out with a wheelchair and assisted Edwin into it. Caitlin went back in to registration and did her best to give them the information they required about a man she hardly knew. There was identification on him, which helped and Edwin was able to speak, which helped fill in the blanks.

It seemed like forever before the doctor was able to look at Edwin. He decided it would be best to keep him overnight for observation. Still in a slight daze and a lot of discomfort, Edwin gave no argument.

Dominic had waited to see what would happen with Edwin and insisted on driving

Caitlin back to her home, taking advantage of the ride back by steering the conversation toward the possibility of them getting together some time for a drink. Caitlin was delighted with the prospect of seeing him again and readily agreed. Dominic explained that he had commitments elsewhere, but promised to look her up as soon as he was able.

Emma came racing along side Dominic's car as it swung into Caitlin's driveway. Caitlin watched him carefully as his eyes took in her house and its surroundings. There seemed to be a glint of pleasure in them that was quickly masked again with that aloof manner he had been prone to display most of the afternoon.

"I just moved in this last spring. It's going to be lovely when I am finished." Caitlin did not know why, but she wanted Dominic to admire her home as much as she did.

"It's a charmer now." Dominic mused. "I was just noticing how peaceful and secluded it is. You must enjoy that. I know I would."

"Oh, I do."

After a short silence between them, Caitlin grabbed the handle of the door before stating, "But, I'm not really alone. So it isn't as peaceful as it might appear."

Dominic raised is eyebrows quizzically, "Oh? For some reason I was under the impression you where unattached."

"Oh, I am!" Caitlin turned away blushing after her all too eager response and got out of the car.

The amused look swiftly left Dominic's face when he spotted Linnie coming across the lawn. She stopped briefly to speak to Caitlin and then continued on to the car. As she approached Dominic, she extended her hand. He reached through the window and took it hesitantly.

"Linnie's me name. 'Tis grand what ya did to help out the lad and the lass and I thank ya." Her eyes locked his unflinchingly.

Dominic nodded his head in a slight acknowledgment, a look of concern flashed across his face. Then, as quickly as it left, his amused look returned. "It's a pleasure to meet you Linnie, I'm Dominic. And I'm glad to have been of service."

Still locking eyes, Dominic slowly retrieved his hand from Linnie's solid grip and excused himself. He told her he was heading somewhere when he stumbled on Caitlin and Edwin and now he would continue on that route. Linnie smiled but kept her eyes locked on him and he shuddered visibly before he touched his brow lightly with his hand in a form of a salute and backed the car out of the drive. Linnie stood watching long after Dominic's car disappeared.

TWELVE

The afternoon sun peaked through the leaves of the trees as the cab weaved its way down the winding country lane toward Caitlin's house. Edwin took in the beauty of the ride as he rolled down the window for some air. The cool evening breeze felt good on his throbbing head. He raised his hand to the bandage the hospital had secured, giving him the appearance of a battle worn soldier. The tender bump protruded out amongst the soft gauze.

A scowl crossed his face as he tried to remember what had happened just a few days earlier in that field, but he had no recollection of how he fell, or much after that, really. He remembered waiting impatiently for Caitlin to cross the field. Then, he saw her working her way out of the grove on her chestnut mare and then everything went black. The next thing he remembered was waking up in the hospital with Caitlin next to him, talking to a member of the hospital staff. As hard as he tried, he could recall no more.

As the cab turned up the drive, he smiled

to see his black gelding racing through the paddock with the chestnut mare close behind. They made a beautiful sight. Each had long silken manes and tails that flowed with the movement of their powerful muscles. The setting sun peaked through the leaves on the hillside with a reddish hew, adding a sense of exotic mystery to the scene.

At one point the drive edged the fence and the cab and horses were side by side. The cab driver fell into competitive mode, and the race was on. He laid his hand firmly on the horn, with a devilish grin on his face, as he stepped on the accelerator. While the startled gelding jumped sideways in response, Emma took on the challenge. She tossed her head high, with nostrils flared, as she gathered her muscles for the push. Little did the driver know that this was her favorite game, and she seldom lost.

As they approached a precarious bend in the drive that led to the final stretch toward the house, he slammed on his brakes. "Damn! There's a crater in the middle of this drive the size of a meteorite! I'm afraid the race is off. I can't believe I was racing the damn beast to begin with." The driver was speaking more to himself, than to Edwin.

Edwin reached to steady his bandaged head as he jolted across the seat. A dark scowl crossed his face, giving him a sinister appearance, as he glowered silently at the cab driver. Seeing the look through his rear view mirror, the cab driver guiltily cleared his throat. He straightened his back somberly and remained focused on easing the cab around the large pot holes in the drive. They finished the drive in silence.

As the cab pulled up along the circular driveway in front of the house, Caitlin stepped out onto the porch. Edwin admired her slender silhouette in the dusky light. Her long hair fell in firelight wisps around her face and over her shoulders while her pale skin, that had been baked golden in the sun, gleamed against a white gauze peasant dress; exposing just enough flesh to make you desire a little more.

Caitlin felt uncomfortable under his intense stare and quickly looked away. She tugged at the bodice of her dress in an attempt to cover her burning flesh. There was something about this man that excited, yet frightened her. Edwin noticed her discomfort and smiled. She certainly was a beautiful woman. He looked forward to getting to know her better.

"I'm glad to see you found the place okay." Caitlin blurted out in an attempt to camouflage her uneasiness.

"It was a beautiful drive out here. You're most fortunate to have such beauty available to you on a daily basis." Edwin eased himself out of the cab. The injury to his head required that he move cautiously.

As he leaned in to paid the cab, Caitlin struggled unsuccessfully to hear their brief, muffled conversation. When Edwin moved away from the he cab and it drove off, she looked on in puzzlement.

Edwin chuckled , "Is something wrong?"

"Well, uh... he left... without you!" She blushed at the obvious panic in her voice. The thought of being alone with this man made her shiver with excited anticipation that she was desperately trying to hide.

"Yes he did. I can't fit my horse in the back seat." Edwin grinned broadly, displaying a set of perfect, brilliant white teeth. "I want to thank you for keeping him here for me."

"It was no problem at all. Emma loved the company."

"Emma?"

Caitlin grinned, "My mare."

"Oh, yes. That's right." Edwin chuckled, "I thought you had someone else here with you."

"I... I do." Caitlin blurted out and then instantly regretted it. Edwin's reminder of their isolation made her suddenly nervous and fearful. After all, she really did not know this man. But, now she would be expected to produce a companion of some sort, and there was no one.

Caitlin quickly turned away from Edwin

and busied herself picking up some empty clay pots that she had left on the porch earlier after transplanting the flowers into the window boxes along the front and side of the house. Concerned that she would be found out, she changed the subject . "What do you call your horse?"

"King." He replied, but not to be swayed he continued, "you said you have a companion living here? Hmm. For some reason I thought you where single."

"I am. But I have a companion. Do you plan on riding King home tonight? Is that wise?"

"Well, I don't know how wise it is. But, the old boy is a devil when it comes to being trailered. So I think it's the lesser of the two evils."

Caitlin caught her breath as Edwin flashed his seductive smile her way.

"Ah. There ya be lass. I was looking for ya quite a while now. Ah, who is this? Be ya the man I last saw lying in the grass?" Linnie stuck her hand out to shake Edwin's in a not too gentle manner.

Caitlin looked on speechless. Linnie had moved home that afternoon and she had not heard her return.

"Sorry lass, did I frighten ya? I heard ya speaking so I thought I'd check to see who the company was!" Linnie pushed past Caitlin toward Edwin with her hand extended.

Edwin flinched under the jolt of Linnie's handshake and his smile looked a little weak as he greeted her; politely acknowledging his pleasure in finding her there. Neither Caitlin or Linnie were certain that he meant it.

Caitlin was delighted to have Linnie show up like she had, since it solved her dilemma of producing a companion. She invited everyone to join her on the back patio.

Caitlin had developed the habit of admiring the moon in the early evenings with a glass of wine. Edwin seemed eager to join her, but Linnie declined. She said she had only stopped to retrieve a few things that she had left behind that afternoon and needed to get back to Samson.

Disappointment filled Caitlin as she watched Linnie go back into the house. She turned to Edwin, who stood quietly watching her. Her heart beat against her chest so hard that she was sure he could see. Taking a deep breath, she walked past him toward to back part of the porch, eager for that wine.

"Shall I pour?" Edwin asked, after noticing how her hands where fumbling with the bottle.

"I can't seem to get it together! It's been that way all day!" She was lying, of course, but did not know what else to say to cover the nervousness that permeated her whole being. Handing the bottle to Edwin, she walked over to the railing and looked up at the sky. "The moon is so beautiful. I remember when I was a little girl, I used to look for the man in the moon and wish I were him. I thought how lucky he was to be living on such a big bright ball and be able to look over at the stars like that. Did you believe in the man in the moon?"

"I still do." Edwin chuckled as he handed her a glass of wine and raised his to a toast.

"In some ways, so do I." Caitlin touched her glass to his and drank eagerly. The liquid was smooth and soothing. Within moments she felt calmer and more relaxed. "Do you ride King often in the moonlight?"

"Never."

"But... Do you mean this is your first attempt; with your injury like that?"

"You guessed it. There's a first time for everything, right?" Edwin kept his tone light, but even he had some concerns about how wise it was to try to ride King in his condition. He would have liked to have waited a few more days to allow his head to stop pounding, but he did not want to start a new relationship with Caitlin with the imposition of forcing her to care for King. He was very attracted to Caitlin and wanted to be in good standing with her.

"But... Edwin... do you think that's wise?" Caitlin's concern was genuine.

"I'm not really sure whether to call it wise or not, but it seems like the only choice. It's a shame they released me so late today. I would have preferred to ride in the daylight."

"How long a ride is it?"

"Hmm, I'm not really sure. I think I should stay on the roadside, since King's not as brave as he looks and the woods can be confusing. So, no short cuts. I've never traveled on the road, but I'm guessing it's probably close to an hour's ride, if I take that route back to the boarding stable."

Caitlin sucked her breath in quickly as Edwin finished his conversation. She was looking past him into the grove. He turned to follow her gaze and stepped back when he saw the creature that was slowly approaching them; its teeth bared. It had the head of a vicious looking dog and the body of a pig.

After opening and closing his eyes several times to be certain he was actually seeing what he was seeing, Edwin put his glass on the patio table and stood in front of Caitlin. "Move away slowly Caitlin. Take your time, and don't turn around. Get into the house. Go now."

Caitlin followed Edwin's instructions while he stood firmly in place; not certain what he should do next.

Once inside, Caitlin rushed to find Linnie. Gasping for air, she babbled on about the creature that Edwin was facing outside. Taking a few moments to comprehend what was being said to her, Linnie went to the back porch where Edwin still stood, motionless. She looked out at the dog-pig creature and spun back into the house.

It was less than a minute later, (but to Edwin, an eternity), before Linnie returned with a small pistol. She held it at arm's length and closed one eye to focus before shooting at the beast. It exploded on impact and its shards disappeared into nothingness.

Linnie quietly returned to the house while Edwin and Caitlin stared at the space that the beast had been only moments before. They remained there until Linnie returned, gun tucked safely away, to reassure them that it was gone.

"What was that?" Caitlin asked hesitantly.

"A demon creature, me love. A nasty thing. There are probably more where it came from, but I doubt they will bother us tonight. Even so, it's not a good idea for any of us to try to leave tonight. It's better to be safe, than sorry, right?" Linnie turned to Edwin, "I Think ya better stay on for the evening and leave in the morning. Better get the horses tucked away as well. Those demons love flesh, so let's not take any chances!"

The uneasiness Caitlin experienced when Linnie offered housing to Edwin quickly switched to horror at the thought of another creature like the one she had just seen getting her poor Emma. She raced past Linnie and Edwin toward the paddock with Edwin not far behind.

Emma and King where kicking around in wild abandonment. Even in the state of panic, Caitlin could not help taking a moment to admire the sheer beauty of these two muscular creatures dancing in the moonlight. King was a full hand taller than Emma and much wider. Emma definitely looked the feminine of the two. King's thick neck arched and his tail was held high as he pranced around her in a seductive dance of nature. Emma reared on her hind quarter, twisting and hopping in the dance of the wild.

Caitlin called Emma to her and the two ceased their display and raced to the fence. As they approached her, Caitlin looked into Emma's eyes. A warm flame glowed within the pupils. She closed her eyes and rubbed them before looking again. The flame was gone. Determining she had imagined it, she decided to say nothing to Edwin and simply attend to the task of securing the horses for the night.

Edwin looked on in surprise as the two animals followed Caitlin into the barn. She had used no means of assistance. She simply told them to follow her and they did. He had never seen his gelding so complaisant before. It was an amazing sight

The glow of the full moon silhouetted the trio as they made their way into the barn. Edwin turned his head toward the tree line where he had seen the dog-pig creature, but all seemed calm.

"Keeping your eyes open, eh? That's a good idea. I know I said they probably won't bother us tonight, but, in truth, I don't think we've seen the last of them." Linnie whispered behind Edwin. "But I wouldn't tell the lass . She's a bit sensitive as it is. Let's you an me be on the look out and say nothing, deal?"

"Deal" Edwin did his best to hide his disconsortment with Linnie's ability to sneak up on people.

"What's a deal?" Caitlin had walked up quietly behind them. Edwin and Linnie turned quickly to her as Linnie answered quickly. "He's agreed to let me have a go at that black giant tomorrow before he leaves. He's a mighty beast that one!"

"Why, Linnie! I had no idea you rode. You could have ridden Emma any time you wanted!"

"That frail thing? Lass, I'm as big as the

horse" Linnie laughed boisterously at the thought of her big bulk on Emma and Caitlin and Edwin joined in. "Well lass. I need me sleep. I sure hope Samson will be okay without me. He's pretty dependant, ya know. But it can't be helped. I'll see ya both in the morning."

"Good night" Caitlin and Edwin said simultaneously.

"Sweet dreams" Added Caitlin.

Stretching in a cat-like manner, Caitlin moved away from Edwin and began walking toward the house. "I know it's early Mr. Holtz, but I'm beat. I hope you don't mind if I retire as well. If you'll follow me, I'll show you to your room. But, please, you're welcome to stay up as long as you like. If you're hungry, there's some fruit in a bowl on the counter and some chicken in the refrigerator or you can look for something else if that doesn't appeal to you. Please make yourself at home."

"I appreciate your hospitality Miss. Thank you." Edwin's formality took Caitlin by surprise.

"Please call me Caitlin." Caitlin's voice was uncertain. She was so confused right now. She wanted to get to know Edwin but wanted to stay distanced from him at the same time. She had never felt the way she felt in his company before and she was not sure how to deal with it. That, compiled with the events of the evening, made her edgy and uncertain.

"And please call me Edwin" He said as she walked closer to her than she might have preferred.

Caitlin stepped away quickly and looked at him. His face glowed in the moonlight. His dark hair and grey eyes gave him a handsome, yet almost sinister appearance.

"I will." Caitlin replied as a shiver ran up her spine. She was not sure if it was from the excitement she felt every time he came close to her or from the powerful dark appearance the mood of the evening and the moonlight gave him.

They walked in silence into the house and he followed her up the staircase to the second floor.

"Your room is just down the hall..." Caitlin stopped short and turned when she realized Edwin was no longer right behind her. He was standing at the foot of a narrow flight of steps that led to the third floor.

"What's up there?" He moved closer to the stairwell and peered past the gate Caitlin had put up to keep the animals from going up it.

"The third floor. I keep it blocked off until I'm able to work on it. This house is quite large for one person; and quite a job at that!"

"You mean two, don't you?" Edwin inquired "You and Linnie? I'm a little confused because she said she only stopped by for some things... but you stated you were not here alone and she is the only person I've seen."

"Oh. Yes, of course, Linnie too." Caitlin resumed her lead to the room she had decided to place Edwin in without looking back. When she reached the door, she opened it and told him to make himself comfortable before quickly excusing herself .

The walk to her own room seemed like eternity as she felt his eyes boring in her back. She had deliberately placed Edwin in a room on the farthest end of the house, as far away from hers as possible. Even so, she turned the lock on her door and then placed a chair in front of it before she was comfortable enough to lay down and sleep.

As she lay there dozing off, Caitlin contemplated on the real reason for her actions. Was it to keep him out, or to keep her in?

THIRTEEN

The moon danced amongst the stars and beams of light trickled through the shutters as Edwin threw them open. He lifted the window to let in the night air. From the staleness of the room, he could tell that it had been closed up for quite some time. He left the light off and looked around at shadows dancing across the furnishings.

He had a sense of not being alone. It was as if there where others in the room. The hair on the back of his neck stood on end and a shiver ran up his spine. He wondered if it was such a good idea to stay her after all. He had felt something different about this place the moment he had stepped foot on it. It was a feeling that he had not felt in a long time; a sense of danger. But of what? The creature, maybe? Perhaps... but he sensed it was more than the creature, but he could not quite put his finger on it.

A soft scratching on his doorway caught his attention and with graceful, silent strides he made his way from the window to the door. There was small thud and then more light scratching. Edwin turned the knob slowing as he eased the door open, not certain what he would find on the other side.

Linnie stood, motionless, holding one finger to her lips, while beckoning him to follow with another. She was holding a single candle. They could have easily found their way without a candle, since the moon beams where pouring through the newly installed picture windows on the east side of the hallway. Caitlin loved the view so much that she had installed a row of windows to allow a panoramic view of the mountains.

Edwin stepped out into the hallway and followed Linnie to the servant's stairwell. The stairs moaned under the weight of the old woman's bulk and they stopped briefly to listen for signs of Caitlin.

Although Edwin had no clue what Linnie was up to, he sensed that it had to do with the beast they had seen earlier and he knew it was best to keep Caitlin out of it. He looked on in amazement as Linnie proceeded down the steps; this time skipping up to three as she stretched her long legs. Edwin was surprised at how agile her large and cumbersome looking actually was.

When she reached the bottom of the stairs, Linnie quickly moved toward the study. By the time Edwin caught up with her, she was pouring them both a glass of sherry. She turned and offered one to him. As he reached out to take it from her large bony hand, their eyes locked.

Linnie's eyes where such dark pools, he felt he could jump into them and go on into eternity. This prompted him to take another long look at the old woman. Her features where large, but quite striking in their own way. He imagined she was quite beautiful in her time. If she would shed the man's outfit and do something with her hair, she would probably still be a looker.

"Ha lad, you're right. I was indeed a looker in my day. But I like the way I am now, son. I have no need to turn a man's head these days. And I am comfortable as I am."

Edwin stepped back, completely thrown off by Linnie's display of abilities.

"Come on now. Ya ain't fooling me with that shocked act. You know what I am, just as I know what you are." Linnie tossed her had back and swallowed the port in one large gulp.

Edwin held his glass to his lips watching her, barely sipping it. "Hmm. Are you some kind of a witch or something?"

"Witch? That's what you're calling me? Witch?" Linnie stood glowering at Edwin with her hands on her hips, her legs spread apart and a large scowl on her face. If she had a parrot on her shoulder and a patch on her eye, she would have easily passed for a pirate; an angry one at that.

"I meant no offense. I'm sorry, I didn't know you'd react like that. It's just that you read my mind and I was trying to figure out why. I apologize." Edwin stepped away from the light of the moon, forcing Linnie to raise the candle she was holding to see his face.

"Quite a player aren't ya?" Edwin's apology did not soothe the tone in Linnie's voice.

"Player?"

Edwin was either a good liar or he really did not know what Linnie was talking about. Linnie scowled with frustration. It was rare for her to not be able to know if someone was good or bad, but with the last two fellas who had come around Caitlin, she was having a dickens of a time. She shook her head in hopes of clearing away whatever it was that was blocking her. "Never mind. We don't have time for these games. But just remember, you aren't fooling me. Not at all. And I'm watching ya. I'm watching ya very closely. Ha... witch indeed."

Linnie put the candle down on the mantelpiece and pulled the black book off the mantle. Holding it lovingly, she walked to the sofa and sat down. After lighting a small hurricane lamp on the center of the coffee table, she opened the book carefully and began leafing through the pages.

"Can I ask why we aren't using the lights? Is there something wrong with the electricity?", Edwin positioned himself in a chair not far from Linnie.

"I don't want to be too noticeable." Linnie's tone was short and crisp.

"Oh, okay." Edwin sounded perplexed as he relaxed back into the chair. The woman obviously was a little off her rocker, but she seemed harmless enough. "Can I ask what we are doing?"

"No" Linnie answered without raising her eyes from the pages. She had found what she was looking for and was running her fingers under the words as she read them.

Edwin looked on in amusement while he watched her lips silently forming each syllable. "Well, can I ask then why I'm here? If I'm not to know what we're doing?"

"Quiet!" Still not looking up while focusing on moving her fingers across the pages, Linnie briskly and flatly made it clear to Edwin that he was to speak no more.

Taken aback by Linnie's outburst, Edwin obeyed her command and sat back quietly. The ticking of the large grandfather clock in the corner of the room echoed in the silence. Its rhythm mesmerized Edwin into a trance like state. He slowly relaxed as he finished his wine and set the glass on the table next to him. His impatience leaving him, he stretched his legs as far in front of him as they would go and sank even deeper into the chair. Suddenly exhausted from the exertion of the day, he fell into a deep sleep, almost immediately.

Linnie looked up at Edwin only after she was satisfied that he was in a deep slumber. She had deliberately ignored him while he drank her special tonic which she placed in his glass of sherry. Its effects should last until the morning; but she decided to be quick, just in case. She had not made that recipe in years and was not sure about the strength of the dosage.

Closing the book, Linnie walked over to the mantle and gently placed it back where she had gotten and moved to the window and pulled back the drapes. The moon glowed like a brilliant flashlight, illuminating the grounds and making it easy for Linnie to see the world outside. She searched for more dog-pigs, but all seemed quiet. This was good. Maybe there would be no more attacks. Although it was very unlikely, she could hope.

Turning back to Edwin, Linnie walked over to him and rolled up his sleeve. Picking up the black bag that she had taken from the back recesses of the closet of the room that Caitlin had assigned to her for when she stayed and had tucked behind the sofa prior to summoning Edwin from his room, she opened it and pulled out a syringe, cotton swab, alcohol and thin scarf. She laid them all down neatly on the table next to his chair and then pulled out two small amber colored bottles. She opened the tops of each bottle and set them down carefully.

A piercing howl came from outside and Linnie froze. 'Not now!' She moaned. This was poor timing, very poor timing indeed! Reaching in her black bag, she pulled out the pistol that only hours before had served her so well. Heaving her body up to full height, she took a deep breath and walked to the front door. She stepped out onto the porch and with no time to spare shot the pistol directly into the chest of a flying dog-pig. If she had hesitated for a mere five seconds longer, it would have reached her. The creature exploded and disappeared. She turned to the left quickly and shot again; grazing another beast, but not killing it. The wounded dog-pig yelped loudly and lunged for her. Linnie shot again and this time hit her mark. Two more dog-pigs came toward her, from seemingly nowhere, simultaneously. She took a deep breath and shot the one on the left first and then the one on the right; watching them both explode with determined satisfaction.

Silence prickled the air as the old woman waited for more. Her chest heaved from the adrenaline that poured through her veins. When five minutes had passed and she still saw nothing, she lowered the pistol and returned to the parlor.

Edwin slept peacefully in the chair, completely unaware of what had just transpired. She listened quietly for Caitlin, certain that she must have been awakened by the shots, but all was quiet.

Linnie poured herself another glass of sherry before returning to Edwin's side. She agilely wrapped the thin scarf around his upper arm and hunted for a suitable vein. When she as satisfied that she had located the best spot, she wiped his skin with an alcohol swab and inserted the needle to draw blood. The blood flowed smoothly into the syringe while she loosened the scarf that had been tied to his upper arm. When the syringe was full, she removed the needle and placed pressure on the spot. Gently laying the syringe of blood on the table, she wiped his arm clean and lowered his sleeve.

Linnie picked up the syringe and slowly dispersed its contents, equally, into the two amber bottles she had set out. Once this was done, she recapped the bottles and put everything back into her black bag.

Edwin stirred slightly and Linnie realized he would not be under much longer. Either he was quite powerful or she had omitted something from the potion because he should have been out for hours! Shaking her head, she extinguished the hurricane lamp, picked up the candle and left the room.

FOURTEEN

Caitlin stopped at the top of the stairs and stared down the hall at the door of Edwin's room. She wondered how he had slept through the night. Her night had been fitful. The moon had been so bright in her room that it was disturbing, and she kept reliving that awful dog-pig snarling at them from the edge of the grove. It had been so scary looking.

In the confusion, she had not had a chance to pull Linnie aside and ask if she knew where it came from or what it was. She was sure it was a breed of wild animal that must have strayed from its den deep in the woods. There was one thousand acres of state land just beyond her property, which was plenty of space for creatures to live in, undetected. The vision of it bursting under the impact of Linnie's shot kept popping into her head and she heard the shots over and over again in her sleep. Her first thought upon awakening was the mess that it must have left after it burst apart; and the chore of cleaning it up. Her exposure to country life and nature still left her a little queasy at times. Thank goodness there was only the one!

Caitlin had stopped at Linnie's designated bedroom and found that Linnie had already risen and gone. So much for her riding King! But, that was Linnie. Caitlin had learned long ago to take Linnie as she was; unpredictable; which was part of her charm.

As she approached Edwin's door, Caitlin wished she had the courage to look in. She longed to see what he looked like while sleeping. Was his face still as disarming as when he was awake and alert? Her heart pounded in her ears and an uneasiness flowed through her groin as she thought about his sleeping body just beyond the thick mahogany door. She could not help noticing the tightness of his form under his free flowing clothes the evening before. His body seemed hard and strong. Shaking the thoughts from her head, Caitlin headed down the steps.

A gasp of surprise escaped her when she entered the kitchen and discovered Edwin at the table drinking a mug of coffee. When he raised his mug in her direction, her heart raced as she struggled to regain herself. His smile was as disarming as ever!.

"Good morning Caitlin. I hope you don't mind. But I was desperate for a cup of coffee. That wine had quite a kick! My head is in one major fog this morning." Edwin stood up and walked over to the cupboard . "Can I get you a cup?" As he turned his head to look at her he winced.

"Sit down... please. I'll get it. That's a nasty wound you have. It'll probably hurt for quite awhile." Caitlin looked at him thoughtfully. "Are you sure it's wise to ride King today? I mean. You just turned your head to look at me and winced. Do you think you'll be able to handle an hour in the saddle?"

Edwin paused thoughtfully. "To tell you the truth, I'm not sure. But I don't want to overstay my welcome, nor do I want to take advantage of your good nature. Plus, I need to get back to work. I've had quite a long vacation."

It had not dawned on Caitlin that Edwin had a life outside of her reality. "Oh. That's right, work; I didn't think about that. What do you do?"

"I'm a photographer"

"Freelance? Or corporate?"

"Freelance. I'm here on multiple assignments for a sports and wildlife magazines. I'm taking photos of these beautiful hills and their wildlife for some time now."

Edwin's mention of wildlife reminded Caitlin of the night before. Her stomach twisted as walked over to the coffee pot. Picking up the cup Edwin had taken out of the cupboard, she poured herself some of the steaming black brew.

"Are you hungry?" Caitlin was anxious to

take the subject into a different direction."

"Starving! I was just thinking about your offer last night. You know, to make myself at home? If you had come down just a few minutes later, you would have caught me whipping up an omelet!"

"Well, I can handle that. You take it easy. And then I'll drive you wherever you need to go. King is fine where he is for now."

There was a long silence while the two exchanged looks; each one trying to determine what the other was thinking. There was something about this man that intrigued Caitlin, yet left her feeling unsettled as well. And those eyes! Oh my, they where alluring. And what a smile. Thank goodness he had it covered with his cup! She looked away quickly, certain he was reading her thoughts.

Feeling her cheeks flush, Caitlin turned back to the coffee pot. "I appreciate that. Thanks."

The two jumped simultaneously as footsteps sounded in the dining room and both laughed at their jumpiness. They where still smiling as William entered the room, stopping short at the sight of Edwin before raising an eyebrow in Caitlin's direction. "Did I interrupt anything?" His face was tense and his smile, curt.

"No... not at all. William. This is Edwin... "

"Holtz" Edwin finished Caitlin's introduction as he stood to shake William's hand. "And you are?"

"William... Caitlin's brother... Who she obviously forgot was coming this morning."

William and Edwin turned to Caitlin as she set her cup down on the counter just a little harder than necessary. "I didn't forget you where coming William. And what are you insinuating anyway?"

"Nothing, sis, nothing at all. It's perfectly natural to come here at seven in the morning to find you entertaining a strange man over coffee. I'm not insinuating a thing!" William's voice sounded strained as he moved closer to Caitlin.

"Whoa! Calm down buddy. This isn't at all what you think." Edwin's voice was equally strained as he watched William near Caitlin.

William's face was clearly contorted with possessive jealousy, mixed with concern and worry over Caitlin's tendency to be too trusting and naive.

In Edwin's attempt to calm William down, he had forgotten about his condition and moved to quickly. His head was throbbing so badly he could not stop himself from holding it.

"What's wrong with him?" William's face visibly relaxed as he watched Edwin cradle his head in his hands.

"He's the man who was hurt in the field the other day. He came by yesterday to get his horse."

Caitlin was irritated by William's actions, but not surprised. He was fiercely protective of her and finding a strange man in the kitchen whom she had not mentioned a thing about to him prior, would indeed raise the hair on his neck. "Linnie was here last night as well, but she left before we got up."

"So, you had a regular slumber party, eh?" William's tone softened. Knowing that Linnie was there during the night was all the reassurance he needed. "Sorry I couldn't make it."

"Well, it wasn't planned, I assure you. Linnie insisted we all stay put because there was some kind of weird looking dog in the grove last night. She killed it, but she was worried there would be more and so they decided to wait until the morning for any traveling on foot or horse. And you know Linnie; she comes and goes as she pleases. I haven't a clue what time she left!"

"I've been up since 6 o'clock and she was already gone, so she must have left at sun up." Edwin walked over to the coffee maker and poured himself another cup of hot liquid. A loud rumbling sound came from his stomach and he looked over at Caitlin with a mild mixture of amusement and embarrassment.

Caitlin smiled back at him and started pulling the makings of an omelette out of the refrigerator. "I think that was my cue to start cooking. Are you hungry William?　We're having omelettes this morning."

"It sounds good, but I ate on the way out here. I think I'll just go up to the office and get started. Join me when you can, okay sis?" William looked over at Edwin and gave a curt nod before he kissed Caitlin's cheek and left the room.

"Please excuse my brother," Caitlin mumbled softly, "He's a bit over protective at times, but he means no harm. And, once he gets to know you, he's a teddy bear."

"No problem. I don't blame him for wanting to keep you to himself. I think I'd be the same way." Erwin looked boldly at Caitlin, leaving no mystery to his meaning.

Caitlin blushed. She was not sure how she felt about this complement or this man. She fumbled with the eggs and a shell fell into the bowl. "Damn it!" She exclaimed, completely frustrated; not with the egg, but with her own body and how it was responding on its own to this man's presence.

"Can I help?" Edwin asked as he helped himself to another cup of coffee.

"Well, as long as you're up. You can set up the table. There's orange juice in the refrigerator. Oh, and can you start the toast? The toaster is over there, by the bread box. Oh yes, and there's a new jar of jam in the pantry; raspberry I believe. Can you get that out as well? I think the one in the refrigerator is so low it won't be enough. I hope I took the butter out of the freezer! Check, will you?"

"Do you want me to make the omelet too?" Edwin's broad smile lit up the room as he went about doing Caitlin's bidding.

In her nervousness, Edwin's joking remark about him making the omelette as well went right over her head. She simply declined and kept working.

They ate breakfast in relative silence. Caitlin was preoccupied with her own nervousness and confusion and Edwin focused on trying to manage the discomfort in his head. He felt a raging headache brewing.

Caitlin broke the silence as just as Edwin had washed his last bite down with some juice. "I need to go and join my brother for awhile. We have some business to attend to. You're welcome to go upstairs and wash up. Make yourself comfortable in the library or walk around the grounds; whatever you choose. I shouldn't be more than a few hours. Is that Okay?"

"That's fine. I think I'll go upstairs and rest a bit more. My sleep was interrupted last night quite a bit and I could use just a bit more rest."

"You didn't sleep well? What interrupted you?

I put you at the quiet end of the house. I'm so sorry..."

Edwin quickly interrupted her, "No, not that... it was nothing in the house. It was my head." He decided not to mention his slumber in the chair after his rendezvous with Linnie. And besides, it was not really a lie. His head seemed to have a constant dull ache in it. "The accommodations where perfect. It's just that .." He raised his hand to point to the bandaged part of his head.

"Can I ask you where you're staying?" Caitlin approached him cautiously and lightly lifted the bandage to peek under it. He leaned forward to make her ministering easier.

"At the inn in town." Edwin responded, wincing involuntarily as Caitlin pulled too hard on the bandage.

"Oh, I'm sorry. You must be incredibly sore." She walked over to the sink and began cleaning up the dishes. "Listen. Maybe you should just stay here for a few days. I mean, you don't have any one to really care for you at the motel and I don't think it's a wise idea to try to travel with that head. I'm sure you'll be fine in a few days." Caitlin could not believe her own words. Was she volunteering to take care of this man until he healed up? Was she mad?

"I appreciate the offer, but I really need to get rolling. I'm behind schedule as it is."

Edwin stood up to help her with the dishes and he waved her away.

Relief, mixed with regret, flooded Caitlin. Thankful that the temptation of having him so close and vulnerable was removed, she also regretting not having more time alone with him in an intimate setting, such as a sick bed would allow. "Well, it's your call. Tell you what. Why don't you go lay down for a while and we'll see how you feel later today? Deal?"

"Deal." Edwin smiled warmly while he stood taking in every inch of Caitlin. She was not sure if she should be flattered or concerned by the way his steel gray eyes consumed her. This man was definitely an unread-able mystery. He turned quietly and left the room. She finished the dishes and went to join William.

Edwin went to his room, eager to clean up. As he entered, a quick flash skirted across the room. He saw it in the corner of his eye, but still, clearly saw it. He turned to get full view, but it was gone. Cautiously, he moved toward the direction he had seen it and opened doors and look behind furni-ture. It had happened so suddenly that he was not even certain how big it was, but he was sure there had been something.

Edwin moved the drapery away from the window, but it was closed. Disappointed and tired he collapsed onto the bed and was fast asleep within moments.

~

The sun was inching its way behind the mountain tops by the time Edwin awoke. Shadows danced around the room from the trees outside his window, indicating that it was early afternoon. It took him a few minutes to get his bearings straight and remember where he was.

As he sat on the edge of the bed, he spotted his reflection in the mirror. His thick black hair was in disarray, dark whiskers sported his face and his shirt was rumpled from sleeping in it. As he ran his tongue across his teeth, the thick film that formed while he was sleeping made him shudder. He definitely needed to clean up!

Edwin walked over to the bathroom across the hall. Its faded flowered wallpaper looked as if it was the original. Small lines and cracks where dispersed throughout it somehow added to its charm. A large claw footed bathtub dominated the room. The toilet was an antique, with the water tank positioned high on the wall and a pull chain hanging for flushing. The large, and rather ornate, pedestal sink had a crack in it. But they room was spotlessly clean and had a soothing fresh flower smell that he could not quite identify. He searched the medicine cabinet on the wall of its contents and was pleased to find shaving supplies and a few new toothbrushes! A broad smile spread crossed Edwin's face as he gingerly removed his clothes. His complements to his hostess's thoughtfulness!

Edwin had always enjoyed antiquities and he took a moment to take in his surroundings. He admired how brightly polished the brass knobs of the faucet were as he filled the squeaky clean, oversized, claw-footed tub with steaming hot water. There was a bottle of bubble bath sitting on the shelf near the tub, so he reached over get it. It was then that he noticed his arm.

Edwin stood motionless, hanging over the tub with the bubble bath in his hand as he stared at a bruise, about the size of a silver dollar, on the inside of his elbow. It was as if someone had drawn his blood; and done a sloppy job of it at that! He scrutinized his other arm, where the hospital had pricked and poked; but their ministries had been clean and well done, with barely a pin prick remaining. No, this was not from the hospital, but how did he get it?

He tried to recall what had occurred the night before, but there was no time, that he could remember, where he had been in a situation to injure his arm like that. It was a mystery.

Edwin lowered himself in the tub and slowly poured the liquid bubble bath under the running water.

His head felt like his brain was playing racket ball against his skull. The strain of trying to remember the night before had brought the pounding back full force. He decided to try to figure it out later and just relax for awhile.

Sinking deeper into the tub, Edwin reveled in the feel of the warm bubbles all around him. It had been a long time since he soaked in a bubble bath and three days since he had even showered! The hospital only provided him with a wash down from the nurse; and an ugly one at that! The water felt soothing and comforting.

Edwin reached for a wash cloth and drenched it with the warm soapy water. Pulling his bandage gently from his head with one hand, he drizzled the warm liquid over it with the other, creating shivers of pleasure down his spine; it was sheer delight. Not certain how his head would respond, he slowly immersed himself until only wound was above water. His wound throbbed for a bit and then subsided. All of the muscles in his body relaxed and he felt a sensation of peace within him for the first time in days.

A new sense of freedom overtook Edwin as he climbed out of the tub. The gurgling of the draining water mixed with his humming, creating a primitive sound that echoed off the walls.

Edwin stood naked while he leaned into the mirror to inspect the wound on his head. It was fairly deep and ugly and had required a considerable number of stitches. The doctor had assured him that it should heal with little, if any, scar. But, looking at it now he wondered about the accuracy in that statement.

Pulling out the shaving supplies from the cabinet, he took out a toothbrush but, unfortunately, there was no toothpaste to be found. He shrugged and put the toothbrush down tackling his whiskers with the shaving supplies. The scraping sound of the razor against his brittle whiskers seemed abnormally loud; something he had never noticed before.

A cool breeze swept across Edwin's back and he turned to see if the door had popped open, but it was secure. The window was closed as well. Spotting a large crack in the corner wall next to the window, he made a mental note to mention it to Caitlin before he left. The house was very old and in need of repair, but she had done a great job with the sections she had already tackled and he had no doubt that the entire place would be beautifully restored before long. Caitlin would have to take care of the leak before the cold weather set in, whether it was on her list or not!

Edwin finished the task of shaving and started rummaging deeper into the recesses of the cupboards for some toothpaste. He finally found a small travel size tube in the far back of the cupboard and went to work on the thick film that had accumulated over the last twenty-four hours. Feeling refreshed and new he walked to the door and stopped as he felt another cool breeze sweep over his back. He turned toward the corner of the wall to inspect the thin crack in the plaster and paper. But as hard as he tried, he could find no sign of a breeze. He decided to simply report it to Caitlin and leave it up to her to find the source.

A loud growl rose up from his stomach and his attention immediately turned toward the matter at hand. He was hungry.

Edwin had a habit of remaining naked after a shower or bath for fifteen minutes or so before dressing. It was a habit his mother had instilled in him with her old world belief that the body needed time to breathe before smothering it with clothes for long hours at a time. Peeking out the door down the hall first, Edwin slowly emerged from the bath-room. His lean naked body filled the door-way as he stepped through it and into the hall. A loud gasp reached his ears and he paused, not sure what to do.

Caitlin stood at the top of the stairs. Her shocked gasp had stopped him in his tracks. Now, there he stood, and there she stood with neither one knowing what to do next. She cleared her throat with gusto, breaking the stillness, and he quickly shifted his body to camouflage as much as possible; not as much for his sake as for hers. She was ob-viously as embarrassed as a schoolgirl!

"Ex... excuse me. I.. was... Just.." Caitlin stammered.

"I'm sorry, I didn't expect you upstairs. Forgive me." A twinkle shot from Edwin's eyes that did not match the sincerity in his voice.

"No.. No prob... no problem. I'll just... go down to my room. Sorry" Caitlin scurried off to her room without waiting for a re-sponse from Edwin, who stood motionless, watching her leave.

Edwin smiled with amusement as he looked down at the primary focus of Caitlin's stare. Although he had done his best to turn his body while still addressing her, he appar-ently had not turned enough. Her shocked mannerism had not camouflaged her intrigue and pleasure at what she saw; something he could tell by the look in her eyes as she surveyed him completely.

Edwin thought sadly about the circumstances that had brought the two of them together and wished things were different. It seemed that they had gotten off to a rough start and her wall of reserve was up high and strong. He wondered what type of relationship they would have had if things had happened differently. She truly was a beautiful woman. He heaved a heavy sigh and walked back into his room. The sound of Caitlin's door closing rang down the hall as he gently closed his.

Caitlin stood leaning against her door. Her heart filled her ears as she tried to calm her trembling legs. The surprise of seeing Edwin standing nude in her hallway in the middle of the afternoon, was enough to shake her to the core. But it was more than that. There was a longing mixed with the stunned sensation. She could not identify what was happening to her. It left her feeling hollow and unsettled and she could not understand it. She had been with men before, so what was different about this man? What was it about him that made her blush like a schoolgirl as well as tremble like a prey avoiding a predator?

Maybe William was right today when he

said she should not have let him stay. He did not like the way Edwin was looking at her. He said it made him uncomfortable. But then, what about the way she was looking at him? She wondered what William would have said if he had seen the way she was looking at him just now! Caitlin cringed with embarrassment as she recalled the twinkle in Edwin's eyes. He was aware of her feelings, she just knew it!.

Caitlin listened at her bedroom door at William's footsteps as he climbed the steps and knocked on Edwin's door. She heard her brother offer to take him to town and Edwin requested assistance with Samson.

As William approached her room, she feigned a migraine and asked him to excuse her to Edwin and to assure him that she would care for King, if he wanted to leave him behind for a little longer. She just could not face him after what had happened. Ten minutes later, she was at the window watching William and Edwin struggle to get Samson into the horse trailer. With graceful teamwork they coaxed him in and were off down the drive. Caitlin stared out the window long after they had disappeared. She could not get the image of Edwin's nakedness out of her mind.

FIFTEEN

A broad smile flashed across Dominic's face as Caitlin pulled the door open. Her childlike look of delighted surprise tugged at him in earnest. It took all his reserve to refrain from taking her in his arms and holding her close. The firelight curls that hung in disarray around her face and her flushed cheeks accentuated the blue in her oval eyes. They were so rich and deep that he could see his reflection in them.

Caitlin was acutely aware of her appearance. She had not expected company, and had invested her day into fixing the crack in the wall in the bathroom that Edwin had reported. It was not going as well as she had expected and just as Dominic had knocked on the door, she was actually standing back debating about the prospect of calling in a professional. William had suggested it several times and this was a time where she was sorry she had not listened.

"Did I interrupt something?" Dominic questioned after surveying her boldly.

"Actually, yes. I was in the middle of making the major decision of whether or not to call in the troops for this project or still try to go it alone." Caitlin decided to go with the flow and made light of the situation. "I'm surprised to see you here. To what do I owe the pleasure of your visit?"

"I was back in the neighborhood and I thought I'd pop over and make sure everyone was fine. Your friend, the one with the injury to the head, is he well?" Although his voice had a note of concern, the twinkle in his eye gave Caitlin reason to think otherwise.

"I guess so. I haven't seen or heard from him in a few weeks. And, actually, I hardly know the man." For some unexplainable reason, discussing Edwin with Dominic left Caitlin feeling agitated. She felt an unspoken form of competition between the two. It was more than just for her attentions. It went deeper. Yet she was certain they had never met before the accident. And, although Edwin had vocalized gratitude for the help Dominic had given him the day of his fall, he never did express a desire to meet him and thank him personally.

"Really? Hmm. The way you cradled his head on the way to the hospital... I got the impression you two where close." Dominic's eyes bore into Caitlin as he awaited her response.

"I'm a compassionate woman. And I didn't

realize I was cradling him." Caitlin was extremely uncomfortable with the direction their conversation was going. The last thing she wanted was for Dominic to discover how she reacted to the mere mention of Edwin.

"Oh the female heart", Dominic chuckled, "I guess perhaps I was misinterpreting the natural female tendency to nurture for more."

"Perhaps you where."

The two stood in silence for a bit longer before Dominic shifted his weight and looked out onto the fields. "It's really pretty and peaceful out here. How are the winters?"

"I'm assuming they're cold. I've only been here since early spring, so it was warming up a by then, but it was still pretty cold and the house had a lot of leaks that let in the air. There has been a lot of work done on the house since then, so we'll see what happens this year. I'm shooting for cozy."

"Ah, yes, cozy" Dominic craned his neck to look past Caitlin into the foyer. "It appears you're on the right path from what I can see."

Caitlin stepped back from the doorway, suddenly aware of her rudeness. "I'm sorry, I'm being rude. It's just that I wasn't expecting any company." Caitlin absent-mindedly smoothed her hair. "You took me by surprise. You're welcome to come in, but I warn you... I've got it torn up today."

Dominic bowed slightly as he walked passed Caitlin into the foyer. He stopped at the doorway to the sitting room and stared at the direction of the fireplace. Caitlin joined him and followed his gaze to the gilded framed portrait over the mantelpiece. A dark foreboding portrait of an elderly woman bore stark contrast to the seemingly new framing hung precariously over it.

"I found it in the attic and had it cleaned up. I felt an odd attachment to her." Caitlin muttered as she made her way toward the kitchen.

"Who is she? Do you know?" Dominic's voice was distant in thought.

"Hmm... I think she was a former owner of this place, from several generations ago."

"Really?" Dominic's eyebrows raised in concentration while he poured over the portrait inch by inch, as if to absorb the woman into memory. "Not very happy, was she?"

Caitlin looked at the portrait more closely. She had actually fallen in love with the frame, not the portrait, and planned on putting something different in it at some point. "I agree." Caitlin chuckled. "Would you like a cocktail or coffee or tea? Take your pick."

"I'm not much of a drinker in the afternoons. But for some reason, it feels right. What do you have?" Dominic's mood lightened as he followed her toward the kitchen. The coziness of the decor and the bright sun gleaming through the french doors she had installed almost as soon as she had moved in gave a welcoming effect.

"Brandy... or sherry?" Caitlin asked as she opened the pantry door.

"Brandy would be great! Thanks." Dominic replied as he settled himself into a bistro chair Caitlin had strategically placed next to the south window. "And you? Will you join me in a glass?"

"It's just what I need, actually. It's been a hectic few weeks. Brandy would be delightful?" She smiled as she handed him a snifter and lifted hers in a gesture of toasting. They sipped in silence, listening to the sound of nature outside. The thick leaves on the trees blanked the mountain side in rich shades of green that swayed in the strong wind that had picked up outside. The heavy branches of the ancient oak tree outside scraped lightly across the roof as it unburdened itself, little by little, lending to the sensation of coziness in the room.

"Oh boy. Look at that wind pick up." Caitlin's mannerism displayed concern.

"Yes," Dominic smiled and stretched lazily, "I love the fall weather. Death can be so beautiful. Don't you think?"

"I suppose. But I wasn't thinking of the beauty. I was thinking about the fact that I have a huge mess upstairs in the one end of the house and I'm at a loss as of how to correct. And with the carpenters around here being so busy, I'm afraid I won't get it fixed before my sister arrives for her visit. I'd hate to have her see this mess. Not to mention the fact that the outside is actually coming inside and the cold weather will be here before we know it."

"Hmm. I have a small amount of knowledge in that direction. I can't guarantee anything, but maybe I can provide some assistance. Do you mind if I take a look?" Dominic stood up and placed his snifter gently on the counter. He walked toward the servants stairs without waiting for Caitlin. "Is it this way?", trailing behind him.

Caitlin stared at the man in startled disbelief, only, briefly before scurrying to catch up. She stopped at the top of the narrow stairwell, surprised and relieved to see that Dominic had removed his jacket and was rolling up his sleeves. Saying nothing to her, he immediately set to task correcting some of the poor patching she had done.

Dominic's hands moved diligently, as if with a mind of their own, and three hours later he had smoothed down the last of the plaster. "This will have to be tackled from

the outside as well you know. I'll leave you a
list of supplies I'll need and I'll stop back in
a few days to do the job. We need to wait for
a less windy time. I don't know how to fly."
Dominic chuckled as he cleaned up the work
space. Caitlin nodded her head as she gratefully joined in.

"Oh gosh, that's so wonderful. I can't thank
you enough. You're my knight in shining
armor! And... of course I have to pay you.
Please, let's go downstairs in my den and I'll
get a check." There was no price too high to
pay this wonderful man who had come to her
rescue and saved her the agony of finishing
a job she should never had tried to do on her
own.

Caitlin's body lightly brushed against Dominic as she scurried past him to lead the way
to the den. A strong surge of energy burst
brought her senses alive and she sucked in
her breath. She excused herself, quickly looking away, certain the color that was rising in
her face would be noticed. What was wrong
with her lately? First she could not control
her reactions to Edwin and now Dominic; it
did not make sense. She had been around
plenty of handsome, charismatic men in her
lifetime; what was so different now? Is this
what happens when you live in seclusion?

Dominic smiled broadly as he rested his
hand above her elbow. Caitlin stopped, still
looking away. He pulled her chin gently un-

til she was facing him. Their eyes met for what seemed to Caitlin to be eternity, but was in actuality only a matter of seconds, before he softly placed his lips to hers. She fell against him, wrapping her slender arms around his neck as the kiss grew more and more passionate.

Without realizing how it happened, Caitlin found herself walking backward, in unison with Dominic while he embraced her passionately, until she was in a guest bedroom and on the bed. Her head was swooning too much to recognize that they were in the room Edwin had only recently occupied.

Dominic's strong hands roamed wildly over her body and she could not hide her growing desire; nor did she want to. Every inch of her body cried out to be touched and loved by this beautiful man.

Caitlin moaned in wild abandonment as Dominic's sensuous kisses covered her body. His complete abandonment in lovemaking was infectious and it was not long before she found herself reciprocating. His moans matched hers in appreciation for her own skills in the art of lovemaking. The two where so lost in their passion, they did not hear the front door open and Linnie call out for Caitlin.

Having searched the downstairs for her friend, Linnie was just starting up the servants steps when she stopped short. Her ears strained to identify what she was hearing. It was undeniably the sounds of two people in the act of sensual pleasure. But, they did not seem to be coming from Caitlin's room, Was it the guest area? Had Edwin lured the lass into his lair?

Tempted by curiosity, Linnie slowly ascended the narrow stairwell. Her large bulk moved with surprising ease, as if floating, in her desire to not make a noise that might divulge her presence.

Moving swiftly, Linnie placed herself outside the doorway of the guest room, unnoticed, as she watched Dominic's lean muscles move in unison with Caitlin's. The sunset was peaking through the window, giving the scene an exotic glow. It was like a work of art that Linnie felt privileged to view.

Feeling suddenly guilty for invading Caitlin's privacy, she slowly made her way back toward the stairs, taking a moment to admire the handy work on the wall in the bathroom. It had to be the man's handiwork because she knew that Caitlin's skills did not lie in that area.

Linnie proceeded down the stairs and out the front door. She had not checked in on Emma in quite awhile and now seemed as good a time as any.

SIXTEEN

Caitlin stretched across the bed in a cat-like manner as she slowly stirred from her afternoon nap. The afternoons were growing more and more lazy, while the days turned into weeks of passionate love making. Since that very first afternoon of what Caitlin reflected upon as sensual spontaneity, Dominic had made it a point to drop by every day at about the same time. Not only had Caitlin come to expect it, but she found herself almost needing it!

Although Linnie was consistent with her visits as well, she grew quiet and distant while she observed the relationship between Dominic and Caitlin unfold. The lass seemed almost too dependant on him. It was definitely not something her character had ever portrayed and Linnie grew suspicious about the relationship; but when she pointed this out to Caitlin, the lass responded with a gentle laugh and brushed Linnie's concerns away as over protectiveness.

Linnie did her best to be civil and polite to Dominic, but the growing strain between them was apparent.

The days turned into weeks as the two

became more and more bonded. It did not come as much of a surprise to Linnie when Caitlin announced that she was going to ask Dominic if he would be interested in moving in with her.

Although this news was not a surprise, it was definitely a concern. Linnie listened intently to Caitlin's musing about how wonderful it would be to have Dominic as a companion in the home. Caitlin was so engrossed in the concept of Dominic living with her, that she failed to notice the frown on Linnie's face, or the sense of determination in her walk as she made her way across the meadow toward her own home.

~

Linnie moved like a graceful cat about her kitchen, pulling out herbs and spices and mixing them in a large wooden bowl. When the herbs and spiced were blended to her satisfaction, she slowly poured a hot liquid she had been simmering on the stove into the center of the mixture. A vaporous, aro-matic cloud arose from the bowl and filled the room.

Linnie stood motionless and stared into the bowl while an image formed in the mixture. Then a whole scene formed, clear and distinct. She saw Dominic standing amongst wolves, pigs, snakes, dragons and bats. His face was distorted with rage and evil. Mice and rats scurried all around him. Linnie jumped back from the vision as it suddenly shifted to Edwin Holtz. He was coming out of the darkness on his large black gelding. There was a sense of authority about him and as he grew larger, his body glowed with brilliant light.

"Oh dear God. I was wrong!! I had the wrong man! Lordie be!!" Linnie wailed.

Having sensed evil around Caitlin, Linnie had taken the blood from Edwin's arm and had found nothing abnormal about him. Shortly after his visit, the energy around Caitlin seemed to have shifted, so she felt the evil had gone. But it had not. It was there all the time, right under Caitlin's roof. Rooted more than ever in Dominic.

Linnie threw her hands to her head. The impact of her discovery was so powerful she felt her head would burst. Feeling overwhelmed with energy, she flung the bowl with her arm, wanting to get it as far from her as possible before she fell to the floor. Linnie lay, totally devoid of energy or even the desire to move, as she watched the contents of the bowl slowly ooze onto the floor. It was several hours before she was able to arise and clean up the mess.

As hard as she tried, Linnie could not get the image of Dominic, encased in vile rodents, out of her mind. She sat on her porch that evening and sipped a glass of brandy while she pondered on what course of action to take next.

Linnie knew what Dominic was and she knew what she had to do to eliminate him. But the problem was Caitlin. What was she to do about Caitlin? The lass been sexual with the evil beast and from the love scene that Linnie had witnessed, she was certain that Caitlin was not careful about using condoms or any other form of protection.

The tea Linnie had slipped into Caitlin's cupboard to replace her regular morning tea had been a salvation more than she had bargained for. She had only thought to thwart off a pregnancy that was bound to happen before its time. She had not thought that she was saving Caitlin from the prospect of being sucked up by the evil of this creature. Bearing his child would be her doom. But Linnie also knew that if she did not do something soon. Caitlin would be lost anyway. The simple fact that she was sexual with him was slowly ebbing her natural life force from her, and replacing it with his false one. Similar to that of a vampire from the old folklore.

Linnie threw the last of her brandy down her throat and rose out of the rocker. The sun was just resting on the edge of the mountain top, casting shadows on its lush shades of green. It added to the sense of mystery she had been pondering. As she peered out over the fields toward the edge of the woods, her gaze stopped on a small form.

Running into her house, she grabbed her binoculars to get a better look. As she raised them up in the direction of the form her suspicions where confirmed. It was another one of those dog-pigs that she had killed while at Caitlin's house the night Edwin had been visiting. She now understood what they were and why they were here.

Linnie calmly put down her binoculars and went back into the house to retrieve her rifle. When she returned outside, the number of beasts had increased. "Ah, I know who ya are", she mumbled, "and it appears you've discovered me as well. Well, if 'tis a fight ya want, 'tis a fight you'll get."

Linnie put her rifle down and grabbed a broom to sweep the porch; as if not to notice the evil creatures as they inched closer and closer toward her. Samson found his way onto the porch next to Linnie and snarled threateningly at the beasts.

Linnie watched the creatures until they were close enough to see clearly without the binoculars. She counted six in all, but she sensed there where more. Reaching for the box of ammunition she had set on the small table by her rifle, she loaded the rifle and prepared a spare clip which she slid into her pocket.

With the accuracy and ease of someone who is very familiar with weapons, Linnie shot at the beasts. One by one they burst into oblivion. They moved with surprising speed and there was barely enough time to exchange the empty clip with the full one before the last three beasts reached the porch. Samson attacked the leader with fervor while Linnie shot the other two and turned to the battling duo.

Samson's blood was everywhere as the beast slowly got the better of him. Linnie's heart twisted as she realized her long time friend was close to death. She took a chance and shot. Samson screeched as the bullet caught him in the hip. She had missed her mark, but it was enough to get the attention of the beast away from Samson and back to her.

Linnie had barely time to blink before the creature raced toward her. His hot fowl breath assaulted Linnie as she was knocked to the floor by his weight. She fought, struggling to keep his long fangs from reaching their mark. The beast was bolted to the side as Samson was again on the attack.

With lightning speed, Linnie was back on her feet, this time determined not to miss her mark. The beast exploded and Samson fell to the floor, no longer able to find the strength to move.

Linnie kicked aside bits and pieces of the beast as she made her way to Samson. His labored breathing accentuated the blood that was flowing out of his neck and hip. She ran into the house and returned with a large towel. Slowly, she rolled him onto the towel and pulled him into the kitchen in front of the sink.

Linnie filled a bowl with clean water and went about the task of cleaning Samson's wounds. It was the better part of an hour before she was confident that he was stable enough to lift onto the table. His eyes told of his weakness as she cradled her loving companion in her arms and gently laid him on the kitchen table. She moved about the kitchen intent on completing her task as quickly as possible, Samson's life depended on it.

It was almost midnight before the bullet had been removed and Samson lay, bandaged and comfortable, next to Linnie on the mattress she had pulled off her bed and placed in the corner of her bedroom. She snuggled up next to him and wrapped her arms around him possessively.

"We go together when we go old boy. Do ya hear me?" Linnie whispered. "You're not to leave me here alone. No, we go together when we go." Samson feebly licked Linnie's face as if to acknowledge the deal and the two dropped off into a deep and undisturbed sleep.

The clock struck three o'clock in the morning when a large glowing ball entered the room. Lael stepped out of it and stood over the woman and her dog. He waved his hand several times as if writing something in the air and then returned to the ball. Within seconds the ball was gone.

The following morning, Samson nudged Linnie to wake up. He had managed to get out of bed and was limping toward the door. She opened her eyes in surprise and immediately leapt up to open the door. Samson hobbled off the porch and went to his favorite tree to relieve himself.

Linnie went into the bathroom to do the same. The shocked look on her face was still there when she returned to let Samson back inside. She had expected him to recover, or as least she had hoped that he would. But this was far better than she could ever have hoped for. It was indeed the help of the spirits, she just knew it.

Linnie closed her eyes as a tear slid down her cheek and she whispered, "Thank you, whoever you are. God Bless ya always." A mild breeze blew through her house, even though the doors and windows where closed and she smiled.   Her words had been received.

Linnie sat down with Samson for a hearty breakfast of eggs and steak. When he had cleaned his bowl and she her plate, she cleaned up the kitchen and braced herself for what had to be done next. With the fear and worry of Samson out of the way, she could now concentrate on the issue at hand, which was how to get Caitlin away from that evil man.

Linnie pulled out her books and leafed through the pages. After looking through the third book with no results she closed her eyes in frustration.

"Ah great grand Mamie, where are ya now when I need your advice?   What to do for the lass, eh? 'Tis a serious thing it is. Please hear me, Grand Mamie. I'm needing your help." Linnie moaned as she stared at the closed book.

Within moments the book opened on its own and the pages fanned until they settled on one. Linnie smiled as she read the words that were almost jumping off the page.   It was not long before she was empowered with the right spell and got up and began to collect the items the book called for. She knew now what she had to do.

The day turned into evening before Linnie had completed her task. She eased her bulk

into her favorite wooden rocker on the porch
as Samson hobbled up to place his head in her
lap. Linnie stroked him affectionately. "'Twas
a long day me laddie, eh? But we've done it.
Now, let's see what happens from here!"

The exertion of the day, combined with the
stress and trauma of the day before had left
Linnie feeling old and tired. She longed for her
lost youth. As she continued to rock on the
porch she slowly drifted into a trance like state
where she was able to revisit her past. She saw
herself back in Ireland.

...The rolling green hills surrounded her, their
beauty unsurpassed by anything she could ever
imaging; and she was a young girl again, all
dressed up in her Sunday best. The tiny black
patent leather shoes that she loved so much glistened in the dew of the grass as she danced her
way across the lawn with her collie dog. Collies
had a special meaning to her father and were the
only breed of dog he would even consider for the
family.

Her mother stepped out onto the porch and rang
a large bell as a signal to call her in. She moved
with ease toward the house as she pretended to
be a ballerina. She could feel the love her mother
had for her as she stroked her hair while she guided to a table on the porch and washed her face
with a cloth she had dipped in some cool water
that was in a bowl on a wooden stand her father
had made. Linnie could still feel the coarseness of

the homespun fabric on her face as it was being scrubbed clean for breakfast...

Linnie was startled back to reality by Samson's frantic barking. She struggled to focus on the darkness. A loud clanging was coming from the direction of the shed out back. Linnie stroked Samson, to settle his wounded body down, and then scurried inside for her rifle. She picked up a large flashlight and headed to the back door to take a closer look.

She was extra alert after the events of the night before as she peered into the darkness, wishing old age had not taken such a hold on her eyesight. When a tall staggering form stepped out from behind the shed, she called for him to stop or she would shoot; but he ignored her warning and kept moving forward. Linnie set her flashlight on the porch in a manner that would aid with her visibility and raised her rifle to shoot, but hesitated. It was clear that the form was a man, not a dog-pig and there was something familiar about him. As recognition set in, she proper her rifle against the port post and flew off the porch to help him.

"William me lad. What are ya doing here, eh? And stumbling like ya are" Linnie rambled as she reached William just in time to catch his fall. She lay him on the cool grass and stretched his limp form to make him as comfortable as possible. Her hands were sticky from the warm blood that was oozing from his body. Regretting the fact that she had to abandon him for even the briefest moment, she head back to the house to get her flashlight so that she could evaluate his situation better.

She rushed back into the porch to retrieve her flashlight and then made her way back to him in record time, surveying the shadows for whatever had attacked him the entire time. The gaping hole in the side of William's neck was oozing blood at a steady rate. If Linnie did not stop the bleeding soon, it would be too late.

She rushed back into the kitchen and pulled down an old tin container from the corner shelf. It was coated with dust; a sign of its lack of use. Scowling, she opened the lid and sniffed for freshness. She wanted the bleeding stopped before she assisted him in taking one more step and this powder, one of her mother's recipes, was the quickest way to do it. Thank goodness it was still fine.

Grabbing a towel from the sink, Linnie returned to William to tend to his wound. The bleeding stopped on contact with the powdery herb. William wailed and writhed from the burning sensation that was created on contact, but Linnie never faltered. Within moments she had transformed the towel into a bandage and was pulling him up onto his feet. He was a lot heavier than Samson and there was no way she was going to be able to carry him into the house.

As they entered the bedroom, she realized that the mattress was still on the floor in the corner and all that was left was the box springs. 'Oh well," she muttered "'twill have to do for now". As she eased William down onto the box springs, blood from a lesser wound soiled the fabric. "Aye! This man is full of holes!" She gasped as she scrambled for more of the herb powder and cloths.

Linnie finally got his bleeding to stop from all wounds and cleaned him up where she was satisfied. She stood back and shook her head at the blood soaked box spring, there was no saving that!

Samson came up beside her and nudged her gently. She realized that neither of them had eaten since breakfast! She stroked his head and made her way to the kitchen. There was a little left over stew in the refrigerator that would do just fine. She split it between herself and Samson and the two dove into the cold fare. The old woman was simply too tired to bother to heat it up. When their bellies where content, the two made their way to the mattress on the floor and fell into a deep slumber.

SEVENTEEN

Caitlin paced back and forth, the full length of her porch, while wringing her hands. William's argument with Dominic had been severe. She had not expected such a violent reaction from William when she him that Dominic was moving in and they were considering marriage. She did not understand. All of her life William had promoted happiness for Caitlin. It seemed a sincere desire of his. So, why would he be so against her happiness now? She just did not know what to think.

She had to admit that William had brought up some very valid points; such as the fact that she really did not know much about Dominic. She had never even been to his home. In fact, she really had not been any- where with him except to bed! But it did not matter. Caitlin felt so close to Domi- nic and she just knew they where meant to be together. Not everyone courted the same way. William's paranoia was unfounded. He would get used to it... He had to!

Linnie's figure coming across the lawn caught her attention and she raced down the stairs to greet her. She met up with her on the patio, just off the kitchen and, breathlessly, relayed the events of the night before. Linnie listened intently, without interruption.

"It was just awful Linnie," Caitlin wheezed the words as she struggled to catch her breath. "The two were circling each other. Literally circling each other! I couldn't believe it. William was so set on having Dominic leave and never come back. And Dominic! Oh Linnie, he looked so mean. I've never seen him look so angry and mean before. His beautiful blue eyes had a dark and sinister look to them. It scared me a little! And then he stormed out of the house; just like that, without a glance back in my direction! I argued with William a little. I mean, when Mark married on the spur, William had just laughed. But me? Me? Heck Linnie, Dominic and I have known each other intimately for some time now. I know it's not a long time, but it's long enough. Do you understand? I feel like we're bonded in a way. Can you understand? Can you?"

"Yes lass. I understand more than ya realize." Linnie clicked out as she moved past Caitlin to sit on the patio. The early morning walk had taken the little bit of strength she seemed to have left out of her. "Fetch me a cup of tea, will ya lass? I'm a bit feeble this morning."

Caitlin did Linnie's bidding and calmed

down in the process. When she returned with the hot tea, Linnie sipped it gratefully, while staring at Caitlin over the brim of the cup.

"He left here for a walk last night. He was so angry. And he hasn't come back. That's not like him. I mean, he's left before when we've argued but he's always returned after a few hours. He likes to walk and think. It clears his mind."

Are ya talking about William or Dominic lass?" Linnie knew it was William, but was not ready to tell Caitlin where he was. She decided to keep that to herself for a while longer while she sized up the situation.

"Oh, sorry... William. I'm a little nervous. He must be really angry not to come back all night. I wonder where he stayed. It was pretty chilly last night so he couldn't have camped out anywhere. And his car is still here..." Caitlin's panic level was rising again.

"Not to worry lass, I'm sure he's fine wherever he is. Now, tell me about this Dominic fella. Why did he get so mad at William, eh? Didn't he expect to have some trouble with the family? He's pretty new and all." Linnie set her cup down on the table and stretched out her bulk, awaiting Caitlin's answer.

They talked for almost three hours while Linnie pumped Caitlin for as much information as she could get. Whether Caitlin was aware of it or not, she did not seem to mind, and she answered freely. By the time they had finished, Linnie had drawn a pretty clear picture of what had happened to William while on his way through the woods. This Dominic was bad news. And he had to be stopped. Linnie silently prayed that the work she had done would be effective.

Morning turned into afternoon before Linnie rose to leave. She stopped half way across the lawn to observe the large white taxi that was pulling up the drive. Emma, feeling the electricity in the air from an oncoming storm, felt more energized than normal and seized the opportunity for a run and kick and squeal her challenge to the vehicle for a race. Linnie smiled, finding Emma to be a genuine treat.

As the cab approached the front walkway, Caitlin stood on the porch, a look of surprised curiosity came over her as she watched Edwin Holtz climb out, pay the driver, and send the cab away as he seemingly ignored her. When he finally did acknowledge her, it was in a calm and matter-of-fact mannerism while he walked up to her slowly, tilting the cap on his head.

Caitlin looked abnormally tense and Linnie decided to stick around a while longer and returned to her cup of tea and comfortable chair on the patio. She left the two of them on the porch but made certain she was able to hear enough of their muffled voices to understand what was happening.

"Hello there!" Edwin's smile was captivating.

"Well, this is a surprise. What brings you here?" Caitlin's confusion was genuine. She had not seen nor heard from Edwin since she had encountered his naked body in the hallway. Although she still remembered the encounter vividly, he apparently did not."

"Would you believe I was in the neighborhood?" He smiled sheepishly.

"Okay," Caitlin drawled as she stepped aside to allow Edwin onto the porch. You were pretty confident you'd find me home?"

"Why do you ask that?" Edwin's innocent tone of voice in no way matched his devilish eyes.

"Well, for one thing, you let the cab go right away." Caitlin chuckled, suddenly finding humor in the situation.

"I'm psychic." He laughed as he strolled into the house without waiting for a reply.

Linnie found them in the living room and quickly approached Edwin, extending her large rough hand for him to shake. The enthusiasm in her movements was exceeded by her greeting.

Caitlin stood back, watching curiously. She had never seen Linnie this excited about meeting up with anyone. And she really did not think that Linnie harbored any type of fondness for Edwin, which made her wonder on why the sudden change. Her curiosity so absorbed her that she forgot completely about the argument between William and Dominic the night before and the fact that William had not returned.

The trio talked and laughed about any topic that came to mind throughout the afternoon. When Dominic arrived, at his usual time, Caitlin jumped with a start. She had completely forgotten about him; which was very unusual. Normally she spent her hours watching the clock with anticipation.

The surprised look on her face when he entered the house did not go unnoticed by Dominic and he glowered at Edwin inappreciatively while motioning for Caitlin to come with him. She excused herself politely, and to both Linnie's and Edwin's surprised, followed Dominic obediently upstairs to her bedroom.

"Do you really think this is a good idea?" A wave of guilt swept over Caitlin as she reached the top landing of the stairwell and she was feeling uncomfortable about leaving Linnie and Edwin like she did.

"What do you mean?" Dominic's voice was almost a growl as he urged Caitlin into her bedroom. His movements very closely resembled pushing.

"We have guests, sweetheart. It doesn't seem right to go to the bedroom while they are sitting downstairs. What will they think?" Caitlin kissed Dominic on the cheek and made move to leave the room. "Let's go back downstairs before they get the wrong idea."

"And what idea is that?" Dominic grabbed Caitlin's arm and prevented her from moving. "The idea that we are two people in love?"

Caitlin giggled as Dominic wrapped his arms around her, pinning her motionless. "Well, you could look at it that way. But you could also look at it as being incredibly rude."

Caitlin tried to free herself but Dominic only tightened his hold on her. She did not like the feeling of being trapped like this and struggled even harder. "Dominic, please." Her voice was a thick whisper.

"Please, what?" Dominic brought his mouth to Caitlin's so forcefully that her lips pained and she was sure they were bleeding.

Caitlin's body hardened in defiance of her lover's actions. But instead of easing up, he kissed her even harder, almost cutting off her breathing.

Dominic fought back the urge to force Caitlin to do his bidding. Things were not going well and time was running short. Between his fight with William and the arrival of Edwin, the threat of Caitlin changing her mind about having him move in was strong. And it did not help that the old woman was down there getting cozy with Edwin. Did she think he did not know what she was up to? Dominic cursed himself for not finishing off Edwin that day in the clearing when he had the chance. If he had not been so worried about Caitlin catching him in the act, he would have finished Edwin off and be free of his threat. Maybe if he had not offered to help Caitlin get him to the hospital... Well, what was done, was done. He needed to worry about what to do instead of what he should have, or could have, done. He was running out of time and could not afford to have any more set backs. The eve of the thinning of the veil was coming soon and it was vital that he have Caitlin conceive his child by then. He was mystified as to why she had not done so already. He knew she was fertile and he had read her mind to make sure she was not taking birth control; so what was the problem? He suspected the old woman was linked to it somehow. She would have to be reckoned with as soon as possible.

Dominic eased his grip on Caitlin and put his lips gently to her ear, "Just a moment, my love. Give me just a moment and then we can go back, okay?"

Caitlin shuddered with delight as Dominic's lips gently caressed her ear as he spoke. She felt herself melting in his arms and forgetting about all else. She loved being in his arms. He had a way of making her forget the world outside.

Happy to have accomplished his mission,

Dominic gently released Caitlin and walked to the mini bar he had suggested she set up in her room. "Let's just have one drink alone before we rejoin our guest, can we? Just one drink. Call me selfish, but I hate to share you. I love you so much."

Caitlin felt like a giddy schoolgirl as she readily agreed. They had only been gone from Linnie and Edwin a moment or two, so taking the time for an intimate drink with her lover would not be a problem. They would still return in time for their guests to realize that nothing else went on. Caitlin giggled as she realized she was placing Linnie in the category of guest; how odd.

"It feels a little chilly in here. We won't be here long enough to justify a fire, but can you pull the drapes closed? Those windows leak some." Dominic was not in the least bit cold, but he needed some reason to occupy Caitlin's attention so that she would not see him reach in his pocket and pour the contents of a small vile into her glass of brandy.

To his delight, Caitlin fussed over the draperies in an effort to seal the windows as much as possible before joining him for their drink; providing him ample time to mix the potion thoroughly.

Dominic place a soft kiss on Caitlin's lips while he slid the glass of brandy into her hand. He held his up to indicate a toast and they gently clanked their glasses together before bringing the burning liquid to their lips.

The potion was strong and it took only one or two sips of the brandy before Caitlin's head grew light and disorientation set in. Dominic grabbed the glass, that still contained the drugged brandy, and set it on her dresser before gently guiding her toward the bed.

Caitlin fumbled a little as she robotically removed her clothes, while Dominic stood and watched her with a satisfied grin. Today would be the day it would be done. He had brought the oil of fertility to seal the deal. He wanted to leave nothing up to chance. Today would be the day he consumed her body and soul. Today she was guaranteed to conceive his child. Today he would make certain that she was his forever.

When Dominic had first met up with Caitlin in the grove, he had looked upon her merely as the potential mother of his child. His actions had been for the strict purpose of impregnating her with his seed. But, as time had gone by and he had coupled with her over and over again, he had also developed a feeling for her that was foreign to him. Could it be love? He was not sure, since he did not really understand what love was. But, one thing was for certain, he knew that he liked this feeling and he did not want to lose it. He would keep Caitlin with him long after the child was born. She would be his queen for eternity.

Caitlin removed the last of her clothing and

walked over to stand seductively before him. He took a different vial out of his pocket and poured a yellowish oil into the palm of his hand. Reaching into her most private area, he gently massaged her with the oil.

Caitlin moaned passionately as all her senses came alive. She had never experienced such ecstasy before she had been introduced to these ancient love oils Dominic enjoyed using. He had introduced them to her that very first time of passionate love making, presenting a different oil each time, and she had grown to look forward to them ever since. They took away all her inhibitions and she found herself performing sexual acts that at one time would have made her blush. Dominic told her that the oils only brought out the true desires of the persona and that this wanton side of her was in her all along. She believed him completely and felt surely that she only would perform such acts of lovemaking with the right man. And since she was doing this with Dominic, then he must be the right man.

It no longer seemed wrong to leave Linnie and Edwin waiting downstairs.

Dominic's irritation from the night before had only been accentuated by finding Edwin laughing freely with the two women. His frustration, jealousy and fear of losing Caitlin effected his love making, causing him to be more aggressive, and rougher, than normal.

Caitlin looked at Dominic, stunned. He had

never been thoughtless and cruel in his love making before. The headiness she felt made it difficult to focus and almost impossible to do anything more than moan from both pleasure and pain as her lover took her over and over again. His love making shifted from sensual and pleasurable to hurtful and unbearable. She longed for him to stop but could only moan her protests.

"You are bound to me for eternity now, my love; remember that!" Dominic burst out when, at last, he rolled off her and zipped up his pants. Caitlin only then realized her lover had never even undressed! "Go back and tell your brother that he loses. Got it? He loses. And that old woman downstairs. Well, let's just say things are going to change around here, shall we?."

Caitlin too her time rolling off the bed. She felt as if she was in a nightmare and prayed to wake up soon. Every part of her body ached and there was a small amount of blood coming from her vagina. Although still foggy, her head was clearing enough for her to speak and register what was happening. She looked again at the snifter with the laced brandy then over at Dominic. He seemed not to notice.

"Why?" She asked shakily.

"Get yourself cleaned up now. You have guests downstairs, remember? And not a word, do you hear me? Never a word, never!" Dominic stated as he ran his fingers through his hair, grabbed the vials off the dresser and left the room. Caitlin stood in disbelief as she listened to him go downstairs and out the door before darkness consumed her.

~

It was ten minutes later when Edwin and Linnie entered the room to check on her, only to find her naked body limp on the floor.

"Ah, first the brother and now the sister!" Linnie gasped. Without taking the time to explain her remarks to Edwin, she bent down to pull Caitlin off the floor and over to the bed. Normally Linnie had the strength of two men, but for reasons she could not explain, she felt as weak as a puppy.

"Help me lad, I'm feeling old today." Linnie groaned as she pulled Caitlin onto her feet.

Edwin regained his sense and pitched in to help.

As they eased Caitlin's slender body down on the bed covers, Edwin could hardly contain his admiration for the beauty her nakedness displayed. Her body was perfectly formed. Her large firm breasts sported perfect pert nipples, and her stomach curved smoothly and tightly into trim hips and thighs. He was hoping that Linnie was so involved with her task at hand that she would not notice the way he was admiring her young friend. She was a work of art.

"I'll be back in a minute. Watch her, okay?" Linnie blurted out as she left the room, closing the door behind her.

Outside the room Linnie stopped and took a minute to compose herself before starting to chant, almost inaudibly. With steady rhythm she danced down the hall, chanting all the way. When she reached the end of the hall, she turned and continued back up toward Caitlin's room, only to turn and continue again.

~

The longer Edwin stood over Caitlin admiring her beauty, the more he noticed the marks left by Dominic's violent encounter. Feelings of rage crept over him as he struggled for a way to make it better for her. One of her taught nipples was a deep purple and faint teeth marks could be seen. He looked at the blood trickling out onto her inner thigh. It was obvious she had been wounded and he wondered why she never cried out for help. He gently pulled her legs apart so he could better see the extent of her injury. Although there was blood and a distinct scent of semen, he saw no visible scars.

He wanted to kill Dominic.

Deciding that keeping busy was the best thing he could do to help overcome his rage, Edwin went to the adjoining bathroom and pulled out a small basin from the large cupboard that was built in the wall. Filling it with warm water, he grabbed a washcloth and returned to begin the task of cleaning her up.

Edwin started with Caitlin's face and worked his way down, wanting every inch of her cleansed from the contact she had just had. She moaned quietly and worked her lips as if they where parched. Looking around, he spotted a glass of brandy that she must have been drinking earlier. Brandy was probably the best thing for her right now. He grabbed it and held it to her lips and she swallowed without opening her eyes. A faint smile spread across her face as she slowly took in a deep breath, causing her breasts to graze his arms; which sent an electric tingle sweeping through him.

Taken aback by the sudden wave of excitement that flooded him, Edwin downed the remains of the brandy in one large gulp before he went back to the tortuous job of cleaning up Caitlin without getting aroused himself.

As he swallowed the liquid, a warm heady feeling came over him. Doing his best to stay focused, he gently continued to wash her, but was unable to prevent the arousal within his groin. He looked toward the door, willing Linnie to return to stop what he was about to do, unaware that she was just on the other side of the door, chanting and dancing with all her will.

His headiness grew stronger and he jumped up away from Caitlin as he fought for control of his body and his actions. Beads of sweat formed on his forehead. It was like something was overtaking him and he was no longer in control. He struggled with the urge to pounce upon her luscious body as she lay there with a seductive smile pursing her lips.

A lustful moan escaped Caitlin's lips. It was more than he could bear. The room seemed fuzzy and faded and all he could see was her pink flesh and pert nipples raising and lowering with her aroused breathing. Feelings of sexual desire arose in him uncontrollably. He found himself moving toward her, as if not by his own doing.

Unable to resist any longer, he eased his manhood into her. Her body stiffened only briefly before it joined with his and they moved in rhythmic unison.

Sensations of wild abandonment swept over Edwin as he consumed Caitlin. To his surprise and dismay, he reached his peak all too soon.

Edwin lay limp on top of Caitlin's soft body only briefly before the realization of what had just occurred hit home. He got off the bed and went into the bathroom, ashamed of his actions and eager to cleanse himself. He showered, leaving the curtain open and never taking his eyes off the still limp form on the bed. Scrubbing his body with a vengeance he gave thanks that the hulk of a woman named Linnie had not entered to see what he had been doing. He could not understand what had gotten over him. Shame consumed him and he prayed Linnie would remain gone until he had time to clean up and figure out what to do. A feeling of sickness ran rampant through his body and he fell to his knees vomiting. He remained motionless with the shower pouring water on him while it washed his vomit down the drain.

Linnie had stopped chanting and dancing and stood silently outside the door. Although she was very aware of what had just occurred between Caitlin and Edwin, she also knew all too well the necessity for it. She hoped with all her might that Edwin's actions had been enough to undo the work of that devil man, Dominic. The only counter for Caitlin's conceiving the devil man's child, that she knew of, was for the seed of another to be planted immediately afterward; and that was still no guarantee. It was in the hands of the almighty now. Only time would tell whose seed was the most powerful to take hold within the womb of the dear lass.

Linnie gave thanks to the spirits for their help in manipulating Edwin and she prayed for the salvation of her young friend.

The energy Linnie had expelled for a ritual she had only done once before had taken its toll. Feeling spent and craving a drink, she headed for the den.

EIGHTEEN

Linnie was sitting in the den sipping on her third glass of brandy by the time Edwin had cleaned himself and Caitlin up. He had removed the top cover off the bed in disgust and tossed it down the laundry shoot Caitlin had installed in the main hallway. Her body looked frail and weak and he hastily covered her with a quilt that was thrown over a chair, before leaving the room. Waves of disgust flowed over him as his head grew more and more clear and he recalled fully what he had done. The look of self loathing was still on his face as he passed by Linnie and poured himself a drink.

"Ya did what had to be done, lad. Let it go." Linnie's words roared in Edwin's ears and he was not sure he had heard her correctly.

"What?" His voice sounded high pitched and strained.

"Have a seat lad; right there." Linnie pointed to the chair opposite her. Edwin settled himself silently; not certain he wanted to be in her's, or anyone's, company right now. Anguish and agony shrieked from him and Linnie felt compassion for his situation. It could not be easy for a good man, such as he was, to understand or accept his recent actions.

"When I was a wee lass back in that old country we used to have monthly visits from the town's wise man. He was old. I remember that well. But strong. There was a rumor he lifted a house one time." Linnie paused a moment to quietly laugh. "Me dad was a bit jealous of that one, indeed he was. But, he was gracious and always offered the man the best of hospitality whenever he came around."

Edwin shifted in his chair. He was not sure where Linnie was going with this story, but he had no interest. He wanted to be left alone to wallow in self hate and misery.

Linnie ignored Edwin's obvious body language and continued. "He came to see me ma because, no matter how wise he was, and he was that, me ma was is equal. She knew the ways of the mysteries. Do ya understand that mysteries?"

Edwin sat motionless, not offering a reply.

Linnie looked at Edwin long and hard before continuing. "Of course ya do. When I met ya, I knew that there was something about ya that felt odd. Because of that, when I felt the ick around Caitlin and blamed ya! I'm sorry about that, really I am. But, ya arrived at the same time as that Dominic demon and I got confused. You're not evil at all."

"Think again dear woman." Edwin growled as he tossed back his whisky.

Linnie continued, refusing to acknowledge his comment. "The wise man would come to the house once a month and spend an afternoon and into the morning with me ma. She would close herself up with him in the parlor an we would sit outside waiting to see them when they came out. Me ma was a special lady, she was. She helped all who came her way, no matter what. And so, when the wise man asked her for some help with his scientific project, she agreed. She had the knowledge, and the gifts. Like you... gifts like you."

Edwin looked at her quizzically.

"Ya see, that old man had gone to Egypt and brought back some ancient books. In them were some spells and rituals of the gods. The spells and rituals were for both good and evil. Without knowing what he was doing, the old man had read some pages that brought forth some pretty dark forces. And like a curse, they attached to him and became alive at the same time every month. Me ma wasn't schooled in Egyptian and didn't understand the writings, but she was smart and, even though she couldn't get rid of them, she figured out a way to subdue them when they came alive."

Linnie paused briefly to make sure Edwin was paying attention. Satisfied that she had finally captured his audience, she continued. "So, each month that old wise man would come to the house and me ma would take care of him. In exchange, he shared books and other knowledge with her to help her grow even stronger in her craft." Linnie pointed to the book that she had given to Caitlin. "Do ya see that book up there on the mantle? 'Tis old. Older than the hills. 'Twas given to me ma from her grandma. And to her grandma from her grandma, skipping generations.

I got it, even though I shouldn't have, because I was special. More special than the rest of me siblings. I've got the gifts strong; and I didn't need to be taught them. I used to stand outside the door of our parlor and tell me siblings what me ma was doing with the old wise man. I didn't hear the words too good, but I could see the actions. When me ma and the old man discovered this, they started bringing me into the parlor with them and teaching me. Soon I was creating and cooking and helping me ma with all kinds of things. Some people called us witches. Well, maybe we are. But I never thought of meself as that. I'm just an old woman who has been given a gift and I've done me best to help me pals with it."

Linnie pulled her bulk out of the comfort of the chair and walked over to take the book off the mantle. "I gave this book to Caitlin a while back, now. I think I made a mistake, because she wasn't ready fur such a responsibility and, like the old wise man, she read from it even though I told her not to... and she unleashed the dark side."

Edwin shifted uncomfortably in his chair.

"I thought you were part of it. Especially after that night when ya was visiting and the woods was filled with the dog-pig beasts. But, when I studied your blood sample it showed me nothing. So I got confused."

Edwin grabbed his arm with a scowl on his face. He had never figured out what had happened to his arm during his visit here. Now it was making sense. "How did you get my blood?"

"I gave ya a sleeping sedative in your drink and, when ya were sound asleep, I took it. But never mind, that's not important now."

Although he was outraged by her actions, Edwin kept quiet; wanting to hear the rest of her story.

Linnie nodded her head toward the upstairs where Caitlin lay sleeping. "Just before she met ya, she read from the book and brought forth the dark side. It ripped up the place, it did. But, her spirits helped to hold it back. Thanks for that." Linnie heaved a sigh. "But, it must have got loose anyway. Its mighty strong, stronger than I thought in the beginning; and it wants her. It wants her to carry and bring the next demon child into this world. And not only does it want her, it wants this place because 'tis quiet and secluded and the perfect place to raise the child until he comes of age to use his powers."

Edwin's eyes grew larger as he listened with disbelief to the story Linnie was telling him. It all seemed so incredible, yet he somehow believed there was truth to it. He sat on the edge of his chair while the old woman continued.

"I think Dominic is the leader. He's damn good ya know. He had me looking in your direction for the bad, he did. But I was beginning to get suspicious. His actions where odd. Like how he never took her out of the house. The man drives a Mercedes and wears fine clothes. I find it hard to believe that he couldn't have afforded to take the lass out to dinner or a movie once in awhile. But instead, he only visited for a few hours each afternoon at the same time. And these visits were upstairs in her bedroom, behind closed doors. He had her under some sort of spell, of course. The lass would have never tolerated such actions otherwise. So, you can imagine the chaos that went on when she announced to her brother that she was going to have him move in with her. Lord be, the chaos that went on then."

"Chaos?" Edwin shifted in his chair.

"Her brother, William, had a wicked time with Dominic and nearly caught is death! And the lass. My oh my. She's not herself, not at all. 'Twas hard to watch her changing like that. I finally pulled out one of me ma's books and did what I had to do to help the situation."

"And what was that?" Edwin asked, still not clear on what she was telling him.

"I summoned you. Or should I say that I summoned the one person that could help; not knowing who it would be." Linnie sat back and studied Edwin's body language. It was clear that he was beginning to believe her words, but was not comfortable with what was being discussed.

"What do you mean you summoned me? I don't follow" Edwin was growing more and more uncomfortable.

"Now relax and stop looking like your getting ready to take flight any minute." Linnie's voice was stern but gentle.

"I am." Edwin could have never been more serious. After the episode in Caitlin's room, this conversation was making him even more confused and a strong feeling of revulsion was overtaking him. While he had thought the drink would help him to feel better, it was doing just the opposite and he felt like he could vomit at any moment.

"Sit back Lad. It'll all make sense to ya in a minute." Compassion rang through her words as Linnie realized that, although Edwin was very gifted, he was not aware of the fact. Like her protégé, Caitlin, he needed study, and lots of it . But there was no time now. She would have to have faith in his instincts..

"I hope so ma'am. I really hope so." Edwin felt suddenly exhausted as he fell back into the chair to finish listening to Linnie's story.

"Ma'am? Hun?" Linnie raised her eyebrows. "Oh, never mind." She waived her hand in dismissal and continued. "Why did ya come here?" Her tone was so demanding that it took Edwin by surprise.

"I'm not really sure." Startled by her blunt question, he answered as honestly as he could. He was not really sure why he had come. He just woke up that morning, an easy hundred miles south, and decided to pay Caitlin a visit; just like that. So, without giving it much thought, he had hopped the train and then taken a cab from there; abandoning his projects for the day without giving them a single thought. He now realized that he would have a mess to deal with when he got back, since his associates would be wondering why he had not shown up for work and had dumped the burden of the deadline in their laps.

"Ya came because ya where summoned by the spirits to help her. You're connected, ya

know, on a soul level. Have ya any understanding of what I'm saying?"

"Yes, I believe I do." Edwin had spent
some time in the south sea islands and
had learned of the beliefs of the pagan re-
ligions enough to understand their thought
process. Although he was not completely
convinced that they were correct, he could
not deny them either. Especially since his
strong Catholic upbringing somehow did
not sit well with him. So, he was searching for something, but not knowing what.
Something in between perhaps.

"I know ya do. I know it. Deep inside ya, ya
have the knowledge. You and Caitlin both
have it. She's like a flower waiting to bloom
and you're like a gardener tending her soil."
Linnie paused a moment as if to contem-
plate what she had said. She walked over to
pour herself more brandy. It was unlike her
to drink so heavily this early, but these last
few days had been unlike any she had ever
experienced before. It was the time she had
been preparing for all her life. She knew it
now. And she also knew what was waiting
for her at the finish line. With calm deliberation, she continued. "What ya did upstairs
was necessary."

Edwin jumped back, startled by Linnie's
incredulous remark. He had just taken a
sip of his own drink and choked uncontrollably.

Linnie beat Edwin soundly on the back until he could breath normally before continuing with her story. "That demon fella, Dominic, was possessing her. Little by little, day after day, he slowly was sucking her will from her body until she would eventually become like a zombie to do his bidding. Oh, don't get me wrong, lad. She would be alive, but she would have no will of her own and would answer only to his desires and wishes. I could see that it was already starting to happen. And, when her brother reacted so violently and things came to a head like they did, he decided to hurry and finish the job. To make sure she couldn't get away. William tried to stop him and was almost killed."

The shocked look on Edwin's face caused her to pause before continuing. "He's Okay. He's over at my place." Linnie lowered her voice to a hush tone, "And the lass doesn't know yet. I didn't want her to tell that demon fella where he was so that he could finish him off."

Linnie tossed down the remainder of her drink and went back to sit in the chair she loved so much. She eased her bulk into it slowly, as if she had suddenly aged a lifetime, before continuing. "Anyway, he's got his hands full with you here. He'll be wanting to be rid of you so the lad's safe now, I'm thinking." Linnie leaned forward and looked directly into Edwin's steel gray eyes.

"You are the one to end it all. You have the power. It's there, deep inside ya. Just follow your gut like ya did when ya came here. And like ya did when I left ya alone in the room with her. I knew what ya was going to do. I knew. But, I also knew it was the only way. The only way I can figure, anyway. Ya released her lad. In an ugly way, no doubt. But he's an ugly demon. Ya had no choice, the way I see it. And we don't need to speak of it again."

"Oh God!" Edwin held his head in his hands and felt the moistness of his tear filled eyes. Never had he felt so horrible; like a sick animal. And now this woman was telling him what he did was okay. She was equally as sick! How could she sit there and look him in the eyes and tell him that it was necessary? Nothing made sense. He needed to sleep. He wanted to go somewhere far away and sleep until he forgot.

Getting up hastily, Edwin excused himself and left the room. Finding his way to the room he had stayed in before, he stopped at Caitlin's doorway to look in on her. She was resting peacefully, as if nothing had happened. A shudder ran through him as he remembered his actions not an hour earlier and he hastened to the guest room. There was something different about the feel of the room, but he did not take time to figure it out. Flinging himself on the bed in despair, he tossed and groan until he finally fell into a blissful deep sleep.

~

Linnie remained in the den until early evening. She knew she needed to go back to her place to check on William, but she also felt she was needed here. It was a difficult decision.

The brandy was kicking in and was making her a little heady. She decided that William would be fine for a while longer. He had Samson there to keep him company. She called on her guides to watch over the young man and her beloved dog, just in case she was wrong, and then moved over to the sofa to lay down. Not certain what the night would bring, she decided she had better get some rest now and allow the brandy to wear off. She might need her faculties about her later on.

NINETEEN

Caitlin laid in her bed feeling safe and secure for the first time in a very long time. She had slept long and hard, not quite remembering the events of the day.

As she lay cuddled under the covers, she looked out the gap in the draperies and discovered it was early evening. Quickly looking over at the clock on the dresser, she was shocked to see it was seven o'clock! What had happened to the day?

Leaping out of bed too quickly caused the blood to rush from Caitlin's head, forcing her to hold firmly to the bed post until she could regain her composure. The muscles in her body felt tired and sore as she made her way into the bathroom.

Little by little pieces of the events of the day came back to her. They seemed like a far away dream. Throwing a wrap around her, Caitlin hit the intercom button for the downstairs speaker and called out for Linnie, not certain if she was still there. She had only recently had the system installed and this was the first time she had tried it out. She was not sure if it was even working properly. After a few minutes with no response, she decided that if Linnie was still waiting for her downstairs, she could wait a little longer. She felt a strong need to soak in a hot bath before going down stairs to get a light dinner.

Confusion swarmed as she filled the tub with hot bubbles while sporadic, dream like memories of the day's events floated through her mind.

Finding a soothing CD, Caitlin placed it in the player and lit a scented candle. Easing herself down into the bubbles, she allowed the warmth to soothe her muscles and hopefully wash away the fogginess from her brain. Although she was still unclear as to what she had dreamt verses what had actually happened, Caitlin was not terribly bothered by it. She felt a strange sense of peace and contentment. It was a different kind of peace than the cozy one she was used it. It was a deep, solid, peace. Something she could hardly explain to herself, let alone anyone else.

The music from the CD seemed to drift off into the distance as a large glowing ball appeared before her. Caitlin was growing used to Lael's graceful entrances and remained calm and still as he stepped out of the glowing ball in a semi transparent state that radiated light. *'If someone asked me to describe what love and beauty looks like, I know I couldn't. I'd just have to ask them to look at*

Lael. He's the essence of love and beauty. I just know it.' Caitlin mused.

Caitlin said nothing as she watched his glowing figure move gracefully about the room until he had positioned himself where she could see him without straining her neck. After a few moments of silence Lael stepped closer. He was so close that Caitlin could smell a faint scent of Jasmine. She had earlier learned that Jasmine was Lael favorite aroma.

"Greetings my beloved. I am Lael."

Lael's introduction brought a smile to Caitlin's face. It seemed the standard greeting from this light being. She wondered why he felt it necessary to give his name to her each time, but decided it would be rude of her to ask.

"I have come to speak to you this evening of the day's events."

Caitlin sat up, suddenly more alert. Although she had a multitude of questions running through her mind, she asked none.

Caitlin kept her torso immersed in the bubbles and her ears alert and eager to listen as Lael continued. "We have been watching with interest during the recent events that have been occurring in your life. Your associations have been less than perfect. Although this is a very good lesson in judgment for you, we fear the consequences may be dear. For this reason, we wish to extend

our assistance to you as much as we are allowed. You have near you very dear souls
who, together, with you, will be able to stop
the evil that has been unleashed. We are in
hopes this can be done without the need of
our assistance. But, if not, you are to simply call. You must remember, please, that
we can not interfere unless you ask. So you
must call. Say my name three times and
help will be available. You are loved my beloved." Upon completion of his statement,
Lael immediately returned to the glowing
ball and was gone.

Caitlin lay still in the tepid bath water long
after Lael had disappeared into nothingness.
She had so many questions that needed answers, yet she was not given the chance to
ask even one. And now he was gone. Who
are the dear souls to help her? Is it Linnie?
William? Dominic? Who would it be? And
what was the association that was less than
perfect?

Caitlin closed her eyes again and saw herself lying in bed with Edwin moving his body
over her. Events of the afternoon flashed before her and she shrieked in disgust, throwing water violently all around in an attempt
to wash away the memory. It was Edwin
Lael was talking about! She must have fall-
en asleep after Dominic left and Edwin came
in and raped her! She scrubbed her skin until it was raw, sinking completely under the

water in an attempt to clean away the sensation she felt. Her skin was shriveled and almost bleeding by the time Caitlin felt satisfied enough to climb out of the water.

Feeling a hollowness in her stomach, she wrapped herself up in a soft robe and started downstairs toward the kitchen. When she reached the doorway, Caitlin stopped short. There, at the kitchen table just as cozy as you please, were Edwin and Linnie.

Deep in conversation, they stopped when she entered.

"Ah, lass. There ya be." Linnie seemed relieved to see Caitlin up and around.

Caitlin ignored Linnie's greeting and rushed toward Edwin. She could not contain the rage she felt for this man and what he had done to her. Bile rose in her throat as tiny flashes of memory haunted her. She closed the space between them with lightening speed and her clenched fists pounded heavily on his body. Shocked and taken by surprise, Edwin crouched to the floor in an attempt to escape her blows. Caitlin kicked and punched until she was weak. Even Linnie's strong grasp was not enough to stop her.

"Lass!" Linnie bellowed, "Stop with ya now! Come on now, lass, calm down!" Linnie's words where barely audible over Caitlin's screaming as she continued to pound as hard as she could on Edwin's body. She escaped Linnie's grasp enough to reach over and grab a cast iron frying pan that was hanging on the wall and flung it, with all her might, in Edwin's direction.

Edwin lay sprawled flat on the floor, barely managing to dodge the pan that only lightly skinned across his back. Linnie threw her body toward Caitlin just as she had gotten momentum with yet another cast iron frying pan. She was successful in weakening the blow, but Edwin still suffered the impact, even if it was to a lesser degree.

"Now enough!" Linnie howled with such authority that it brought Caitlin to a startled halt. "I want ya to calm down for a minute and let's talk about this. Okay?"

Caitlin's chest was heaving from the exertion and she stood in a silent, stubborn stance while she watched Edwin struggle to get up.

Linnie grabbed a bag of frozen vegetables out of the refrigerator freezer and handed it to him. "Here, put this where it hurts. It should help to keep the swelling down."

Edwin took the frozen vegetables sheepishly. He was not able to look at Caitlin and he certainly could not blame her for being angry. What he had done was vile. He disgusted even himself. And the worst part was that it was not like him to do such a thing. He could not explain his actions to himself, so how could he justify or explain them to poor Caitlin. He had violated her, plain and simple; and it was an unforgivable act. He deserved all the pain Caitlin could inflict upon him.

Linnie had talked to Edwin about spells and rituals. But it sounded like the fantasies of an old superstitious woman. Linnie told him he was special and that he had special powers. He did not have a clue as to what she meant. Thinking her a bit senile, he had politely listening to her while he searched his mind for a solution to the problem. He knew he would have to face Caitlin and that what he had done would also have to be faced. He wished he could undo it all, to go back in time and change everything that had occurred. But, before he could come to terms with it all, or find a way to smooth things out, Caitlin had come racing into the room like a wild animal attacking him and he could not blame her. And now, he had to face her and he could not even look at her.

"Get out!" Caitlin shrieked. "Get out, you filthy animal!"

Edwin he rose to leave and Linnie interrupted, "Stay where ya are, lad. No one is going anywhere. Not just yet, anyway." Linnie made her way past an angry Caitlin toward the stove. She had placed her bag in the corner of the kitchen upon arriving and had searched it while Edwin was with Caitlin for her potion, sensing it would be needed later. And now, it was definitely needed. She poured two teaspoons of the potion into a cup of tea with some honey to ease the bitterness and handed it to Caitlin, motioning her to drink it before she motioned Edwin to sit down in the far corner of the room and did the same for him. The two obediently drank; Caitlin, never taking her angry eyes off Edwin, while Edwin never taking his eyes off the floor.

Satisfied that they had both emptied their cups, Linnie took the cups back, in case Caitlin decided to use one as a weapon before the potion had a chance to settle in, and motioned Caitlin to sit across from Edwin.

Feeling a little more subdued, Caitlin followed Linnie's instructions.

"What I gave ya both was a potion for truth." Linnie took a deep breath before continuing. "It will help ya to understand what I'm about to say. I've been trying to tell this lad here, but I know he thinks I'm a crazy old fool."

Startled that Linnie had stated exactly what he thought, Edwin shifted self-consciously.

"Never mind, lad. If I where ya, I'd think the same thing." Linnie chucked. "Now I want ya to both sit there and listen to me for a bit while I try to explain what's been going on here. It's a bit hard to understand, so I'll take me time. But ya gotta listen good because 'tis serious what I'm going to say!"

Caitlin and Edwin nodded in agreement. They both felt the urgency in the need to know the facts of what had been going on and they both somehow knew that Linnie's words would shine a light on these facts and help them to understand them.

Linnie spoke of the times of old, with demons and witches and sorcerers; times in her country when people believed in the undead and of possession. Instead of laughing , which would normally be his first inclination, Edwin listened with interest. There was the ring of truth to her words.

Caitlin and Edwin listened intently, with not so much as a sound, until Linnie reached the topic of Dominic. As she firmly worked her way up to saying that Caitlin's lover was a demon in disguise, Caitlin sucked in a breath of shock.

Edwin jerked his body to attention. It was somehow all making sense to him.

Caitlin, on the other hand, rejected the information vehemently. "How can you say that? How? You know I'm in love with him. I couldn't fall in love with a demon, Linnie. You're wrong. You're terribly, terribly, wrong about him! I just know it."

"Know this lass, and know it well. Dominic is a demon. He is! And what he's been doing to ya every afternoon is leaving is seed inside ya to make some demon offspring! But I fed ya the tea to stop it, I did! Not because he was a demon, I didn't know it then, but because I had a feeling he was up to some kind of no good. It just wasn't right the way he was coming over here only to take ya in that bedroom and leaving again. And you, lass, allowing it like ya did! No, oh, no, it wasn't right. I knew something was wrong. I just didn't know what."

"No. You're wrong! You have to be!" Caitlin fled from the room, tears of frustration and rage gushing down her cheeks.

Linnie stood in silence looking at Edwin. It was going to be harder than she had thought to break the hold the demon Dominic had on her young friend. Her body felt the strain of the last few days and she suddenly remembered William and her beloved Samson. "Come lad," her voice sounded a little more gruff than intended, "I need to go an check on some things and I don't think 'tis a good idea to leave ya behind."

"No.. No", Edwin mumbled, "I'll go. I have to go anyway. I.. I need to go."

"The hell ya will! Ya will stick this one out buddy! You're going nowhere, do ya understand?" Linnie pulled Edwin onto his feet with the strength of an angry bull. Shocked he nodded and followed her out the door.

TWENTY

Caitlin stretched her body across her bed as she stared at the antique lace canopy above. Frustration mixed with panic filled every fiber of her being. Something was wrong, she knew that, but what was it? Was Linnie telling the truth? Why did she not remember Dominic making love to her earlier. Why did she only remember Edwin raping her? Linnie had to be wrong. It was Edwin who was evil. He was influencing Linnie in some way. That had to be it!

Caitlin got up and paced around the room, unsure of what to do next. She had to see Dominic. She had to talk to him and get some things straightened out. He needed to sit down with Linnie and let her get to know him. Then Linnie would be able to see for herself what a wonderful man Dominic really was. Yes, that was it. She would go to Dominic and have him straighten things out with Linnie and then help her get rid of that horrible evil man, Edwin Holtz.

Caitlin threw on a pair of jeans and a sweater. As she stood before the mirror running a brush through her long curls she stopped for a moment and let the memories of the afternoon run through her mind. As hard as she tried, she could not remember Dominic's visit; but she remembered Edwin all too well. Her body shuddered with revulsion as she put the brush down and pulled on a pair of socks. Her mind was racing with questions. What would Dominic say when he found out how Edwin had violated her? Should she even tell him? She hoped he would defend her in some way.

A faint smile crossed her face as she thought how silly she was to even doubt that Dominic would come to her rescue. After all, he was her love. Of course he would be there when she needed him.

As Caitlin closed the door behind her, the cool fall air filled her lungs. The bright stars surrounded the full moon, lighting up the night and affording easy visibility. She walked past the den and peered in the window. There was no sign of Linnie and Edwin. She decided they must have remained in the kitchen after she had run out.

Happy to have gotten out without being noticed, she headed for the paddock and Emma. The mare stood in the moonlight, majestically watching her mistress approach. Caitlin stroked Emma's mane and nuzzled her neck as she tried to decide what to do next.

The confusion and pain of Linnie's words permeated her being. *Dominic is a demon, he*

*is!.. It just wasn't right... him coming over here
only to take ya in that bedroom and leaving
again. And you lass, allowing it like ya did!"*
A cool breeze swirled around Caitlin's head
and suddenly Linnie's claim seemed to reel
with reality.

Caitlin's eyes grew wide and her heart
picked up pace as she absorbed Linnie's
words. Dominic truly was a mystery and she
really did not know anything about him; not
really. They had talked a little during his
afternoon visits, but mainly about her. And
Linnie was right when she had pointed out
that Dominic had not taken her anywhere
but to her bed.   And she could not go to
see him because she did not have a clue
where he lived! The absurdity of it all was
overwhelming. How could she have been so
blind; so foolish? This was not like her at
all. She needed more answers. She needed
help in understanding everything that had
happened since Dominic had arrived at her
house that afternoon. It all seemed a blur;
like a dream. She needed Linnie.

Caitlin kissed Emma's muzzle quickly
and returned to the house. She was finally
ready to listen to what Linnie had to say.
She would sit down quietly and give the old
woman her full attention, without interrupt-
ing her.

Caitlin still could not perceive Dominic
as a demon. There was a misunderstand

or Linnie was exaggerating a bit there. After all, she was very into the magic world and believed so strongly that it would make sense she would jump to that type of a conclusion. No, Linnie was wrong about her love being a demon.

He may not be a demon, but, Dominic was up to something. Caitlin was certain of that. Visions of his visits started rushing to her now. If he wanted her simply for a lover, then why would he want to set up house with her? He would lose his freedom and would have to eventually take her someplace other than her bedroom if he lived with her.

She should hear Linnie out. The old woman was dear to her and she trusted her completely. There must be a reason she distrusted Dominic like she did; a bigger reason than the fact that she did not like how cheap he was.

But, why was Linnie defending Edwin? Was it because she did not really have the facts and details of what Edwin did to her? Caitlin moaned at the prospect of telling the horrors of Edwin's actions. She wanted to forget them, but, she had to make Linnie understand the reason for her actions.

Caitlin called for Linnie as she entered the kitchen, but all was silent. She checked the patio, knowing that Linnie enjoyed sipping brandy in the moonlight, but there was no sign of her, or Edwin for that matter. It soon became clear that Linnie had gone and since she had not noticed any vehicles coming up the drive to take Edwin away, she concluded that he must have gone with her. Knowing how private Linnie was, Caitlin wondered why she would take Edwin to her home, but it appeared she did just that. Caitlin did not understand any of this.

She made her way back out to the barn where Emma stood waiting, as if knowing her mistress would be back shortly. Slipping Emma's bridle on with ease, Caitlin decided to forego the saddle and ride bare back. It had been a while since she had done it, but impatience was prompting her. As she slung herself onto Emma's back she winced, the unforgettable events from the day made her instantly regretful that she had not use the saddle. After mulling over the advantages of getting off and putting one on, she opted to stay riding bare back, deciding that she would be uncomfortable no matter what.

Emma's flanks spurred into action as Caitlin dug into her heels into her sides. With a jolt, horse and rider were through the gate and moving swiftly across the field toward Linnie's home. The cool wind blew through her locks while they raced with the moonbeams. Shadows darted all around them, giving the night and eerie sensation.

As they approached the grove of trees Caitlin slowed Emma down to a graceful canter

and then to a steady walk. The crunching
of the leaves and twigs under Emma's hoofs
rang out as they made their way along the
path through the trees. An owl hooted overhead, giving Caitlin quite a start. And when
she jumped, so did Emma, causing her to
lose her balance and almost fall off. While
she regained herself, she looked over her
shoulder and discovered a pair of large green
eyes staring at her from the distance through
the darkness. Emma seemingly noticed at
the same time because she shuddered and
picked up speed; tension clearly mounting
in her body.

Caitlin regretted her decision to ride Emma
to Linnie's in the night, especially after the
incident, not so long ago, with the mysterious dog-pig creature that Linnie had killed.
She considered returning home, but determined that she was midway and there was
no difference in distance. So she moved on.

Just as horse and rider reached the other
side of the grove, a loud howl sounded behind them. Caitlin kicked Emma forward
and the two sped across the open field toward
Linnie's house. The lights in the distance
seemed miles away, as the howling grew
louder. Sounds of hoofs pounding on the
ground approached behind them. Fear took
over when Caitlin looked over her shoulder
at the large dark figure racing toward her on
horseback. Her heart pounded wildly, com-

peting with the pounding that was closing in on them.

Wild with panic, she kicked her heels into Emma, instantly regretting her decision not to use a saddle as she slid from side to side trying to regain her seating. As Emma pushed to her limit, the pounding of the hoof beats behind them grew fainter while the lights in Linnie's burned brighter and brighter.

Caitlin felt indescribable relief when she reached the lawn and Linnie came out on the porch to see who was approaching. Linnie rushed forward just as Emma slammed her hoofs into the ground, causing Caitlin to finally give up her seating and tumble onto the cool grass in a large ball. Linnie helped her up and, without hesitation, and pulled her into the house. To Caitlin's surprise, Linnie immediately went back out for Emma and coaxed her into the house as well.

"I haven't got a barn", Linnie explained to the shocked people in her kitchen, "and the beast is out there. 'Twouldn't do to leave her out side."

Seeming to understand the situation, Emma made her way over to the far side of the room where the furnishing where more sparse. Samson approached the mare cautiously, but with a warmth of acceptance.

Caitlin looked around the room. She was

surprised to see William and Edwin sitting next to each other with a game of chess between them.

Caitlin gasped when she saw her brother's bandaged body. He ignored his sisters reaction while he looked at her with concern in his eyes. He released the breath he did not even realize he was holding when he was satisfied that she was fine.

Edwin avoided Caitlin's eyes, too embarrassed by his actions to face her.

Fury still coursing her veins over his vile actions, she ignored Edwin and went over to William. "You're hurt! How?" Caitlin jumped back in surprise at William's painful reaction from her mere touch.

"Ouch! Be careful sis. I... I'm not sure what happened. I was walking through the grove and... I don't really know. Something attacked me!" William's face was pale and gaunt as he told his tale to the room. "It was this ugly, indescribable... thing! It had the head of a dog and the body of a pig. What would you even call something like that? A dog-pig? I'm not sure."

Caitlin gasped as she recalled the beast at her house that evening. This sounded like the same kind of creature.

Linnie stepped across the room with interest. There had been so much going on that she had not had the time to question William about the source of his injuries. "Go on lad", she prompted.

"I know it's hard to believe, but that's what it looked like! I rolled on the ground with it and luckily there was this big bolder. We slammed against the boulder and this... thing... took most of the blow which must have knocked the wind out of it or something. Its grip weakened on me and I slipped free. I took another big rock and threw it at him as hard as I could and just ran. I don't know what happened after that. I ran blindly through the grove and then, the next thing I remember is Linnie taking care of me. God! That was an ugly thing!" William shuddered as he reached up and touched his bandage. "I hope it didn't have anything contagious like rabies or something."

"Hmm, I didn't think of that." Linnie mused. "I doubt it. But we better get ya on something to prevent an infection. Some of those wounds are quite deep. Did it bite ya or claw ya? It was hard to tell"

"Both. It was full of claws and teeth. Its teeth felt like knives going in me. And the stench! Oh God, it was putrid!"

Edwin popped into the conversation. "It sounds like those creatures we saw the night I stayed over. I was beginning to think I'd had a bad dream that night. But it sounds like them for sure!"

"Yes it does." Caitlin took her attention away from William and turned to Linnie.

"Please, Linnie, can you please give me an idea of what's happening? Do you know?"

"I know, Lass." Linnie looked into Caitlin's eyes and did not speak until Caitlin looked back at her. "So... you're ready to listen, are ya?"

Caitlin lowered her head as she recalled rushing out of the room earlier. "Yes. And.. I'm... I'm sorry about my actions earlier. It's just that..."

"Never mind and sit," Linnie interrupted, "it's not important now. What is important is getting something into your brother to prevent any infections of diseases. It should've been done earlier, but I've had me hands full! Look at Samson over there, will ya? He had a similar encounter. 'Tis the demon's doing, it is. Believe me."

Linnie's chest heaved heavily as she thought of the work ahead of her. Her tired muscles longed for the comfort of her bed. But it did not look like that was going to happen any time soon. "Caitlin, lass, get my book down from the shelf for me, please. The one with medicines written on it, and I'll clear away the table. Let's fix up your brother and then we'll sit down and I'll finish telling what I started earlier."

Caitlin immediately obeyed Linnie's request. She had been an eager student since she had met the old woman and was, by now, quite familiar with Linnie's quirks and pattern of action.

They worked in unison, with Caitlin second guessing Linnie's needs and request prior to her asking. A smile of satisfaction spread across Linnie's broad face as she watched her long hours of schooling and preparation with Caitlin come to bloom before her eyes. The lass would make anyone proud, as she moved about with the skill of the women of the old world.

Linnie focused on Caitlin's energy. There was something changing right before her eyes. It was as if she was becoming a different person. Linnie stepped back, mildly startled, as she saw the barely visible, almost transparent figure of a man standing behind the lass. He was in what appeared to be biblical robes with glowing light emanating from his being. It was clear Linnie was having the privilege of glimpsing Caitlin's main spirit guide.

Without warning, the figure of a woman stepped out of the robed figure, as if housed within him and encompassed Caitlin. It was two women in one body!

Caitlin looked up at Linnie as she awaited more instruction. The face of the spirit showed clearly on Caitlin's face. It was the face of Linnie's great grandmother. Tears of recognition flowed down Linnie's face as she stood silently looking. Not sure what was wrong, and not feeling comfortable asking, Caitlin stood silently, waiting.

Edwin cleared his throat, not meaning to break the silence, but Linnie had closed the windows after bringing Emma in and the room felt hot and stuffy; not to mention that the scent of horse was beginning to fill the room.

Linnie recomposed herself and focused on the task at hand. Within minutes she and Caitlin where standing in front of William offering him spoonfuls of the herbal medicine. He coughed and gagged as they pushed several heaping spoonfuls of the thick porridge-like mixture into his mouth, barely affording him time to swallow. A long shutter ran through his body and he struggled to get down the last spoonful. "Water!" He gasped. "Please... it's stuck!"

Edwin quickly ran to the sink and drew a glass of water and handed it to William, thankful he was not having to swallow any of the muck the women had thrown together. It smelled foul, even from where he was standing.

"You'll be fine, ya will. I know it's a bad taste. But it'll kill anything trying to live in ya."

"Are you sure it won't kill me too? Damn it tasted bad! It was like swallowing puke!"

"Oh William! That's disgusting!' Caitlin's stomach turned as she thought about William's comment.

"You're damn right it was disgusting! Try some!" William was still trying to get the last of the mixture to go down his throat and into his stomach.

"I'll pass thanks." Caitlin walked behind her brother and put her arms around him gently. She bent down and placed her cheek against his and spoke softly, "But I trust Linnie, William. And, by the look of your bandages, I'm thinking those wounds should have been stitched. You're oozing blood!"

"Let me see lad" Linnie pulled Caitlin back away from William to allow her to move in closer. She gently pulled a bandage away from him so that she could look behind it. "Nope, you'll live. But ya need to stay as still as ya can for another day or so. Go lie back down on the springs will ya?"

"Springs?" Edwin looked puzzled.

"Yes, springs," William chuckled. "Poor Linnie's overridden with patience. She and Samson have the mattress on the floor and I've got the box springs." William looked at Linnie and smiled warmly. "And I have to say, dear lady, it's fit for a king. 'Tis the best sleep I've had in ages.!"

Linnie chuckled at William's remark and attempt at an Irish brogue. She was glad to see that he was able to project humor into the situation, easing the panic that could have easily mounted as the reality of the severity of the situation set in.

The sound of beasts howling outside brought their chuckling to a halt. They all knew that sound by now. Edwin ran to the window while William turned gray. Caitlin and Linnie looked at each other briefly before Linnie ran to her shelf of books, replaced the book marked medicines and pulled down one labeled spells.

The spell book seemed to open on its own when Caitlin pushed Linnie out of her way. The image of her great grandmother grew stronger as Linnie watched Caitlin run her finger down the page until she had found the section she was looking for. Caitlin tapped on the page lightly and swung the book toward Linnie so that she could read the page.

"Yes, lass. That's the one. Good. Very good!" Linnie rushed to the corner cupboard in the pantry room and returned with a small box. She gently took off the top to expose a neatly packed array of candles and incense. Disappearing back into the pantry room, she returned with an armful of candle holders and four challis. Selecting some black candles and a large white candle, Linnie secured them in the holders. Pushing furniture out of her way, she placed the large white candle on the floor in the center of the room and then the black ones in the four corners of the room before lighting a long twig and handing it to Caitlin.

"Go lass and say these words as you light each candle." Linnie took a loose piece of paper from the back of the book that had been placed there by her great grandmother years ago. It was brittle and yellowed with age. She handed it gently to Caitlin, who seemed to understand the reverence of the words.

Caitlin did not hesitate, but went immediately to the black candles and began lighting while she read the words the paper. "I bring forth the power of light, the power of the heavens. Mine to do with as I choose. I light the candles of protection. Enclosed are we within these boundaries. No evil can penetrate. It is said and it is so!"

Linnie stood before the large white candle and lit it with another small twig. She spread her arms out wide and looked up to the ceiling. With a firm voice, much louder than Caitlin, who was working at a low methodical mutter, she bellowed to the heavens. "Oh come all ye spirits of protection and divine energy. Come... enter this space with us. Keep us from harm as ye give us the strength and wisdom to do what need be done to cast out the demons! Here me, oh great ancestors, and join your children in this battle between good an evil. Bring your knowledge and put it into the lass so that she may work on your behalf. Come... come... cccooommmmeeee!"

The room heated up to the point of being almost unbearable. Edwin longed to open a window for some air, but knew better than to actually do it. To his surprise, he had a small understanding of the ritual Linnie was performing and found himself humming, in monotone, a few long notes as a way in assisting her.

William sat quietly observing. He was not quite as comfortable with the happenings as

Edwin seemed to be, but he did not argue. The entire events of the last few days seemed absurd to him and this just fit right in with it all.

Caitlin had completed her part and Linnie was just finishing up when a loud pounding on the back door filled the room. Linnie walked cautiously over to it and called out "who's there?"

Linnie's house was set back away from the road. In fact, it was so far back that you had to know it was there to even find it! There had been no sign of a vehicle of any type coming up lane. They looked at each other, immediately on the alert.

"I've come for Caitlin" Dominic bellowed from the other side of the door.

"Dominic?" Caitlin got up and moved toward the door. Edwin grabbed her arm to stop her. At his touch, she flinched and ripped away, backing herself up to the sink. "Keep away from me!" She spit. Her tone brought concern to William, who was not aware of the reason behind it.

"No Lass, stay where ya are now, please. Just stay put an I'll explain later." Linnie looked pleadingly at Caitlin.

"I've come for Caitlin. Now, open up!" Dominic roared.

"Get yourself gone demon! You've no business here! Be gone with ya!" Linnie's voice was equally powerful.

"Careful, old woman. Mind your business, if you know what's good for you!" Dominic growled the words.

"The lass is my business, as ya well know, demon. So, be gone with ya!" Linnie was not deterred by Dominic's threats.

"Caitlin! Can you hear me?" Dominic pounded again on the door and softened his tone. "Caitlin my love. Let me in!"

Caitlin struggled within herself. Part of her wanted desperately to be with Dominic. She longed to have him hold her and caress her body like he had done so many times before. She closed her eyes as she remembered his sensual touches. Visions of their many afternoon of love making traveled through her mind. She was lost in her lustful memories when a deep throated growl sounded from the other side of the door. There was a familiarity about it that she could not place, but it sent rivets of revulsion through her body. She searched her memories in an attempt to remember where she had heard that growl before.

Linnie looked over at Caitlin and the memories flashing around her and Caitlin's struggle to recall certain events. Nodding her head intently toward her, Linnie sent Caitlin a telepathic message *in the bedroom... you heard it in the bedroom this afternoon.*

As Caitlin received the message it opened a whole channel of blocked memories. She relived in her mind the afternoon of Dominic sordid abuse. She again saw the look of evil in his eyes as he cruelly devoured her body. She watched as he left the room coldly after stating that he had won. Linnie's words rang through her head, *Know this lass, and know it well. Dominic is a demon. He is! And what he's been doing to ya every afternoon is leaving is seed inside ya to make some offspring! But I fed ya the tea to stop it! I did! ... It just wasn't right ... Him coming over here only to take ya in that bedroom and leaving again. And you lass, allowing it like ya did! No. Oh no.. It wasn't right.... Dominic is a demon... Dominic is a demon ...Dominic is a demon...*

Dominic's pounding on the door merged with Linnie's words in her head and created such a state of panic that Caitlin was overwhelmed. She screamed out "Stop it! Stop it now!", not certain if her screams were for Dominic to stop pounding or for the memories in her head to cease. But, for whatever reason, it worked and all was quiet; for a moment anyway.

Linnie walked over to Caitlin and held her close. "There now lass, 'tis going to be alright. And that fella over there..." She pointed to Edwin, "He did ya a favor, he did. Not that it appears that way now, I know, but he did. If he hadn't done what he did when he did it, you'd be gone to us all. As it is, can't ya see the hold he still as on ya? 'Tis a strong one, it is. But, we can beat it! You're fighting it already. Ya got the strength inside ya and ya got us to help."

Although Dominic had stopped pounding and calling for Caitlin, the sounds of the beasts howling had grown louder and more insistent. It was clear that Dominic was in some way connected to the dog-pigs. Horror flooded Caitlin's veins as she realized she had been repeatedly intimate with such a vile creature. She fought his pull as she grew stronger and more in control of herself.

Linnie had not had the time to finish explaining everything to Caitlin and Edwin before Caitlin had bolted from the room, but the picture was clear enough. She had been in a love affair with a demon. She had read enough of the books Linnie had provided to know that she had come close to losing her own will, completely, to this demon.

And now, Dominic had come to get her, to finish the job. To bring back his human bride to breed and create more of his kind before he changed her into a demon forever. She had read the stories, but had thought them just that... stories! But this was real; very, very real!

Caitlin looked at Linnie, William and Edwin. William was obviously fading from the strain and struggling to remain upright. She knew instinctively that they where in for a long night. William would be of no help if they needed to defend themselves in any way.

Caitlin remembered Lael's words. *You have near you very dear souls who together, with you, will be able to stop the evil that has been unleashed.* He was talking about Linnie, of course, but who else? He could not have been referring to Edwin, could he? How could he call Edwin a dear soul? Edwin may not be a demon but he had proven himself to be just as evil. It could not be Edwin that Lael was talking about, it just could not be. But, William was in no shape to do anything, so there was no one else.

Linnie was watching Caitlin's thought process closely and interjected, "What he did had to be done, lass. Indeed, it seemed wrong, but it was necessary and he did it with a good heart. Look at him now. He's ashamed of himself. He doesn't even know himself why he did it and that's because he's an instrument of God that's here to help, lass. It was not within his power to stop. He was not in control, I was. So don't be too hard on him. And if you are angry with anyone, be angry with me. Or better yet, with that demon fella outside. He's the reason for it all, he is."

Edwin looked away, knowing full well what Linnie was referring to and wishing he could some how undo what had been done. William sat staring at everyone in confusion.

"Is someone going to clue me in on all of this? What's going on?" William's voice sounded weak.

"Ya better get yourself onto the bed there, now. You're fading fast on us and those wounds are opening a bit. We can't fight what's outside and worry about you as well. There's time to fill ya in later, but not now. Go on with ya now!"

William struggled to his feet at Linnie's words. Edwin grabbed his elbow and assisted him while Caitlin got on the other side of her brother and wrapped his arm around her shoulder. William fell against Caitlin and her knees buckled under the strain. Edwin took William's other arm around his shoulder, relieving Caitlin of her burden, and they walked into the bedroom and, in flowing unison, eased William down onto the box springs.

Caitlin looked over at the corner of the room to see the mattress pushed up against the wall and Samson resting peacefully on it. She was suddenly struck with the fact that the sounds of the dog-pigs outside did not seem to disturb him. It seemed odd for such a fierce protector of Linnie and her home, as she knew he was, would not be responding to the threats that were going on all around them.

Caitlin walked over and looked at Samson more closely. He was too quiet and she could see no signs of breathing. She did not dare try to rouse him in case he was just in a deep sleep. After all, he had been wounded pretty heavily himself. She decided to send Linnie in to check on him instead.

The two returned to the kitchen area to find Linnie loading her rifle. Her face looked taught with concern. "There's a lot of them out there. It looks like he's brought is army!" The old woman's face was gray.

Edwin ran to the window to look. The dark of night was filled with eyes. They stretched as far as he could see. It was like the stars had fallen out of the sky and planted themselves onto the fields.

Caitlin moved beside Edwin and silently look at the sea of fiery eyes. *You have near you very dear souls who, together with you, will be able to stop the evil that has been unleashed.'* Lael's words seemed weak. There where only 3 of them who were able to fight. Look out there! There where so many!

"How much ammunition do you have?" Caitlin asked shakily.

"Not enough to pick off that many, I'm sorry to say", Linnie's shoulders looked slumped and she suddenly looked old and tired. Caitlin walked over to her and laid her hands on her shoulder. Linnie looked up into her face lovingly. "You have the power lass. If we need it. Use it!"

Caitlin nodded in agreement, not wanting to admit that she did not understand what Linnie meant.

"Why are they just circling the house?

They're not advancing and trying to get in."
Edwin asked.

"We made a protective vortex." Linnie explained. "As long as we stay here, we're fine.
But we can't stay here forever. And even
though he can't come in. He can get outside
and raise hell with the place. It wouldn't do
to wait around and find out what he's got in
mind. We need to attack"

Linnie got up and walked into the pantry
room. Within minutes she was back with
an old box containing long barreled pistols.
She pulled them up and held them lovingly.
"These were me dad's. They're old, but good
enough in a pinch. Each of ya take one and
aim it well. There is barely any ammunition
for them." She pulled a small box of bullets
from her sweater pocket and shoved it beside
the guns. "That's it."

"I.. I've never shot.." Caitlin stuttered.

"Well, you're about to now! Grab one and
let's get started!" Linnie did not wait for
them to get there guns. She got up and positioned her body across the sink. She opened
the small window over the sink and poked a
hole in the screen "Use the small windows
please." She stated flatly, not offering an explanation.

Wails of beasts rang out through the night
as Linnie steadily aimed her rifle and in the
direction of the eyes. It was more difficult
than the night she had been at Caitlin's. The

moon had shone bright that night. It seemed to have disappeared now. For some reason, it wasn't illuminating like it had been earlier in the evening.

Caitlin and Edwin went to the back window next to the door that Dominic had been pounding on. Caitlin's heart beat wildly as they lifted the window and she peered out into the darkness looking for signs of Dominic. The field of eyes made her gasp in horror. "Oh my God, they're everywhere!" She whispered.

Edwin took out his knife and slit the screen to make a small hole to shoot through. Linnie called out for them to stop wasting time and within no time they where shooting into the darkness and listening for the sounds of dog-pigs wailing in a confirmation that they had hit their mark. It was not long before they where out of bullets and looking to Linnie for the next step. She too was running low and thinking hard about what to do next.

"Let's take a minute to think." She wheezed, noticeably exhausted. "We need to think of something else. There are too many of them. You're out of bullets and I'm almost out. If I keep shooting I'll be out of bullets before ya know it and then we'll have no defense."

They sat in silence while they each worked out in their mind a possible solution for their situation.

"I've never seen them in the daytime, have

you?" Caitlin asked.

"I've only seen them once before, at your house. And it was dark" Edwin responded.

"They disappear at daylight. They go back to their den to rest 'till night again" Linnie pitched in. "They're creatures of the night, lass; evil beasts that would scare themselves in the light of day." Linnie's face twisted with disgust. "They're damned ugly creatures."

Edwin was so taken aback by the look of disgust on Linnie's face and the power in her voice that he burst into laughter. When they did not join in, he apologized and awkwardly got up to stroke Emma, who moved nervously away from him.

"'Tis going to be morning soon." Linnie muttered.

"Good!" Exclaimed Caitlin.

"Not so good, lass. They'll be working even harder now to get at ya. They're running out a time." Linnie got up and drew a glass of water from the sink. She stood drinking it until the glass was empty. After releasing a loud belch and excusing herself, she walked back over to the window. "I'm thinking we need to trick them somehow. Like making them think she's leaving when she's not. Hmm. What to do?"

Linnie paced back and forth for a bit while she wrestled for a solution in her mind. She stopped and stoked Emma's silky neck, getting small comfort from the mare. Feeling the need to embrace her faithful Samson, Linnie turned and looked around the room, but saw him nowhere. "Where's Samson?"

"Oh, yes. In all the fuss I didn't get a chance to tell you that Samson seems awfully still. I checked on him when we took William in there, but I was afraid to touch him for fear I'd hurt him. Maybe you should check on him yourself, Linnie." Caitlin's voice was hesitant, as if she was holding back something.

Linnie nodded and left the room. A few minutes later she came back with tears streaming down her cheeks. "He's gone. My lovely companion left with out me. Ah, 'tis a sad thing." She lowered her bulk into a chair and stared at the floor in silence for a few moments. Then, with a look of determination on her face, she wiped the tears away with her shirt sleeve, she got up and went back into the room where Samson lay peacefully on the mattress. William's light snoring added life to an atmosphere of death and doom.

Caitlin rushed to help Linnie as she carried Samson and laid him on the table. She stretched him out lovingly and then walked silently into the pantry room.

It seemed to Caitlin like an eternity had passed before Linnie returned with a long broom handle. She called for Edwin to help her and the two huddled together while Caitlin stood watching, puzzled as to why they where securing a broomstick to the long stretched out back of Samson, but knowing that now was not the time to ask questions.

Tears continued to flow down her cheeks as Linnie steadily completed her task. When she was done, she told Caitlin to take off her shirt. Shocked, Caitlin obliged. Edwin turned away while Caitlin removed her shirt and put on one of Linnie's baggy flannels. While she rolled up the sleeves in an attempt to make it a more comfortable fit, she watched while Edwin and Linnie put her shirt on Samson. Linnie took a pair of jeans from her closet and tied them on the lifeless dog as well.

When they where finished, Linnie looked at Caitlin with eyes that were filled with sadness. "Lass, sit down for a minute. We need to have a serious talk."

Caitlin sat next to Linnie. Linnie took Caitlin's hand and, in a voice that Caitlin found surprisingly gentle, she spilled her idea to Caitlin. "There's nothing more precious to me in this world than Samson. He was my companion for years and years. He far outlived the normal life of a dog. Did I ever tell ya that?" Caitlin shook her head no. "Yes. He made it to twenty, he did! But, he's gone now and that makes me sad." Linnie took a moment to wipe the tears from her face with her sleeve before continuing. "But what would be even sadder would be if they got ya. Them devils! I don't know if I could bear that. I mean it, lass. You're like me own kin. Did ya know that? I'm so proud to have ya near me!"

Linnie squeezed Caitlin's hand while Caitlin choked back the tears that were threatening to gush forth. She did not know what Linnie was about to say, but she got the feeling it was something that she would not want to hear. "Now, that mare over there. She's your love like Samson was mine, right?"

"Why.. Yes... I guess so." Caitlin's heart started to pound as the fear of what was coming mounted. What was Linnie leading up to?

"Lass, this is serious. There's a field full of demon beasts out there and the leader is out there looking for a way to get ya away just like we are looking for a way to keep ya safe. They'll kill ya. Ya know that, right? If they get ya, you'll be like them in the end."

Caitlin shook her head yes, her eyes were wide with fright as the impact of Linnie's words hit her.

"Lass, I don't know what to do. 'Tis almost daylight an they'll be pushing hard to get us out. If they don't find a way, then they'll burn the house. I heard their thoughts in my head, I did. He will kill everyone to get to ya. Once the house is on fire, we'll have to leave. And once we leave, they've got us. Do ya understand?"

Caitlin again nodded as she waited to hear the solution Linnie had come up with.

"Lass. I ... I'm sorry. But I just can't think of anything else. We've got to make them think you're running for it. We've got to get them to chase ya so they'll waste what little time is left before the sun comes up."

Caitlin could hardly contain her heart in her chest. She looked at Samson and then over at Emma. It was starting to become clear. "No!... You can't mean..."

"Lass. 'Tis the only way. I just can't think of anything else. Please, try to understand." Linnie was in a rage of tears now as she lifted Samson off the table and carried him over to Emma. Edwin followed close behind her. They propped Samson up and used ace bandages to tie him in a sitting position on the mare's back.

Caitlin had to admit that, from a distance in the dark, Samson could possibly pass as a person on horseback.

"Oh Linnie..." The groan came from deep within Caitlin's throat.

"'Tis the horse or all of us. Your brother could never make it out. Ya know that lass. We've no choice!"

Caitlin walked over to Emma and buried her head in the mare's neck. She felt as if her heart was being ripped from her body. Pain seared her chest from its deepest core. Emma nuzzled her mistress lovingly, as if to comfort her. Caitlin burst into tears, unable to contain them anymore.

"Maybe she'll make it Caitlin," Edwin whispered, hesitantly. "You never know. She's pretty fast!"

"That's true lassie. Ya don't know about these things. And 'tis the only thing I can think to do!"

"Oh God! Oh God! Oh God!" Caitlin chanted, her face buried deep into Emma. "No... please no. Oh God!"

"Child, please." Linnie's heart ached for her friend. She wished with all her might she could think of another solution. But this was all she could come up with; and it was a weak solution at that.

"Caitlin," Edwin walked up behind her and stroked her head lightly. It reminded her of when her mother was around. She would do the same thing whenever she was upset.

As the heat of Edwin's hand penetrated her scalp, Caitlin slowly grew calmer. She thought of William lying on the bed, weak and torn. She had brought this on them; all of them. And now, her loving Emma was going to have to pay the price. She could not let them do this. There had to be another way.

"No. I'm sorry, but I can't. Please... take Samson off Emma. I can't do this. I just can't." Caitlin ripped at the bandages around Emma's girth and Samson's lifeless form started to slide off. Linnie rushed to catch her companion and gently lowered him to the floor.

"Well, lass. It wasn't my favorite idea. But,

I'm at such a loss at what to do!" Linnie did not look up as she removed the rest of the bandages from Samson and released the pole from his back. His body was still soft and supple.

"Let me think for a minute, please. There has to be another way." Caitlin begged.

The howling of the beasts grew stronger and closer. Edwin went to the window to look out and jumped back, startled, when he found himself face to face with Dominic.

Dominic's eyes burned in the night, reflecting the anger and rage that welled within him.

"Damn!" Edwin shouted as he backed off. Dominic pressed his face against the glass, accentuating his rage.

Caitlin cringed to think that she had actually thought she was in love with this man. What had she ever seen in him? Looking at him now, she felt noting but revulsion. She walked over to the window and closed the curtains.

"The sun's starting to come up Linnie. I can see the pink over the trees". The panic in Caitlin's voice was shared by Edwin and Linnie. The sun was coming up and Dominic would be going in for the serious move. Something needed to be done, and soon.

Linnie grabbed her book of spells again and quickly leafed through the pages. Without a moment's hesitation, Caitlin joined her.

Dominic had resumed pounding on the door and was shouting for her to come out. Every nerve in the room was worn thin as the tension mounted. Linnie finally came to a page and stopped. She took in a deep breath as she read and then just as quickly let it out.

"What's the matter?" Caitlin asked, not missing how quickly Linnie lost had her enthusiasm.

"Damn, it calls for fresh flowers of jasmine." Linnie wailed.

"You don't have any?" Caitlin was shocked. She had never known Linnie to be without any ingredient needed, no matter what page they turned to.

"I do. But 'tis outside, growing in the garden." Linnie wailed. "What to do.. What to do..."

Linnie book marked the page before proceeding to leaf through the others. When she had combed through the book and had not found a suitable replacement, she returned to the book marked page.

"This is the only one that will work. I just know it." Linnie was almost shouting over the howling and pounding that was growing more intense from outside.

William came to the doorway of the bedroom. The noise from Damian's pounding and the dog-pig's howling was overpowering and he leaned against the door frame trying to collect his wits. He felt groggy, as if he' had been drinking all night.   Caitlin rushed to help him to a chair.

"He's feverish" she shouted as she wiped the beads of perspiration from her brother's brow.

Linnie left her book and went over to the refrigerator. She pulled out a jar of brown liquid and measured some into a small glass. "Hold his head back and I'll pour this down him. It'll help with the fever."

Caitlin did as Linnie asked as the old woman practically threw the liquid down William's throat. He coughed and gasped for air as he pushed the glass away from his lips. Within moments he was still again, staring at the door that was visibly trembling from Damian's pounding, which was getting increasingly more insistent.

"I'm going to have to go out for the jasmine. There's no other choice." Linnie started for the door.

"You can't!" Caitlin screamed as she grabbed Linnie's arm to keep her from moving any further.

Linnie had been growing progressively weaker as the day wore on. She could not explain the reasoning for this except to say that it was her time and her soul was doing its best to leave her body. She prayed she could stay alive long enough to make sure the lads and lass were safely out of harm's way. Then she would happily go to her maker. *We made a deal, Samson, and my soul's planning on honoring it. But please let me stay long enough to keep these geer folks safe. That's all I ask.*

"Let me go! You stay here." Edwin piped in.

Both women looked at Edwin. They where so engrossed in finding a solution for the problem that Caitlin had forgotten all about his being there. Linnie raised her hand and shook her head.

"What does it look like, lad? Eh? Can ya tell me?" Edwin lowered his head and shook it slowly. He had no idea what it looked like. He could hardly tell one flower from the other. "That's what I thought."

"But they're all over! They're everywhere! You'll never make it!" Caitlin threw herself between Linnie and the door, trying once again to stop her.

"I'll wear my cloak. It'll work for a bit anyway. Hopefully it will give me enough time to get the flower and get back in. I see no other choice, lass. Now, step aside." Linnie pushed Caitlin gently but firmly out of her way as she pulled a long black cloak off the hook by the door. It felt like it weighed a ton as she positioned it over her shoulders and pulled the hood up over her head

"What will the cloak do for her?" William asked weakly.

"It will hide her, sort of make her invisible. The only problem is that when the sun's rays hit it, it will sparkle. They'll be able to see it then. Oh, please Linnie... hurry!" Caitlin peered into the gray morning.

The sun was just coming over the top of the trees and Dominic was pacing around the house and looking like he was getting ready to do just what Linnie had warned them about. He had a can of gasoline in his hands and was pouring it around the parameter. Caitlin saw no sign of Linnie.

"That son-of-a-bitch is going to burn the house down!" Edwin exclaimed. The anger in his voice superseded any fear he may have felt. He wanted to run out and rip the can out of Dominic's filthy hands, but common sense took over.

"Oh, hurry, Linnie... Hurry!" Caitlin moaned as she peered at the flower bed in search of any sign of her.

Dominic noticed Caitlin's searching looks and followed the direction of her eyes. A sinister smile spread across his handsome face as he saw the grass giving under Linnie's weight while she made her way toward the flower garden. The sun beams were faint, but strong enough to give off a tiny glimmer from the cloak Linnie was wearing. He raced toward her while letting out a thunderous roar.

"Linnie!" Caitlin screamed as Dominic flung himself onto Linnie, ripping her cloak off, as she fell to the ground.

Edwin's grip felt like a vice, holding Caitlin in place while she looked on, helplessly.

Linnie heard her bones snap as she rolled under Dominic's weight. His breath had the smell of death. She struggled for air as he bore down on her more heavily. The most intense pain she could have ever imagined seared through her bones as they crushed beneath his weight. Tiny flecks, like stardust, danced before her eyes and the world began to spin. Visions of her childhood days in the old country passed through her mind and she heard her mother's voice singing in the distance while she skipped in her patent leather shoes through the dew.

"No! Linnie!" Caitlin ripped at her arm as she tried to free herself from Edwin's grip. William came up behind them and grabbed her other arm.

"No sis. No. You can't go out there." William winced from the effort of holding his sister back, but he stood firm and did his best to calm her down. As the result of their struggle, one of his wounds opened and blood started to ooze out onto the bandage. "Please sis... listen... you can't help her. It's in the hands of God. Stop sis. Please."

William's words echoed in Caitlin's head as she watched Dominic get up and kick Linnie for signs of life, but she lay still. The anguish Caitlin felt for the loss of her friend was all consuming and she was numb with despair.

The three watched in horror, frustrated at their inability to do anything, as Dominic backed away from Linnie allowing the dog-pigs to circle in. Soon Linnie was covered with dog-pigs as they tore at her flesh. Traumatized by what she was witnessing, Caitlin fell faint to the floor.

Edwin ran to the sink and vomited. His legs were shaking and the room was spinning. With white knuckles, he held onto the edge of the sink, forcing the darkness that was threatening to consume him away.

Only William was strong enough to maintain composure. "Sis... I know... I know what you're going through. But now's not the time to break down. He's coming back! Look!" William hobbled over to the window to point to Dominic, who had resumed his task of pouring the gasoline. "We're going to be burned alive if we stay in here! And we'll end up like Linnie if we go out there!"

"It doesn't look like there's much of an out for us here, now does it?" Edwin sounded cold and resolved as he looked from Caitlin to William. His eyes swept the room until they rested on the rifle Linnie had left propped against the wall. "I don't know about the two of you. But neither one of those options sounds good to me. I think I'd rather go by that than by fire or... or... them!"

Caitlin groaned with despair. What had

she done? It was her fault that Linnie was dead and it was her fault that she and William and Edwin would soon follow. Maybe she should have listened to Linnie and put Samson on Emma and used them as a decoy. Maybe Linnie would still be alive and they would all be free right now. But then, Emma would have died. Yes, Emma was a horse and Linnie was a human being, but Emma was her family too. She was a living, breathing creation of God who trusted and depended on her. How could she do that? How could she deliberately send her mare to her death? Waves of anguish flooded Caitlin as tortuous thoughts consumed her, *instead I sent Linnie to her death..* "Oh, how did it get to this?"

"What do you say?" Edwin looked into Caitlin's eyes. The seriousness of the situation mirrored back to her. She looked up at William, who was now preoccupied with trying to stop the blood that had begun to flow steadily from his recently opened wound. His words pounded in her head. *Please sis... listen... you can't help her. It's in the hands of God... It's in the hands of God...*

Suddenly, Caitlin remembered Linnie's words ...*'You have the power lass. If we need it. Use it!...* What power? What was she talking about?

Caitlin ran to the book that Linnie had left

open on the table and read down through the ingredients. There was nothing she could do there. If Linnie did not feel they could improvise, then she could not.

"Think, think, think!" Caitlin shouted as she slapped her forehead with the palm of her hand, as if that would help her think better.

Edwin made his way to the rifle, picked it up and walked over to William. "What do you think? I know this is the way I want to go. What about you?"

William looked at the rifle in silence and then looked at Dominic who was just finishing pouring out the contents of the gasoline can. The sun was almost up now and it was easier to see the field of ugly beasts, as well as what was left of Linnie. The seriousness and gruesomeness of the situation finally hit home and bile filled William's throat as he quickly turned away.

"No Edwin," Caitlin shouted. "No! There's another way. I feel it!"

"Well? Tell us then." There was urgency in Edwin's voice as well as finality, "And hurry! That son of a bitch has lit the fire!"

Caitlin ran to the window to see the flames following the gasoline all around the house.

"I want you, Caitlin!" Dominic bellowed with blood curdling laughter. "I want your body. But if I can't have that... I'll have your soul!"

Leaning against the wall, Caitlin frantically

searched her mind for a solution. She felt it was at her fingertips, but she just could not think what it could be.

She moved to Emma and wrapped her arms tightly around the mare's neck, feeling this was their last moment together. The air seemed hazy as Emma's telepathic words penetrated her forehead. *Call upon your friend, mistress. Remember? Call upon your friend. The one who helped you before. Try to remember.*

Her friend? Who was Emma referring to? What friend? Linnie was her only friend in this area and now Linnie was gone. Who else was there. Who?

Smoke started to penetrate the room as the flames shot around the house. William struggled to keep his coughing at bay, so as not to disturb his wounds and Edwin grew more insistent that they use the rifle. "Well, you two can stick around if you want. But I don't want to go this way! I'm using this!" He reached over for the box of ammunition to load the rifle.

Suddenly Caitlin remembered. She knew what Emma was trying to say. She recalled Lael's message... *We are in hopes this can be done without the need of our assistance. But if not, you are to simply call. You must remember, please, that we can not interfere unless you ask. So you must call. Say my*

*name three times and help will be avail-
able.'*

With a voice as loud as she could possibly muster, Caitlin cried "Help us Lael! Please... Help us!... Lael!... Lael!... Lael!"

Instantly the room was filled with light and free of smoke. Edwin dropped the rifle and stared with disbelief. Outside, the field around was filled with exploding dog-pigs.

Caitlin ran to the window and looked through the flames and watched as Dominic, panic stricken, shift himself into the shape of a large wolf. Caitlin recognized it as the wolf she had encountered on the roadside.

But it was too late. Lael stood before him with outstretched arms while the wolf slowly transformed back into Dominic's form and he lay twisting and writhing while he fought off the energy that was destroying him. Within a matter of minutes, which seemed like hours to the onlooking trio, the field was empty, the fire was out and Lael had disappeared.

Caitlin, William and Edwin stood in a room so silent that you could hear a pin drop in it.

"What just happened?" William broke the silence as he stood in disbelief looking at his bloodless bandages. "My wounds are healed. How could that be?"

"A miracle," Caitlin stated. She rushed

over to Emma and hugged her tightly. "Thank you my friend. Thank you for reminding me. Thank you." Her tears of relief flooded onto the horse's silken neck.

"Let's get out of here, shall we?" Edwin was standing behind Caitlin. The heat of his body in such close proximity reminded her of what had occurred between them. A faint shudder ran through her. Noticing her reaction to him, he backed away. "I'm sorry."

William walked over to Caitlin and pulled her close. "Come on sis. Let's go home."

TWENTY-ONE

William and Edwin returned that afternoon with the police to retrieve what remained of poor Linnie. They did not tell the truth, of course; feeling that no one would believe them.

Linnie's body had been mangled, so the police wrote the report up stating that she was the victim of a wild animal attack. After all, there had been multiple reports from around the county about sightings of a strange looking wild animal. Some said it was a wild dog and other claimed it to be a pig. It must have made its way to the old woman's house.

The singed circle around the house was passed off as some queer ritual that she more than likely had been doing. It was no secret she was a bit odd and there were also rumors of her practicing witch craft; if you believed in that stuff, of course.

Caitlin went straight to bed and slept. By the time she had awoken, three days had passed and Nora was bending over her adjusting her covers. Caitlin reached up and pulled her close; hugging her so tightly that she had to gasp for air. Hearing her struggle, Caitlin loosened her grip, but did not let go. Nora adjusted herself so that she could lay comfortably next to her sister and the two of them remained there, eventually falling into a gentle slumber.

By the time they had awoken, the house was full of activity. Nora jumped up to investigate, but motioned Caitlin to stay put. She wanted her sister to take it easy for just a bit longer. William had told her everything, not missing a detail. And what he could not tell, Edwin did.

Although William was shocked at Edwin's admissions of his own actions, he claimed he understood why it happened. It was obvious to Nora that the horror of the last few days had created a type of bond between her brother and Edwin. And, although it would not be not considered an admirable action under normal conditions, the events of the last few days had been anything but normal. His sister was alive. Who knows where she might have been if Edwin had not been there. William shuddered to think.

Although Nora believed the story that had been told to her, she did not as readily accept the need for Edwin's type of participation in Caitlin's salvation. The thought of her sister enduring that type of treatment and then housing him as an honored guest was hard for Nora to accept, but she did her best to hide her feelings and be as warm and as hospitable as she could, for William's sake. Her brother had been through enough. It was a shame Edwin had done what he did. Under different circumstances, Nora felt she would have like him very much.

In an attempt to bring normalcy back into their lives, William had opted to do some long awaited repairs for Caitlin. Edwin decided to hang around for a few days to help. He was still a little shaken and not quite up to facing the world. William and Nora understood completely and graciously accepted his offer.

The better part of a week had passed before Caitlin came out of her room. Still not up to talking to anyone, she made her way quietly toward the barn to visit Emma. The air was crisp and moist. It felt like the upcoming rainstorm could easily turn into snow if the temperature dropped just a few more degrees. Fall was in the air.

Emma snorted puffs of moist hot air as she watched her mistress approach. Caitlin made her way into the stall with the intent of doing a little cleaning. She was sure that neither William or Nora had taken readily to the task and did only what they absolutely needed to. To her surprise, the place was cleaner than she had ever known it to be.

"I hope you don't mind, but I took the liberty while you where resting. It gave me something to do." Edwin's voice came from the shadows.

Caitlin searched , and could barely make out the outline of his lean body. "No, it's fine... and... thanks. You did a far better than I've ever done." Caitlin could feel her body going tense.

"Don't mention it. I have a method, you

know. I grew up around horses and I enjoy working around them. I find it therapeutic. I'll show you sometime, if you like." Although his words where friendly and casual, his body ached with anxiety. He could hear the strain in Caitlin's voice as she tried to be cordial. How she must hate him. His heart was heavy as he wondered what it might have been like under different circumstances. She was so beautiful and vibrant, even after all that had happened. She looked like a young flower, waiting to bloom. He longed to hold her close and tell her how sorry he was for her pain. He wanted to tell her how lovely she was. He slowly moved out from the shadows, hoping to possibly bridge the gap that circumstances had created, but Caitlin stepped back quickly.

"I won't hurt you Caitlin. I never meant to hurt you, honest."

Although she could hear the pain in his voice, his words where blocked by her revulsion and fear. She could not get past the memories of that horrible afternoon.

"But you did." Although he had left her nothing to do, Caitlin picked up a rake and started cleaning anyway.

"Oh God. Please forgive me. I... I wasn't myself. I swear!" Edwin pleaded.

"Forget it. Let it go." Caitlin put the rake down and started for the door. Edwin jumped in front of her, blocking her path while he grabbed her by the shoulders, desperate to make her listen. Her heart raced with fear.

"Don't be afraid Caitlin. I just wanted you to know that I'm sorry. Really I am. And... I know you hate me. And I really don't blame you. But I hope some day you'll understand what happened and forgive me." He let her go and she left the barn, not looking back.

Edwin stood, heavy hearted, as he watched Caitlin make her way up the path to the house. He had stayed on as a guest longer than planned while he waited to see her, in hopes that he could get her to understand; but it did not work. There was no reason to stay any longer.

Edwin waited for Caitlin to enter the house before he sought out William and Nora to inform them that he had decided it was time for him to leave and to thank them for their hospitality. William tried to talk him into staying, but the pain and anguish of being in the same house with Caitlin, knowing how she felt about him, was more than he could bear. He refused an offer from William to take him to town, insisting, instead, on calling a cab.

The cab was scheduled to arrive at seven, which left time for dinner. Nora quickly threw together a light meal and pulled out a bottle of wine from the wine cooler. She wanted to make Edwin's parting meal as pleasant as possible. As they sat at the table, conversation was difficult. Each one wanted to say something, but there seemed to be nothing to say.

William finally broke the silence. "Hey buddy. I can't tell you how sorry I am to see you go. I wish you'd stick around a bit longer."

Edwin shook his head. "I have to get back to work, but thanks for the offer. I'll swing back off and on."

"Oh, please do." Nora joined in. She hoped she did not sound as phoney as the offer she was making. She, for one, was happy to see him leave. Although she found Edwin to be pleasant enough, she knew how much distress having him here in the house brought to her sister and she felt that the sooner he was out of the house, the sooner things could get back to normal.

Although he sensed she did not mean it, Edwin thanked Nora with genuine warmth. He could not blame her for feeling the way she did about him; especially when she was not there through it all. The whole story must have sounded pretty crazy to a level headed woman like Nora. He had been impressed with her attentiveness and lack of criticism as she listened to William tell her the story the first night she had arrived. It was a perfect display of family bonding. Something he had never known.

"I hope you mean that," he heard William saying. "I'd hate to lose touch with you. I'm serious man."

"We won't lose touch, I promise." Edwin smiled as they all clanked their glasses together in a toast to solidify the promise.

TWENTY-TWO

Caitlin sat at the window looking out at the stars. It was getting dark so early now that fall was approaching. It could not be more than six o'clock. She had declined joining them for dinner, feigning a headache; although everyone knew the real reason she had stayed in her room.

Caitlin remembered Linnie's words about how it was necessary that Edwin do what he did to counteract what Dominic was trying to accomplish. But, even understanding it, she could not accept it. The thought of being under the same roof as him was bad enough, she just knew she could not be at the same dinner table. Nora had brought her some food on a tray and she sat nibbling at it now.

Memories of Linnie flooded her mind and she wondered if she would ever find peace in her heart again. The pain of separation was intense. She wanted to hop on Emma and go to Linnie's house and find her there sitting on the porch with Samson, like she had done so many times before. What would life be without her good friend? How would she pass her days?

She found herself wandering the house and

finally settling in the upstairs den. The black book Linnie had given her lay in its usual resting on the mantle. She walked over and picked it up, holding its bulk to her chest lovingly. It had the smell of Linnie. She inhaled deeply, trying to fill her being with its aroma. It was all she had left of the old woman. It was her book of memories.

Opening up the pages, Caitlin landed on the section of angels. Surely Linnie had become one. She was such a good soul, she had to have.

"People are spirits my dear one. They are different than angels. She will incarnate again, my beloved. But fear not, for she is in a good and loving place now."

Caitlin turned to see Lael standing in the shadows of the room. There had been no glowing ball to announce his arrival and he did not seem as bright as he had the other times he had appeared to her, although he still had a mile glow.

"Greetings, my beloved. I am Lael. You are wondering about my brightness?" Lael chuckled at Caitlin's surprised look. "Yes, my beloved, I can hear your thoughts. It is simple. I am standing amongst the shadows in time. It is the plane of shadows that rests between your time and mine. It is the space where all travel is done. I have not fully come to you and not fully left where I have been. I have come to bring to you a message from the beautiful spirit you befriended. The one who spent this last incarnation as the persona of Linnie. She has asked that I relay to you that she is with her loving Samson and they are happy and whole. She wishes you to retrieve her family secrets from the ashes of her home before they are discovered and taken by others ... And to continue with your studies. There is a will to be read, in the safe deposit box at the bank. She has willed all her earthly belongings to you, my dear one. It is her desire that you find peace within yourself and with the one who worked selflessly to help you in your time of trouble. You must see that sometimes help comes in strange ways. She is entering sleep state and will remain there until her spirit is well rested from the release of the bonds of a human body. If you were to measure it in earthly time, it would be a variance of time between one and twelve months. The length of time depends entirely on the soul and how much rest and transition time is needed. After that, she will be back to work with you and continue with your lessons, for she wishes you to carry on the mysteries of the ages. That is, of course, if your free will chooses. She will be of spirit of course. Until then my beloved, I am at your disposal and will do my best to help you with your journey through life. You need only ask. I am with you always."

This time Lael remained, as if to await her response. Caitlin had never actually spoken to him, with the exception of calling to him during the crisis and a few times in her dreams. She stepped toward him hesitantly, but he remained motionless. Clearing her throat she asked, "Can I enter the dimension of the shadows in time? Is that possible?"

What Caitlin was asking to do was something that very few humans were able to do; and those who had accomplished it had found themselves wrestling with their desire to stay in the shadows in time and ignore their obligation to return. Lael was silent for several moments while he contemplated his response. He finally looked at her so intensely that Caitlin felt an energy wave so powerful that she was sure she would fall over from the pressure.

Lael's eyes were filled with compassionate warmth as he replied, "Anything is possible... If you believe."

Look for
Book II of the Shadows Series by R. A. Lura

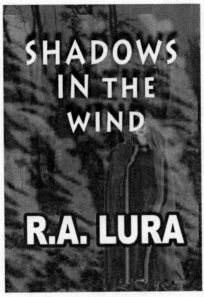

ISBN 978-0-9820562-8-8 (Paperback)
ISBN 978-0-9820562-8-8 (Hardcover)

If you liked book one the Shadows Series,
why not try R. A. Lura's Vampire series?

Vampires in Vegas
(book one of the Vampire Stories)
ISBN 978-0-9820562-0-2 (Paperback)
ISBN 978-0-9820562-4-0 (Hard Cover)

Find out more at www.raularpublishing.com.